Shark Bait

Matt Walker

STEELE

The worst time to get pulled over by the cops is when you have a body in the boot.

I had no idea the pair of headlights in my rear-view mirror belonged to a police car. Bloody typical. And it wasn't just the little guy in the boot. I had a gym bag full of stolen cash on the passenger seat, a handgun in the footwell, and a bullet wound in my left arm. Which hurt like hell.

The blue flashers came on. The siren chirped twice.

"Oh, Jesus *Christ*."

That's all I needed. As if tonight hadn't been hard enough.

No one else on the road. I indicated, pulled over. Put the transmission paddle into neutral. Left the engine running. Hoped the cop wouldn't notice the blood running down my left arm. Or the gun.

He'd freak if he saw the gun. This is England. Police have a can of CS spray, a little baton thing that looks like a squeezy toy, and maybe a taser if they're lucky. They get awful jumpy over guys with guns.

Even guys like me, who are allowed them.

The police car pulled in behind me. Vauxhall Astra. A policeman got out. He was alone. Budget cuts, I guess. He ambled over, admiring my car.

And so he should. It's a Mercedes S500. Obsidian black like the night. Costs about eighty grand.

I wound down my window, and he saw me and gave a wry smile. Of course he did. I look like a car thief. Pasty. Bedraggled. Mid-forties. The sunken eyes of a druggy and an unkempt ginger beard like a Scottish hobo.

I'd taken off my jacket to bandage up the bullet

wound. I stank of sweat and smoke. At least the dots of blood would be hard to see on my black shirt.

"Is there a problem, officer?" I asked. I have a strong, memorable Scottish accent.

The cop raised his eyebrows. "Do you know how fast you were going?"

I did. Sixty-six mph exactly. "No more than fifty, surely."

"At one point you were doing seventy."

Bit of a liberty. "Seventy? Really?"

"I'm going to have to write you out a ticket, I'm afraid."

"Okay." It's not like I'll have to pay it. Better to get this over with before he began asking me questions about my nice car, or my arm, or what was in the boot to make it sit so low.

"Do you have your driving licence?"

"Not with me." I don't carry it when I'm working. No point.

The cop pondered. Then he said, "Can you turn the engine off, sir."

I thought about just driving away, but the borough's chief superintendent was already a bit fed up with me. I'd overstayed my welcome, and he wouldn't appreciate me leading his officers on a wild goose chase after everything else. So I turned off the engine.

"Is this your vehicle?" the policeman asked.

"Yes." It wasn't, not really, but all the documents would say it was. HQ was careful about such things.

"I think I'll just check that."

Be my guest. I just stared at him.

As he turned away he noticed my bandage. "What have you done to your arm?"

The guy in the boot shot me before I could return the favour. I said, "I walked into a door." Cute, I know. But I was getting fed up. I still had things to do tonight, and pandering to the police was not one of them.

"You walked into a door."

"Aye. The handle was sharp."

I don't think he believed me. "What's in the bag?" He nodded at the purple gym bag on the passenger seat.

Money. Lots of it. I don't know how much because it's not mine. It belongs to the guy in the boot. I said, "My overnight bag. I'm staying at a hotel." Hence the Scottish accent.

He weighed everything up. Friday night. Nice car. Fortyish Scottish vagrant. Bandaged arm. Looks high on drugs. "Would you step out of the vehicle please, sir."

There we go. Inevitable, really.

He tried to open my door, but it was locked and he just stood flapping the handle.

I sighed. Time to show my ID, then. I braced my feet, pushed up off the seat and pulled my wallet out of my left trouser pocket. Awkward. Had to do it with my right hand, because my left arm was dead as a plank of wood.

And the cop just stood flapping the handle and saying, "Out of the car, sir, out of the car."

And that's when the guy in the boot woke up.

*

He began banging and calling out.

Me and the cop just stared at each other for a moment, and then, before he could radio in for back-up, I got my wallet open and held it up to his face.

My ID. My LV licence. Black and gold. *Security Service* stencilled on top. My name: John Steele. My photo:

ginger and rugged. Quite like a mug shot. My LV number. Signed by Jacqui Smith, who was Home Secretary when it was issued.

The cop let go of the handle, took a step back. His eyes widened.

Exactly as expected. I have that effect on people.

The guy in the boot kept banging and yelling out, but the policeman didn't look like he heard. Probably zoned out. He stammered, "W-what's that?"

"You know what. I'm sure your duty inspector told you all about me."

The cop swallowed. "Y-you... you're the guy..."

"Yes." I'm the LV. And it doesn't stand for *long vehicle*.

It stands for Licensed Vigilante. A government hitman, contracted as a last resort to take out those criminals the police can't touch. You know the ones - the masterminds with the expensive lawyers who muddy evidence, who silence and intimidate witnesses, who are above the law. They know how to stay out of prison. The Criminal Justice System can't bring them down, so I have to.

I'm a ghost. I don't exist.

And I kill criminals for a living.

The guy in the boot, for instance. One of the Carlucci brothers. Biggest drug barons outside London. Specialists in MDMA. Better known in table form as E, X or XTC. Ecstasy. The party drug. And the Carlucci product would give you a five hour high instead of the usual three and a half.

The Carluccis were untouchable. No hard evidence whatsoever, just rumours on the street and a white tablet stamped with the letter C. Witnesses went missing. Dealers refused to implicate them, or ended up dead in the showers. The Carlucci family lawyer had made a lot of money over the years keeping them out of prison.

Hence the contract. The security service wanted both brothers taking out.

I'd blown up the bigger brother in their den half an hour before. Maybe now I could go on my way and actually finish the job.

And then get to a hospital, because I'm not Sylvester Stallone. I needed stitches.

The cop backed away from the car as if he might catch something. Whispered into his radio, shooting me wide-eyed looks like I might breathe fire on him or something. Then he came back over to me and burbled out, "I... I'm sorry, sir, I didn't realise it was you..."

"Don't worry about it."

"If I'd known I'd have never..."

"Hey, it's fine." I started the Merc's engine. Put the automatic transmission into drive with my right hand. "Just remember: you never saw me. Okay?"

"Okay."

"I don't exist."

"Nope."

"Good."

The guy in the boot was still making a racket, and the cop fidgeted and bit his lower lip and finally said, "Who've you got in there, sir?"

"Oh, just some bad guy." And then I drove away.

*

About five minutes later my phone rang over my Merc's hands-free. I answered with the button on my steering wheel and Dawn Gainsborough, my operations manager from HQ, said, "Steele, have you got someone in your *boot*?"

"Yes."

"*Who?*"

"Little Carlucci."

The drugs den had its own exterior security camera system, and HQ had hacked into it and obviously seen me kidnap the tiny Italian drug baron and drive off with him.

"Why exactly is Little Carlucci in your boot?"

Little Carlucci wasn't his real name, of course. We just called him that because his actual name was something stupid and Italian and unpronounceable, and at least 'Little Carlucci' was descriptive.

"He tripped an alarm," I said. "Or someone did."

"We knew that would happen."

"Aye. Well I couldn't hang around and question him there in case more of his guys turned up."

"They *have* turned up."

"Well there you go. And also the building was on fire."

"Yes, I did notice. The smoke's really thick and the security feed is grainy as it is, but I think I counted six black Land Rovers pull into the car park. About twenty men with guns got out and rushed inside even though the building was on fire."

"They're too late. Big Carlucci's dead. I blew half his head off."

I heard keys clacking. Dawn updating the file. "You want to tell me what happened?"

I summed it up for her in a couple of sentences. Plan worked. Went in. Boom. Got out. Got shot.

"You got *shot?*"

"Only in my arm. No big deal. It's just a flesh wound."

"Well are you okay?"

"Fine. Apart from being shot."

"Do you want…"

"No, I'm fine, really. But I won't be doing cartwheels any time soon."

"Can you estimate the number of fatalities?" Dawn asked.

"No civilians. Enemies…" I counted up as I drove. "Nine or ten. Targets; one eliminated and one remaining, soon to be eliminated."

"Where are you taking him?"

"Somewhere secluded. I want the lab location."

"Be careful, Steele. I recommend you finish this as quickly as possible and get out of there."

"Advice noted." And ignored. "Are the Land Rovers still there?"

"Yes."

"Well let me know when you're sure they're gone. I don't want to let the local police and fire go in and get them shot."

"No problem, I'll let you know."

"Thanks." I hung up. Pulled up in a rundown industrial part of town, in the shadow of a long abandoned factory. Totally deserted at this time of night.

I picked up the pistol from the passenger footwell. This too belonged to the Carlucci in my boot. A Beretta, of course. Italian. One of the 90 series. 9mm calibre. 17 in the magazine, minus the ones he'd shot at me.

Little Carlucci was still banging about back there.

I got out. My arm hurt like a bitch, and blood roses still bloomed up on the bandage. Perhaps I should have wound it tighter. Still. I was in a rush. And it could have been worse. The bullet had barely grazed the bone. Could have shattered my shoulder.

Or hit me in the face.

Still. I needed to get to the hospital as soon as I'd finished up here.

I opened the boot and pointed the Beretta. Little Carlucci lay folded up in there like a foetus. At least he wasn't his brother. Big Carlucci never would have fitted. Not that I'd have been able to lift him, not with my busted left arm. I'd had enough trouble with the smaller brother.

Little Carlucci raised a hand, blinked at the barrel of his own Beretta. His face was a mess, all bloody where I'd hit him with the butt of the gun.

I transferred the Beretta to my left hand, even though I could barely hold it up. I needed my right hand to haul him out of the boot. He slumped to the road and cried out, clutching his leg where I'd shot him twenty minutes ago. It hadn't been a great shot. I'd been aiming for his heart. But in my defence I had been diving through the air at the same time.

The boot stank all coppery. Crap. There was a lot of blood. *A lot.* I must have hit his femoral artery.

That'll take ages to clean up.

I slammed the boot shut.

Little Carlucci didn't even bother trying to crawl away. Just rolled over and stared at me, blood pumping everywhere.

"You die for this," he said, his accent even thicker than normal. I think I'd bust his jaw. "Think my father will let you get away with this, eh?"

'Eh' to rhyme with *yeah*, not *yay*.

I shrugged. "He's in Italy. He won't be bothering me."

"What you want, eh?"

My bonus, of course. "Information," I said. "Where is

your MDMA lab?"

He spat blood. "I never tell you. Bastardo."

My Italian isn't great, but I got the gist. "Now that's just rude."

"You shot me!"

"You shot me, too."

Little Carlucci rested his head back against the road. The blood had drained from his face. Probably out his leg. "Who are you, eh?"

"I'm no one. Just some guy, you know."

"I don't know you."

"That's not what I meant." I pointed the Beretta at him again. "Last chance. Where is your lab?"

He couldn't speak. Just lay there, his breathing getting raspy.

I realised he was already as good as dead. He'd lost too much blood, and even if I'd tried to bandage the wound and call an ambulance he was likely to be dead before it arrived.

Not that I had any intention of calling an ambulance.

He lost consciousness soon after, bled out and died in the street.

"Ah shit," I said. There goes my bonus.

Oh well. He should have gone to prison like a good boy.

I waited for Dawn to phone back, which she did a few minutes later. "They're gone," she said.

"You sure?"

"Positive. The smoke's thick, but I've run the tape again – seven cars go in and seven came back out again."

"Thanks, I'll let Andrews know. Little Carlucci's dead."

"Okay, I'll close the file. Cause of death?"

"Blood loss from a gunshot wound to the leg."

"Did you find out the lab location?"

"No. The bastardo died on me."

"Never mind. Hopefully some of his people will start to talk now."

"We'll see." I hung up and called Chief Superintendent George Andrews, who answered on the second ring.

"Is it done, Steele?"

No greeting. As I said, my continued presence was probably starting to piss him off. He'd obviously been sat waiting for confirmation ever since my last call, two hours earlier, just before I'd gone into the drugs den.

"Yes. Both Carlucci brothers are dead."

Andrews sighed. "Okay then. So – we done?"

"Aye. You can send in fire and the armed response now. You shouldn't have any trouble."

He snorted, because all I'd done is bring him trouble. "I hope not."

"I've got the younger brother with me, though." I checked for a street name on my satnav. "I'm at the end of Upper Mill Road in the industrial estate. Could you send a van?"

Andrews didn't ask why I'd driven into the industrial estate with Little Carlucci's corpse, just grunted an okay and hung up without saying goodbye.

None of this was a surprise. The police have never known how to react around people like me. Licensed Vigilantes. Ghosts. Government hitmen. People who don't really exist, who really *are* above the law. A mixture of awe and trepidation, usually.

The ambulance arrived ten minutes later. No blue lights.

No point.

They zipped him up and loaded him in the back. I got

one of the paramedics to have a look at my wound and bandage it properly, but I was still told to go to the hospital.

The ambulance disappeared, and I returned to my Mercedes. Checked my left arm again. Blood was now blooming through the fresh bandages. I put the Beretta on the passenger seat and opened the purple gym bag. Whistled. Cash, and lots of it. Twenties, in thousand pound bundles. Too much to count now, but probably between forty and fifty grand.

And mine. I could keep all salvage from my contracts as long as they were completed. And this one was, finally, after two weeks of planning, two weeks relocation, two weeks being John Steele. Both Carluccis taken care of in an evening's raid.

I fancied an extended break. After I returned the car to HQ and debriefed I'd have a few months at home. Perhaps just take little local jobs. I'd been away for too long.

I put the Merc into drive and turned on the CD player. Beethoven's Moonlight Sonata, 1st movement. Slow and moody, perfect wind-down music. I pulled away, heading back into town through the deserted side streets.

And then I saw him, stumbling along the pavement and tripping over his own feet. The man who would complicate everything.

BROOKER

Jeremy Peters owed me fourteen grand.

Fourteen.

And the bastard refused to pay me.

He kept saying that he didn't have it or it was too much or he needed more time and generally took the piss.

I mean, was that *fair*? Did he think it was a goddamn *gift*?

Was I supposed to just leave him alone? Let him waltz off into the sunset with his ugly wife and my money?

Hardly.

He *would* pay me. I'd make sure of that.

So at about half seven we picked him up off the street.

You should have seen his face when I pulled up in my Porsche beside him.

"Get in," I said.

"G-Gary..." Jeremy stammered. His eyes flicked to the back seat, because I had Baz and Terry with me. "I... I have to get this home to my wife..."

A bottle of wine. I raised my eyebrows. "You can afford Pinot Grigio but can't afford to give me my money."

"But..."

"Get in."

My guys got out, in case he needed any persuading.

He swallowed. He got in. Terry and Baz squashed in either side of him and Baz took the wine.

"Where are you t-taking me?"

"Oh, not far," I said. "We just need a chat. Iron out a few things. Make sure we understand each other."

"Gary, look..."

"Er, Mr Brooker, I think. We're past the niceties now. We're talking business."

"I'm sorry, Mr Brooker..."

"Later. We'll talk later. When we get there."

"But..."

"You got somethin' wrong with you, Peters?" Baz growled, shutting Jeremy right up. "You keep yer mouth shut until Mr Brooker asks you somethin', right? Or do I need to shut yer mouth for yeh?"

Jeremy fell silent and turned pale, shrank in his seat as if he could disappear.

I smiled. That was more like it.

We took him to Stu's garage. The other mechanic had gone home for the weekend so we had the place to ourselves.

Stu was waiting for us. I drove up the ramp and he closed the roller doors behind us.

"Bring him." I got out. The guys dragged Jeremy after me.

"Right through here, boss," Stu said, and led the way into the garage proper, between shelves of tools and tyres.

He'd put up a chair in an empty corner, and we shoved Jeremy into it. He sat there shaking, drained of colour, his hands outstretched.

Baz had brought in the bottle of wine. "Do you have any glasses, Stu?"

"There are mugs in the kitchen."

"Sound." Baz disappeared off.

The rest of us just stared down at Jeremy, at his wide roaming eyes and the gross film of sweat on his upper lip.

We stood there in silence for five minutes. I was

hoping Jeremy would crack and say something, start grovelling, but he just sat there and shook.

Baz returned, expertly carrying three mugs and the bottle. He passed the mugs to me, Stu and Terry and kept the bottle for himself.

We drank Jeremy's wine in silence and stared at him.

The bastard still wouldn't say anything. Wouldn't apologise. Probably didn't think he'd even done anything wrong. I know the type; my wife is exactly the same.

"*Where's my money?*" I growled.

Jeremy stuttered. "I... Mr Brooker, I told you... fourteen thousand is too much..."

"You shouldn't have borrowed it if you couldn't pay it back."

"But I only borrowed six..."

"The rest is interest."

"... I've already paid you back *eight*..."

"More interest."

"But..."

"Are you arguing with me, Jeremy?"

He fell silent. Looked from me to Terry to Stu to Baz. Baz was tapping the bottle against his thigh, as if he might lunge forward any second and smash it over Jeremy's head.

And if he did I wouldn't be entirely surprised.

"Please... I just need more time..." Jeremy managed.

"Oh, I'll give you time. You can sit here and work out how you're going to pay me."

Jeremy blinked. "H-here?"

"Give me your phone."

He stared at me like I was talking Chinese or something. "My phone?"

"Yes Jeremy, your phone. I don't want your wife to

think you've gone missing and call the police."

He paused. "Please don't bring my wife into it any more…"

"Give me your phone!" And I threw the rest of my wine over him.

One of the guys laughed.

Jeremy wiped his face, dug his phone from inside his coat and handed it over.

"That's better." I scrolled through his contacts, found 'Home' and dialled.

Mrs Peters answered. "Hi Love."

And I said, "Afraid not. Guess again."

"Who… who is this?"

I grinned at the crack in her voice. "It's Gary Brooker. Remember me?"

A long pause. "What have you done to my husband?"

"Oh he's right here, he's fine. We're just having a little chat. I didn't want you to get worried when he didn't come home. The wine was very nice, by the way."

"I'll… I'll call the police…"

"Now that'd be a very bad idea. Like I said, we're only *talking.* And you know what would happen if the police started sniffing round. What we did to you before will be *nothing* to what happens if you start screwing with me, you crazy bitch. And Jeremy. You don't want anything to happen to him, do you? *Do you?*"

And she croaked, "No."

"Right then. But like I said, we're only talking. Tell her, Jeremy." I passed the phone to him.

He said into it, "Honey, I'm fine, honestly. No - we are just talking. I'll sort it out, trust me. Yes. I love you. He wants the phone back."

He handed it over and I said, "Don't do anything

stupid Mrs Peters. He'll be home in a few hours," and then hung up before the jabbering old cow could reply.

Jeremy said, "A few *hours?*"

"Yes. As I said, you need time to work out how to get me my money. I get that. So here it is. Your thinking time. Stu, tie his hands."

*

We tied his hands behind his back and to his ankles with some tubing. Slight strain on his muscles. He'd start feeling it in a while, and that was just fine.

Then Baz blindfolded and gagged him with a couple of rags. He didn't like that. Began shaking and sobbing. And that was fine too.

We left him like that for more than an hour. Terry went and got pizza, and then the four of us sat in the office eating and watching TV with the door ajar so we could keep an eye on Jeremy.

After a couple of hours we untied him. He was moaning and moping and all his muscles had clamped up so he fell off the chair. We left him lying stretched out for a few minutes and then removed the rags from his eyes and mouth.

"P-please…" he gasped. "My legs…"

"What? You want a massage?" Baz laughed.

"It hurts…"

"And it hurts me to have to do it," I said. "But you have my money and I want it back."

"We have some jewellery we could sell," Jeremy gasped. "Gold and silver… I'll… I'll sell my grandfather's watch…"

"Okay. That's better. How much is all that worth?"

"I'm not sure… must be a few thousand…"

I highly doubted that, but he was on the right track. "What else?"

"My car! I'll sell my car!"

"No point, Jeremy. It's a heap of shit. You wouldn't get two hundred quid for it, so you may as well keep it. I'm not unreasonable." I thought for a moment. "Is that it? Some jewellery and an old watch?"

"Er, I... I don't..."

"What about your TV? Computer?"

"We don't have a computer and you've seen our TV - it's about twenty years old!"

That was true. It was a huge brown box of a thing that still had tubes in it. "Well Jeremy, a few thousand pounds isn't *quite* fourteen grand, is it."

His face dropped. "I... But..."

"It's not enough."

"No, please... It's all we have!"

"We'll see about that." Actually, I'd be happy with an extra three or four thousand pounds. I'd leant Jeremy six, and he'd already paid back eight so I could end up doubling my money. Not great by any means, but I'd pushed Jeremy and his wife pretty hard already.

No harm in trying for a little more, though.

"Put him back in the chair."

The guys tied him up again, but left his legs free this time because it's not like we're psychopaths, and then I gagged him myself but left off the blindfold.

"You need to do better," I told him, "or else you're going to make us do things we don't want to do."

And Stu picked up a wrench and tapped it against his palm. *Tap tap tap.* Stu was good with that wrench.

"I guess you'd prefer your legs to stay as they are, in one piece?" I asked.

Stu tapped the wrench against Jeremy's shins.

Jeremy wriggled and sobbed and nearly shat himself.

"It'd be a shame," I continued, "to live out the rest of your life in a wheelchair for the sake of a few thousand pounds, don't you think?"

Jeremy tried to say something. But the gag.

"I think we'll leave you a bit longer to see what you can come up with," I said. "Just to make sure there's nothing you've... forgotten. Okay?"

I blindfolded him, and we left him there again and went back into Stu's office and watched a film and had a couple of beers.

And then evening had become night time. Jeremy sat with his head down as if he were asleep, but he snapped to attention when he heard us walk over. Began shaking.

I relieved him of his gag and before I'd even removed his blindfold he spat out, "There are medals!"

I stepped back. "Medals."

"My father's, from World War II." He dropped his head and sighed. "They're worth about thirteen thousand pounds. We had them valued a few years ago."

And boy my heart! It started racing, I can tell you!

I tried to keep a straight face. "You have medals worth thirteen thousand pounds?"

I knew the coy bastard was hoarding something!

"Yes," he said. "My father was awarded a Distinguised Service Order *and* a Distinguised Flying Cross."

"Jesus Christ. That's more like it!" I untied him and handed him back his phone. "Go home and get them. I'll send someone round to pick them up."

I still had contacts from my bailiff days, and knew I'd be able to sell them on with little trouble if Jeremy had what he said he did. "If I get thirteen grand for them we'll call it quits. How about that? You can keep your jewellery. Stu, open the doors."

Jeremy said nothing as I steered him down the ramp. I don't know why he looked so goddamn miserable - hadn't I just said we'd be quits?

I turned to Baz. "Baz, take Jeremy home and make sure he doesn't arse about."

Jeremy jumped as if he'd been electrocuted. "No - I'll get a taxi. I'm not having him anywhere near my house."

That surprised me. Not the fact that Jeremy didn't want Baz anywhere near him - Baz was nuts - but that Jeremy actually had the balls to *say* it.

"Fine," I said. "Fine. You go. I'll send Jermaine to pick them up. Do *not* mess him about, right?"

"R-right."

"Do not keep him waiting."

"I'll be as q-quick as I can."

"Good." I grinned. "Off you go then."

Baz gave Jeremy one of his ball-shrivelling smiles.

It almost made *me* shiver. I was surprised Jeremy didn't wet his pants.

"Go!"

Jeremy hobbled off into the night, and I watched after him with a warm glow in my chest.

And I thought, *score*.

Baz stood and watched him too, wearing a strange smile. "Gary, I want to kill that dickhead," he said.

I didn't answer, because I thought he probably meant it.

STEELE

My first thought was that the guy stumbling around was probably drunk. Friday night, past 11pm - not exactly unheard of. But then, where exactly had he *got* drunk? This place seemed an industrial wasteland. Hardly a likely place for a nightclub or bar, I'd have thought. Not that I'm an expert - I haven't had anything stronger than tea for years, and I'm pretty sure the clubbing scene has moved on quite a bit without me.

I slowed down, and the guy limped on and then tripped off the curb and fell across the road. I stamped the brake and stopped a few yards away, illuminating him in my headlights. He grabbed at his legs and began rubbing them furiously as if to relieve cramp.

I sighed. All I wanted to do was go to the hospital and get some stitches and pain relief and then get the hell out of Carlucci territory. I could have probably driven around him (and I admit it crossed my mind). Carjackings come in many forms, and this could be one of them.

Thief sees nice car, thinks he'd like to take it on a joy ride. First step: get the car to stop. Many ways to do this. At traffic lights and junctions is the most usual, when the car is already stationary and the job is done. Running out into the road is another. *Falling* into the road is a bit more elaborate, I admit, but it kind of leads into the next step:

Get the driver out of the car.

Even with the popularity of the *Grand Theft Auto* video games, many people don't lock their doors and a thief can get in the passenger seat and 'encourage' the driver out with a knife. Or a gun.

I guess it's easier if the driver gets out on their own accord, so thieves put paper on rear windows, forcing the driver to get out and remove it. Pretending to be ill or injured could work just as well. Guy falls into road, stopping car (step one), and driver gets out to see if he's okay (step two).

Many people wouldn't bother turning off the engine and removing the key, making step three (steal the car) fairly straightforward. Thief, and maybe some friends, appear, jump in and drive off. Perhaps after overpowering the driver. Or knocking them unconscious.

I put on the handbrake. Looked around. Pretty sure the guy in the road didn't have any friends hanging round. But perhaps he had a knife instead, and was just waiting for me to go over and see if he was alright.

He sat up and looked over at my Merc. Raised his hands, maybe against my headlights, maybe in apology.

Maybe asking for help.

Fine. I turned off the engine and the headlights. Beethoven's Moonlight Sonata cut out mid-3rd movement as the CD player powered down. I winced as I pulled my jacket on to hide my bandaged arm. Took the key. Climbed slowly out, on guard for any signs of approaching carjackers. Nothing. I shut the door. Locked it. Put the key in my pocket.

If the guy planned to carjack me he was going to get a shock. I walked over.

He didn't look like a carjacker. He must have been about sixty. Hair greying and thin. He climbed warily to his feet, trembling all over, and I fancied not just from the cold because sweat dotted his forehead and upper lip.

He was as pale as a ghost, and so we stood there looking at each other, two ghosts in the moonlight.

"Are you okay?" I asked. Dumb question. I took another look round, just to make sure no one was creeping up on me.

"Do you have any phone signal?" he asked. Whimpered it, actually. "It was fine in… but... I need to get through to my wife and it keeps cutting off…"

I downgraded him from carjacker to potential phone thief. If I handed him my phone would he try to run off with it on his cramping legs?

I doubted it.

So I handed him my phone. He thanked me, and didn't try to run off with it. Fumbled in a number and put the phone to his ear. Stuttered, "Hi Love, it's me. No, I'm okay, I couldn't get through on my mobile… No, they didn't really hurt me, they just…" He looked at me, looked at the ground and lowered his voice. "They were just trying to scare me. You didn't call the police, did you? Good. Look, I'm going to call a taxi - would you… would you look out my father's medals for me. *Yes*, Love. They're in a box in the wardrobe. No, please don't argue, just get them for me, okay? I'll be half an hour. Bye, I love you." He hung up. Looked back at me. "Could I call a taxi? My wife doesn't drive…"

"Of course." Then, "Who tried to scare you?"

He looked dumbly at my phone. "Oh, just…some guys. Do… do you have a number for a taxi place?"

"No. I'm not from around here."

"Oh."

He said nothing else, just stared down at my phone as if the number for a taxi firm might miraculously appear on the screen.

Oh great. Just what I needed. "Do you need to get back into town?"

"Yes, but I…"

"Do you want a lift?"

He blinked. "What?"

"Do you want a lift home?"

It was a simple question, but my kindness had surprised him. He'd got himself into trouble. Physically, he looked unhurt apart from his cramping legs. But someone, or a few someones, had scared him witless.

"I... I..." he garbled.

He wanted a lift home, but I looked like a serial killer. I *was* a serial killer, technically. But I'd probably keep that to myself.

I remembered the Beretta in the passenger footwell. He'd freak if he saw it. Telling him I only killed bad guys wouldn't make him feel any better, I imagined.

So I took my phone back off him and returned to my car, round the bonnet, unlocked and opened the passenger door. Unzipped the purple gym bag and hid the gun inside, out of his view. And then I noticed in the footwell the dummy watch that had doubled as a detonator, and although he wouldn't know what it was I thought I better hide that in there too. Then I took the gym bag out and put it on the back seat. Left the passenger door open.

"You coming?" I asked him.

I think he clocked that my car was a Merc, and that may have swayed him.

He limped over. "Thank you so much. I don't live far..."

"No worries. I have to head back into town anyway." To go to the bleeding hospital.

I circled round and got behind the wheel.

He got in beside me. "Nice car." A little envious.

"Thanks." I half thought you might be planning to steal it. "Give me your postcode and I'll satnav it. That'll be easier."

He did so. Shut the door. Shivered whilst I programmed it in. "Thanks for this. I'm Jeremy Peters."

"Steele. John Steele." I didn't mean to do a James Bond impression, it just came out.

"It's not too much out of your way, is it?"

The satnav finished calculating, and yes, it was very much out of my way. "Not at all." I started the car and pulled away.

"You live in town?"

"No. I'm staying in a Travelodge. I'm only here on business."

"Ah. You're Scottish?"

"Aye." Hence the Scottish accent. "You want to tell me what happened to you, Jeremy?"

"W-what do you mean?"

"I mean, how did you end up stranded out here? It's nearly midnight."

"I… it's nothing."

"Doesn't look like nothing."

"No, it's... I'm fine, honestly."

He was not fine, honestly. He was a wreck. But he obviously didn't want to talk about it, so we drove in silence. I ran the conversation Jeremy had had with his wife through my mind. Well, his part of it, which was the only side I could hear.

No, they didn't really hurt me...

He'd said that almost at the beginning. So the first thing his wife must have asked him was, *Are you hurt?*

Are you okay? Perhaps even, *Did they hurt you?*

And he'd replied, *No, they didn't really hurt me.*

So she must have known something had happened, that he was in trouble, or she wouldn't have asked. She must have known Jeremy had been with people who might hurt him.

And it wasn't *He didn't really hurt me*, it was *They didn't really hurt me.*

So it wasn't just one guy, it was at least two. Maybe more.

You didn't call the police, did you? Good.

That was the most worrying thing. Jeremy had obviously been frightened for his own safety, but he didn't want the police involved. He'd been worried his wife might call them, I guess because he thought that would make things worse.

You didn't call the police, did you?

Presumably she'd said no, because the next thing he'd said was, *Good.*

And why wouldn't his wife have called the police if she thought Jeremy was in danger? Maybe because she had been warned of the consequences.

Would you look out my father's medals for me… No, please don't argue…

That was intriguing. Jeremy wanted his father's medals for something, and I had a feeling it wasn't just to clean them. It must have been because of the guys who had frightened him - did they want the medals for themselves? Had they been intimidating him into handing them over like some fascist antique dealers or something?

No, please don't argue…

Jeremy's wife hadn't wanted to look out the medals -

she'd argued about it. But Jeremy had insisted.

So who were the guys? Who had Jeremy got himself in trouble with?

I began to find out fifteen minutes later when I pulled up outside his house.

*

There was a white van parked across the street facing us with its headlights glaring.

Jeremy saw it and blanched.

"What's wrong?"

"He's sent... Oh, it doesn't matter. What do I owe you?"

"Nothing."

"Well, thanks very much for the lift, John. I appreciate it." Jeremy got out and made his way across the drive giving the white van a long look.

He's sent... Two words. But I got a lot from them. Whoever the guys were, the ones who were scaring him out of his father's medals, there was a bossman out there somewhere, and the rest of the guys were just his goons.

Like the guy in the white van. I *assumed* it was a guy. Not because women couldn't be tough (some of the women I've come across could pound me to a pulp), but because big bossmen operating beneath the police radar don't often see women as likely adversaries.

Except the Chinese. I've seen *Rush Hour.*

So the guy in the white van. Just another goon. A nobody, cresting on the reputation of his boss.

I don't like goons.

Jeremy was half way across his drive when the driver's door of the white van opened. A huge black guy got out, flopped from the cabin to the pavement like a blob. He was almost the size of a sumo wrestler, and sumo wrestler types make me laugh because of their little heads. "I'm watching you, Peters," said the blob.

Jeremy stopped and turned, hunched his head like a turtle. "I'm just getting them..."

"Well go on then, what are you waiting for?"

God what an arsehole.

"I'm..."

"Hurry up, Peters, Mr Brooker doesn't like to be kept waiting."

And hey presto, the big bossman had a name.

It took Jeremy about ten seconds to get his house key steady and in the lock. He disappeared inside and shut the front door behind him.

The blob was chuckling to himself and shaking his head.

Oh Jesus. I thought about getting out. Nothing to fear from a sumo wrestler type as long as they don't fall on you. Too slow. They move like jelly. And yes, they have enough protection round the middle but remember their little heads. Pop. And once they're down they don't get up easily.

He had left the key in and the engine running. I had a huge irrational urge to steal his van and crash it somewhere.

But I stayed in my car, because I'd just blown up a drugs den and been shot in the arm and I was almost done, running on empty, and I doubted my adrenaline would sustain another confrontation.

Although a part of me wanted to, a large part.

The blob noticed I hadn't driven off and turned and stared at my Merc. I could see his brain working. First he frowned, and then he winced against the headlights and peered closer. And then he said, "That's not a taxi."

I swear he said it out loud. Probably found thinking difficult.

I put my headlights on full-beam. Immature, I know. He shielded his eyes as if from a bomb blast and took a couple of steps back. "What the hell, man?"

I stopped full-beaming him. Perhaps he'd think it was an accident.

He didn't look in the forgiving mood, and for one moment I thought he was going to come right over to my car.

But then Jeremy came back outside. He held an A4 envelope, and brandished it. "Here."

The blob turned his attention to Jeremy. Took the envelope. "Bout time." Opened it, and pulled out an enamelled white cross by the ribbon.

My stomach lurched. Jesus Christ, it was a Distinguished Service Order. They didn't give out those for nothing.

The blob returned the DSO and started rummaging around some more. There must have been other medals in there too, but he didn't pull anything else out. Just said, "This lot's worth *thirteen grand?*"

My stomach again, like I was on a rollercoaster.

"T-that's what I was told," Jeremy stuttered. "We had them professionally valued..."

Thirteen thousand pounds?

Jeremy's father must have been a highly decorated officer. There must have been more than the DSO in there - perhaps an award for gallantry too, or an Albert Medal Group or a Military Cross with two bars, something like that.

And Jeremy was just *handing them over?*

"I hope you're right, Peters," The blob said, unconvinced, "because if Mr Brooker discovers you've been lying to him..."

"I haven't, I swear."

I wanted to put a stop to this. I wanted to get out the car and take the medals back and take the blob down.

Ordinarily I would have done so without another thought.

But ordinarily I felt better than this.

The blob got back in his van, medals in hand. Jeremy stood on the drive and watched the envelope disappear inside the cabin, and then put his head down.

I took off my seatbelt and turned off the ignition.

Oh Jesus.

I hesitated.

Don't, Steele.

The van pulled away. I watched it go.

You can't get involved, I told myself. You have to get out of town. If the Carluccis catch up with you in this state you're *dead*.

I couldn't really argue with that. So I let the van drive off.

Shit.

Mrs Peters appeared at my driver's door, and I wound down my window. "Jeremy said you gave him a lift home," she said. "I just wanted to say thank you. That was very kind." She'd come out without a coat and shivered.

"No problem at all." I smiled at her. She tried to smile back, but I think she'd forgotten how. Her face was thin and gaunt and she had bags like pockets under her eyes. "Who was that guy in the van?"

"He…" She sighed. "Oh, no one."

"He works for Mr Brooker?"

She'd turned back towards the house but my words stopped her. "You know Gary?"

And suddenly the big bossman had a full name. Gary Brooker. I could picture him. A bald-headed builder-type in T-shirt and jeans, holding a can of beer in one hand and a lit fag in the other.

"Not personally." Not yet. "Why did your husband hand over those medals?" I couldn't help myself, I had to ask.

Mrs Peters pursed her lips. "He owed Gary money."

Ah. Of course.

"Jeremy only borrowed six thousand," she continued. "And we've already paid Gary back eight."

I blinked. "You borrowed six and you've already paid back eight?"

"Yes. And now he wants another *fourteen thousand.* Hence the medals. He said he'll leave us alone if Jeremy hands them over."

Gary Brooker was a loan shark, then. Happy to lend you money as long as you're happy to pay back five times as much in the long run.

Jeremy came over then and put an arm around his wife's shoulder. "It's over, love."

She tried a smile, but it didn't reach her eyes. "We've thought that before."

He didn't answer, just turned to me and said, "Thank you again, John, for the lift. I was really in a pickle..."

I said, "Do they threaten you?"

Jeremy paused. "I'm sorry?"

I thought about the blob coming here and how Jeremy had looked when he'd seen him. *Oh no... He's sent...*

"Do they threaten you?" I asked again. "Gary and his

guys?"

They looked at each other without say anything.

So that would be a yes.

Jeremy cleared his throat. "Well, goodbye," he said, and took his wife firmly by the hand.

She gave me a small, pained smile and then disappeared back up the drive with her husband.

I wound up the window and pulled off, feeling anger bubble beneath my skin. I clenched my teeth and my right hand tightened on the steering wheel.

Gary Brooker and his goons had frightened the Peters so much Jeremy was prepared to give away what must have been a treasured family heirloom.

I sighed. Nothing I could do. The Carluccis knew what I looked like and knew what car I drove, and I was exhausted and shot in the arm.

But then I saw the white van again.

It was parked up in a road on my right, and I could see the blob by the glow of a lamp post. He was on his phone, no doubt telling this Gary Brooker that he had the medals and was on his way. That everything was fine and dandy.

I thought of how I would feel if someone tried to steal my own father's medals. He hadn't won anything quite so valuable, but still. I'd be pretty furious, I reckon.

The difference, of course, was that Jeremy hadn't won any of his own. Perhaps if he had this Gary Brooker would never have picked on him.

But I had.

I'd won the Military Cross and Iraq Medal. I had nothing to fear from this lowlife small-time crook.

I shouldn't get involved.

But still.

I wanted to.

So I hung back and waited for the white van to carry on its journey, and when it did I followed him. I couldn't help it.

BROOKER

Jermaine called me just as I pulled up outside the one-room office space I rented.

"I'm on my way, boss," he said.

"You've got the medals?"

"Yes. There's five of 'em." He rummaged about in what sounded like a paper bag. "I don't know how these are supposed to be worth thirteen grand, though."

"But you don't really know anything about medals."

"No, boss."

And neither did I. I'd have to call someone who did. "Did Jeremy give you any trouble?"

"No. No trouble. He didn't even plead any more. Just handed them over."

"That's good." Holding him at Stu's garage had been a very worthwhile trick. Risky, perhaps, but worth it. I mean, *thirteen grand!* Goddamn. I saw myself making use of Stu's garage quite often. "Bring them over, Jermaine. I'll see you in a bit."

"Okay, boss. Bye." He hung up.

I turned to Baz, who blew on his hands to try and ward off the incoming winter cold. "Jay's got them," I said.

Baz nodded.

I'd known the mad bastard since primary school and still didn't have the foggiest idea what he was thinking. His face didn't seem to register emotion. Baz was like a goddamn robot. Anything could be going on behind those eyes.

"Gary," he said, "What if they're not worth what Jeremy says they're worth?"

"They will be."

"Yes, but if they're not. We gonna kill him?"

I felt a twitch in my gut. "No, Baz. We're not going to kill anyone." I got out of my Porsche and Baz followed.

"Even if he's lied to us?"

"He won't have lied." I unlocked the office door, stepped in and turned off the alarm.

Baz didn't say anything, just followed me in and up the stairs, into the room I rented above the launderette.

I turned on the light. So cold I could almost see my breath.

Fifteen minutes later Jermaine arrived. He carried a large brown envelope and handed it to me. "There we go, boss."

My heart began bumbling. I walked over to my desk and opened the envelope. Took out a white cross I imagined was made from ivory and set it carefully on the table. Then a bulky silver cross, not half as impressive as the other one. A tarnished bronze star and two silver coins.

And those five medals were supposedly worth thirteen thousand pounds.

"Is that it?" Baz asked.

I checked the envelope again, even though it was obviously empty just by the weight. "Yes. This is the lot."

"I told you, Gary. Jeremy was taking the piss."

"We'll see."

I'd worked as a bailiff for a short time a few years back, and was still in contact with an independent valuer who dealt in jewellery and antiques. It was Friday night, but it was also nearly 11:15pm, and so I was grateful when he answered.

"Yes?"

"Hi. It's Gary Brooker."

A pause, then: "Gary. Haven't heard from you in a while."

"Sorry to call you so late," I said, "but I think I have something you might like."

"And what's that?"

"Some medals from World War II. I've been told I should get thirteen thousand for them."

"How many medals?"

"Five."

"Five?" The dealer pondered. "You'll have to have something special for that valuation. What are they?"

"I... don't really know. I'll text you through some pictures if that's okay?"

"Absolutely."

"Okay. One moment." I hung up, snapped the five medals with the camera on my phone and sent them over.

The dealer phoned back about thirty seconds later. "You were told right," he said. "They're in good condition. I can see the lot going for between twelve and thirteen thousand at auction."

I exhaled. Broke out into a smile.

"The white cross is the Distinguished Service Order. The silver one is the Distinguished Flying Cross. Very unusual to have both. The smaller copper star is the 1939 to 45 star and the two silver coins are the British War Medal and the Defence Medal. I'll need to inspect them in person, but as I said, they look in good condition."

"That's brilliant, thank you."

"If you can bring them over first thing tomorrow, I'll make some calls."

We hung up.

Bloody brilliant! What a scoop!

"He was telling the truth?" Baz asked. "*Thirteen grand?*" He sounded disappointed.

"Yes! I told you he was." I circled my desk and opened the top drawer. Pulled out the logbook where I keep all my clients' information. It went back a few years now, and I got a kick every time I flicked the pages and realized how much of it I'd filled.

Jeremy's name first appeared on 3rd March 2014. Initial loan of £6,000. His name appeared four more times. Twice in June and once in July and October. His repayments. Two for £2,000 in June, one for £2,600 in July. He'd taken a bit of persuading before he'd coughed up last month's £1,500.

Total repayment so far: £8,100 on a six grand loan.

And now the medals.

Another ten grand for me *at least*, after my dealer's commission.

On a new line I wrote *14th November 2014, Jeremy Peters, repayment of goods (medals) to the value of £13,000 approx.*

And then in block capitals: COMPLETED.

I put the medals back in the envelope, turned to the guys and grinned. "Good score, boys."

I had a warm feeling in my stomach, and thought it would last a pretty long time.

STEELE

Following someone without them noticing isn't easy, especially if there's not much traffic on the road. It's much easier if you have a friend in another car helping, because after a while you can turn off and let them take over. No one ever suspects a second car.

Not that I needed it whilst following the blob in his white van.

Vans stand out. It's not easy to lose sight of them, even in the dark, given the fact that they tower over everything. And he had no rear-view mirror, obviously, having no back window. So I only had to worry about being spotted in his wing mirrors, and how would he recognise a pair of headlights anyway? So I hung back a bit, following at a safe distance.

The van pulled up outside a launderette at the end of a terraced row of shops, and I pulled in further back behind another parked car and turned off my lights and engine.

Houses to my right. A large Tesco behind me.

There was a Porsche already outside the launderette.

The blob got out with the brown envelope. He glanced into the Porsche, then headed to a door in the wall beside the launderette, pushed it open and disappeared inside.

The launderette was dark, like the rest of the row. But the window above it was lit up.

Intriguing. Brooker rented a room above a launderette. Why? To keep business deals away from his home, presumably. But I'd never heard of a loan shark who conducted himself out of a makeshift office before. Usually they'd just visit their victims' houses.

Then again, I'd never heard of a loan shark hiring guys as muscle.

I thought about joining them. Go in and give Brooker and the blob and whoever else he had up there a taste of their own medicine. I would make Brooker cry. Then maybe push the blob down the stairs or something.

But that would be stupid. First, I didn't have a clue how many of them were up there. That wouldn't normally stop me, but I wasn't exactly at full strength. I only had one working arm. And, of course, I couldn't just go in and *shoot* them – being a licensed vigilante doesn't mean I can go round killing people randomly – that would be no kind of justice.

And also, I didn't want them linking me with Jeremy. It was possible that the blob might recognise me. Very unlikely – he'd certainly seen my Merc outside Jeremy's house, but it was dark and I'd stayed behind the wheel, so all he'd seen of me was a silhouette.

Still. Better to err on the side of caution. If I went in and the blob *did* recognise me they might think Jeremy had set them up. I didn't want that. It needed to look like a random robbery. A coincidence. And I knew exactly what to do.

I twisted in my seat and reached for the purple gym bag in the back. Retrieved the Beretta from inside and put it in my right jacket pocket. Not because I was planning on killing anyone, but... just in case.

A few minutes later the door opened again. Three men came out onto the street, and they were all smiling. One was the blob. Brooker was one of the other two, and I knew which one because he held the envelope. I was wrong about him looking like a thug. He wore a grey suit with a white open-necked shirt, like he thought he was one of the mafia or something. I put him around forty, with a clean-shaven, suntanned face and cropped black hair. I watched him stash the envelope inside his jacket.

The other guy was the thug. Muscle. Bald. Looked like a rugby player. Baldy wore a tight T-shirt tucked into his jeans even though it was mid November, showing off his muscles. No gun, unless he had one in his shoe, which I doubted.

The blob got back in his van, raised a hand and drove off.

Brooker went back inside, presumably to set an alarm, then he reappeared and locked the door behind him. He clapped Baldy on the back and said something with his face all lit up like a firework display.

Baldy smiled back, but there was something wrong with it, something cold and distant and... *not all there*.

The two of them got in the Porsche. Brooker was driving. He pulled away and I followed at a distance.

I thought over the three steps carjackers use to steal a car. I didn't want to steal the Porsche, so I was only interested in steps one and two.

Stop the car.

Get the driver out of it.

And then rob the hell out of him.

I wasn't going to put a sheet of paper on the back window, or jack him at a junction, or fall into the road like Jeremy had done.

I had a better idea. And when he stopped at a set of traffic lights, I didn't.

I didn't stop in time.

BROOKER

"I can't believe he actually had them," Baz said. "Jesus Mary."

"Ah, I knew the greedy bugger had something stashed away somewhere."

I knew no such thing. I thought I would make a few grand extra maybe, but *goddamn!* He actually handed over his father's medals – and they were worth nearly thirteen thousand pounds!

"You're a genius, Gary."

I thought maybe Baz was right, and I relaxed in the seat of my Porsche and drove away with a smile on my face. Not the biggest score of my career by any means, but it was still a good one. I hadn't even had to have them seriously roughed up. No hospital visits, and my guys were quite sure no trips to the police. So all in all a great goddamn success.

And now I could start applying more pressure to Kevin West, that weird loner. He definitely had money, I could tell by all the fancy shit he had in his house.

I stopped at a red light. My heart still hadn't settled down and my blood was thrumming and everything was intense like that one time I'd tried coke as a teenager.

And then some arsehole smashed straight into the back of me, into my goddamn *Porsche*. It was so loud, like the inside of my head had broken.

Baz flew forward and head butted the dash because the idiot wasn't wearing his seatbelt.

I looked into the rear-view mirror and saw this ginger dickhead staring back at me with his hand over his mouth.

I hate gingers. They make me so goddamn mad. I

couldn't even bare to watch Game of Thrones.

The light turned green and I stamped on the accelerator so my whole Porsche squealed and pulled over to the side of the road.

The ginger arsehole followed, pulling in behind me, and before I'd even straightened up me and Baz were getting out and I slammed my door and I hate goddamn gingers and I said, "What the hell are you doing?"

He got out and stood there probably crapping himself. "I'm so sorry..." he said, and he was also a goddamn Scot! If there's one thing I hate more than gingers it's goddamn *Scottish* gingers because the ungrateful bastards had that referendum, and so I started shouting again, walked up to him and suddenly I...

Ugh

    aw SHIT

STEELE

Brooker pulled over, revving the engine and making the Porsche scream like a cheap prostitute. I pulled in behind him and got out with one hand covering my mouth. Hoping I looked shocked. Didn't want him knowing I'd shunted him on purpose.

Baldy and Brooker both got out, both red faced, both looking ready to kick out my teeth.

"I'm so sorry..." I started, and for some reason this set him off. Brooker lost it, yelling his head off, and he strolled up to me with his arms out, so I punched him in the face. Hard.

He fell back against his open driver's door and sat there in the road, stunned, holding his busted nose.

I turned towards Baldy, my hand going to my pocket just in case he did have a gun hidden somewhere, but he just lumbered round the front of the car towards me like a bull. No gun, which was good. I'd already got shot once tonight, and that was enough. I didn't bother drawing my Beretta. Bad manners.

I ran to meet him, even though he outweighed me. I'm quick. I ducked aside, ramming my knee into his mid section. His own momentum provided most of the power. He went over. I kicked his head.

Brooker looked up from Baldy to me. His lips curled. "You're a dead man."

"I am so scared."

"You have no idea who I am..."

"You're an arsehole."

"... or what I'm capable of..."

"Ditto. Now give me your phone and wallet."

He just stared at me, so I kicked him in the ribs. Hard.

He wailed like a baby.

"*Phone. Wallet. Now,*" I repeated.

His mouth fell half open, as if he couldn't quite believe he was being robbed by some pasty-faced ginger Scotsman. But he managed to extract his wallet and phone and handed them to me.

I put them in my jacket. Glanced at Baldy to make sure he wasn't coming round, but he was still out cold and dribbling on the road.

"Now empty your coat. Turn out the pockets. Don't make me search you." I kicked Brooker again but with less force, this time in the arse.

He howled. His eyes grew wide. "Please... I have nothing else..."

Is that what Jeremy said to you, eh? How does it feel, you bastard? "Empty your coat!"

He might have liked to think he was tough, but basic training in the army would have had him crying for his mother. He took out the brown envelope with a shaking hand and handed it to me. I pretended to look confused, then put that in my jacket too.

"That it?"

He nodded. Blood came trickling out his nose. He looked bloody pathetic.

The Porsche's driver's door was still open. I reached in and took the keys and then threw them into the night, just in case he decided to come after me.

He didn't like that, and made a sad mewing sound.

Then I got back in my Merc and drove away.

*

It may seem hard to believe seeing as I kill people for a living, but I don't have mental problems.

I never have, unless you count the chronic case of insomnia during my teens. I don't have a primal need to kill. I don't get the shakes like a junky if I go too long between contracts. I don't torture animals or go to illegal bare-knuckle boxing matches or start bar fights.

I'm not a fan of boxing or the Ultimate Fighting Championship, and although I got into one or two scrapes in school I always avoided them if I could.

But there are times when certain people *do* deserve a punch on the nose.

Or sometimes more than that.

I like action movies, but who doesn't?

When I was sixteen I joined the army, but not because I wanted to fight. We had those types, of course. And I wasn't a partizan nationalist either – nationalism is just fascism dressed up in patriot clothes - though I met my fair share of those too. We had cadets who were there because they had nothing better to do, or who were following in their father's footsteps. And then there were the ones who signed up because they wanted to kill someone. Not many, but they were there. This one guy in our squadron – we called him Mad Jim behind his back – he frightened the hell out of me. I could never shake the feeling he might go psycho one night and knife me in my sleep. That didn't do much for my insomnia, I can tell you.

I didn't join the army because I wanted to kill people. I joined because I wanted to protect them. And that's why I do what I do to this day.

Most of the time killing is wrong.

But sometimes it's not.

There are only two instances where it is acceptable to kill: in defence of the self, and in defence of the innocent. And that's all I ever do.

Being a licensed vigilante mostly entails the latter: killing bad people to save innocent ones. Killing in self-defence just comes with the territory.

But I don't kill people if I can help it.

I know. Why didn't I become a newspaper salesman? Or a baker? Then I wouldn't have to kill anyone at all. But that's not how it worked out for me. I don't think I had much say in the matter. The armed forces was in my blood, and I always knew I'd follow in my father's footsteps.

I remember the first time I killed like it happened this morning. It was December 1995, I was seventeen, and I was in Bosnia with the Fourth Mechanised Infantry Brigade. We called ourselves The Black Rats. The Bosnia War was almost done. Yugoslavia was broken up, NATO had intervened after the Serbian massacres, the Dayton Peace Agreement had been signed and Bosnia and Herzegovina had their independence.

The Black Rats were there with NATO's Implementation Force under Major-General Mike Jackson, tasked with keeping the peace and assisting the humanitarian crisis.

We were stationed in Banja Luka, the second city after Sarajevo. All sixteen of the city's mosques had been destroyed, and my battalion was near the rubble of Ferhat Pasha when we were attacked by a group of Serb nationalists.

Some say such events happen in a blur, but that's not how it was for me, not that day. I remember everything - the glare of the sun, the weight of my gun, the shouts of the dishevelled Serbian men as they popped out of the rubble.

Why do they shout? I never understood that. Perhaps if they hadn't the extra split second of surprise would have counted. I would have been shot and killed on the dusty street, I wouldn't be here today and the Carlucci brothers would still be pedalling their E.

But anyway. Call it a primeval thing. They yelled then sprang out and raised their weapons, I think one of them even managed to get off a shot, not that it did him any good.

One of them pointed his gun straight at me, and I shot him three times through the chest without even thinking about it.

The thinking about it would come later.

He fell down dead on his back, and I remember how there hadn't been as much blood as I'd expected, not like in the movies.

I can still remember his face. I see it sometimes, but not as often as I once did. For days after, maybe even weeks, I saw his face every time I closed my eyes, and on the odd occasion I did manage to sleep I dreamed of him.

I'd suffered from sleep-onset insomnia ever since my father died, and one of the most striking things I can remember from my teenage years is lying in the dark at four in the morning, saying *please sleep* to myself over and over. I never mentioned it in the psyche tests, of course. Besides, it got a little better as I neared adulthood, and there were even times when I fell asleep before midnight came around. But killing that Serbian boy made it worse than it had ever been.

He couldn't have been more than fifteen or sixteen. He was just a child, like me. And I'd killed him.

I knew if I hadn't killed him he'd have killed me. But

the *guilt*. It ate me up inside like acid, and I didn't sleep at all for three days straight, and only an hour or two on a good night after that.

That is, up until my second kill.

That's when the guilt stopped.

BROOKER

He knocked out Baz like some goddamn ginger ninja and robbed me.

I sat there and watched him reverse out the arse of my Porsche, feeling like I'd been struck by lightning. He drove a *Mercedes* for Christ's sake, and there was hardly a scratch on it. That pissed me off even more. How the hell could that ginger hillbilly afford a *Mercedes*?

I saw his number plate and started a little. "Baz! Give me a pen!"

Baz groaned and said, "Foggin ay."

"Baz!" I recited the number plate over and over as the Mercedes drove away, fumbled Baz's phone out of his front pocket and after a few seconds of fiddling turned on the goddamn voice recorder. I repeated the number plate into it a couple of times and then said, "A black Mercedes!" and, "He was a goddamn ginger!"

"Are you okay, Gary?" Baz had come round. He wiped the drool from the corner of his mouth and climbed to his knees.

"I... I don't know..." I stopped the recording and set the phone on the road. Dabbed my nose and my hand came back all red and sticky.

"Jesus," said Baz. "What happened?"

"That guy stole the medals. And my wallet and phone."

"H-he took the medals? He robbed yeh?"

"Yes." My goddamn nose wouldn't stop bleeding. It felt like a bakewell tart squashed there on my face. When I moved my side hurt, and when I didn't move my side hurt. "He had a knife..."

"He had a knife? I never saw..."

"That's because you'd gone and got yourself knocked out, Barry. What do I pay you for?"

Baz looked down at the road. "I'm sorry, Gary. He, I mean... *urgh,* I can't feel my head. Is it still there?"

I'm going to kill that ginger, I told myself. I'm going to find him and kill him. No one steals from me. He punches me in the face for no reason and kicks me when I'm down? No sir.

I tried to stand up but my legs wouldn't hold me. Baz had lain back down on the road. "Baz? Are you okay?"

"I just need a few minutes." He clutched his head with his hands.

"I'm going to call Jermaine." My nose had mushroomed so much I sounded like a flight controller. I used Baz's phone but it rang through to voicemail. "Goddammit, he's not answering."

"Try Terry."

"I don't want Terry, he won't know what to do. Have you got Royce's number in here?"

"No. I don't like Royce. Or Johnson. They're both dicks."

Royce and Johnson had both recently been sacked from their jobs as doormen at one of the clubs in town. Apparently they'd got a bit rough with one of the customers, who'd pressed charges. They'd only done one job for me so far, but were more professional than my other guys if I'm honest. "You just need time to get to know them."

"I don't like them. They wear suits."

"So do I."

"You're the boss."

In the end I had to call Terry. A couple of cars went past whilst we were waiting, but by that time me and Baz had managed to scramble onto the pavement and sat against a wall. My nose stopped bleeding, and Baz stopped feeling his head as if unsure what it was.

Terry turned up wearing what looked suspiciously like his goddamn pyjamas. But he'd brought us beer and paracetamol, so he could have turned up in his wife's dress for all I cared. "Jesus, boss – what happened to you?"

I told him about the ginger robbing me at knifepoint between pill popping and swigs of beer. The combination made my head light as a balloon. Terry went hunting for my Porsche keys without even having to be asked. As he did so I played the recording I'd made and jotted down the Mercedes's registration on an empty McDonald's bag from the footwell of Terry's car.

How we were going to find the Mercedes and the ginger ninja I had no idea.

Terry found my car keys a way down the road. That made my night.

And then Jermaine called Baz's phone.

I answered. "Jermaine, it's me."

"Sorry Baz, I was in the shower. B-Baz? You sound different. All nasally..."

"It's not Baz, it's Gary."

"Who?"

"*Gary Brooker.*" I said it as slowly and clearly as I could.

Jermaine gasped. "Boss, you sound terrible."

"I've been robbed, Jay."

Another gasp. "*Robbed?*"

I told him about the ginger robbing me at knifepoint. By this time I almost believed the bit about the knife myself. "I have the registration here – do you have a pen?"

"Yes, but wait – did you say he drove a Mercedes? A black Mercedes?"

"Yes, why?"

"The... the kind with a big front grille and the badge sticking up off the bonnet, what's it called?"

Goddamn my heart almost stopped. "*The bonnet ornament...* How did you know?"

"He dropped Jeremy home!"

My insides began to buzz. "Wait... are you saying that Jeremy was taken home in a black Mercedes?"

"Yes! With a big front grille and a what's-it-called... bonnet ornament."

"He didn't get a taxi?"

"No, it wasn't a taxi."

"Did you see the ginger guy? Was he driving?"

"No, it was dark – but how many more of those black Mercedes are out driving round town at this time of night?"

And I thought, just the one. Just the one belonging to the ginger ninja.

The one that had dropped Jeremy home.

"Goddamn," I said. Jeremy Peters had set us up.

*

I drove Baz to Jeremy's house. It was past midnight by the time we got there. Parked right across his drive. We both got out and hurried to his door. Baz looked around, but there was no one about. Jeremy's neighbours couldn't see us from this angle even if they peered out between their curtains, and there was nothing but trees separating the main road overlooking the front of the house.

I rang the bell twice. Whilst we waited Baz drummed

his fingers against his thighs. He had that cold half smile on his face again.

Jeremy answered the door. He was still dressed.

He wasn't happy to see us.

I pushed him backwards and he fell against the stairs. We followed him in and Baz shut the front door.

"Steady on…" Jeremy started. "Gary, what…"

I punched him in the face. It felt glorious, like I'd flicked a switch and got wired up. I could almost feel my hair standing on end.

"Go and get his wife," I told Baz.

Baz smiled, climbed the stairs, giving Jeremy a little kick as he passed him.

"What, no…"

I lifted him by the front of his shirt and pushed him into the lounge. The light was still on and the curtains were closed. "*Sit down.*"

"W-we had a deal…" He slumped onto the sofa, holding his cheek. He kept staring at my nose. "You said if I gave you the medals…"

"That was before you set me up, you bastard."

He pretended he didn't know what I was talking about. Tried to look all confused. Kept looking from my eyes to my nose. "I don't know what you mean."

Goddamn that made me mad. I felt a throb in my temples, and also in my nose, which hadn't happened before. I'd checked out what the ginger ninja had done to it in my Porsche's rear-view mirror. It looked like a volcano. "*Stop looking at my goddamn nose!*"

"I… I'm sorry…"

"This is what your friend did to me. Do you think I'm happy about it?"

"My friend?"

"Do you think my nose is happy about it?"

"Gary, I really don't…"

I was just about ready to hit him again, but Baz came in at that moment holding Jeremy's wife by the arm. He shoved her onto the sofa next to Jeremy.

"I've told her what will happen if she starts yellin' her head off," Baz said.

She looked from Baz to me, then bloody hell she looked at my nose. She said to Jeremy, "I told you."

Ha! Got him! "You should have listened to your wife, shouldn't you," I said. "Did you really think I wouldn't find out?"

"Find out *what?*"

"That you sent a friend to get your medals back."

Now they both tried to look confused, even his wife.

"Gary, honestly…"

"*Stop trying to deny it.*" My fists clenched all by themselves. "Jermaine saw the ginger guy bring you back here earlier."

"The ginger guy?"

Baz moved before I could stop him. Punched Jeremy so hard he must have almost taken his head off. Mrs Peters began to scream, but Baz clamped a hand over her mouth before it was out. "Don't even think about it, bitch, or I'll kill you. You understand?"

She tried to nod, and Baz released her. Jeremy had got himself upright again, and held his jaw, making pathetic moaning sounds.

"The ginger guy who brought you home," Baz said. "Jermaine saw his car, you old prick, so how about you stop lyin' to us."

Jeremy held up his hands. He already had a huge purple bruise on one cheek. "Yes, okay, the ginger guy who gave me a lift - what about him?"

"He robbed us, Jeremy." I glowered down at him. "Smashed into the back of my Porsche. Took my wallet and phone. And the medals."

"He had a machete," added Baz.

Jeremy was shaking his head. "The ginger guy? *Robbed* you?"

Goddammit, he was still trying to pretend he had nothing to do with it. That wouldn't do at all. I looked at Baz. Nodded.

Baz grabbed Jeremy by the leg and yanked him off the sofa. He made quite a thud when he hit the carpet. Mrs Peters stood up, but I shoved her back down again.

"No, please..."

Baz knelt on Jeremy's chest and hit him again.

I said, "Who is the ginger guy, Peters?"

"H-he said his name was John Steele..." Jeremy croaked.

That was more like it. The lying bastard hadn't wanted to tell me about the medals, either, but I found out in the end.

"...But I only met him today, I swear..."

Baz hit him again, and Mrs Peters tried to get up. This time I grabbed her face and forced her against the wall. "Where does he live, Jeremy?"

"I don't know, I think he lives in Scotland! He said he was staying in a Travelodge in town..."

"Tell us where he lives!" Baz growled, and he hit Jeremy twice more.

There was blood. Jeremy managed, "I don't know..." and Baz went off on one.

For a few seconds I was dumbstruck. It brought everything back. Baz swinging his huge arms. The wet *thwacking* sounds. Jeremy's head bouncing this way and that as if he was watching a tennis game.

"Baz." I didn't raise my voice, but Baz heard and stopped straight away as if he'd snapped out of a trance.

Jeremy wasn't moving. His face was a mess. Mrs Peters was sobbing and clutching at my wrist.

"Oh shit," said Baz. "I think I killed him, Gary."

The electric feeling had turned itself off as quickly as it had turned itself on. I was left with a prickly tingling sensation all over my skin, and I didn't like it. "No, he's... he's still breathing." And he was, but only just.

Baz stood. His knuckles were red, and there were flecks of blood on his T-shirt. "He kept lying to us, man."

"I know."

"He got the ginger guy to rob us."

"I know." I looked at Mrs Peters. "We're going to go now, and you're going to call an ambulance for your husband. Call the police as well."

Baz said, "What? Gary..."

"You're going to say that Jeremy was assaulted by a man in a balaclava, okay? He wore gloves, and you didn't see his face and you didn't know who it was. Okay? It was a burglary gone wrong." She stared back at me, her eyes wide. "Now, if you tell the police it was us, if you even mention my name, I will send someone to Watton."

She heard – *Watton* - and gasped, gave a shudder, and started sobbing again.

"I will send someone to your son's house, and they will kill your grandchildren. Now, is that what you want?"

She shook her head.

"No." It's not what I wanted, either. Don't get the wrong idea, I don't like threatening kids. "So, are you going to do as I ask?"

She nodded.

"Good." I took my hand from her face.

She said, "Get the hell out of my house."

STEELE

The second time I killed.

It was early 1996, and Fourth Mechanised Infantry Brigade was still stationed in Banja Luka, though that day we were passing through the surrounding towns.

Nothing had really happened since the ambush just before Christmas in the remains of the Ferhat Pasha Mosque, although it seemed I relived that day constantly.

The war was over. Slobodan Milosevic and Ratko Mladic were indicted for War Crimes. The Serbs were done, although some of them didn't seem to know it.

We heard gunshots outside Jajce, and followed them to a crossroads. A lone gunman stood at the intersection, shooting civilians in the back as they fled. Three were already lying dead at his feet. A man, a woman, and a child. When he saw us coming he ran to a young woman who had fallen over in her attempt to escape, dragged her to her feet. Used her as a human shield. Shouted at us, the gun shoved to her head.

But he couldn't shield himself from all of us.

I was the one who shot him. Clean through the head. I didn't even think about it. I had a shot and I took it. And the woman lived when she otherwise would have died.

I waited for the nausea, the tightening stomach, the sweating and the light head - everything that had happened the first time. Except it didn't come.

I stood there with my gun still smoking and I felt fine. I felt *good*.

Someone clapped me on the back. Someone else said, "Good job."

And I nodded, because I *had* done a good job.

And for the first time I could remember I slept very

well that night.

I have ever since.

*

I parked in the hospital car park and looked through the medals in the envelope.

Jesus.

A DSO and DFC, along with three more common medals.

I still couldn't believe Jeremy had been prepared to give them up to that lowlife.

Still. I'd taught Brooker a lesson, and he'd be reminded of it every time he looked in a mirror. In fact, he probably wouldn't even need a mirror – his nose was probably so swollen he'd be seeing it out the corners of his eyes for days.

I put the envelope in the glove box. I'd return it to the Peters tomorrow morning. Right now all I wanted was to get my arm looked at and then get some sleep.

I checked myself into the hospital, but even with my ID I was still there two hours later. Friday night. All the gutter drunks puking in the corridors. Well, Saturday morning now.

They cleaned, glued and strapped my arm.

Then they put it in a sling.

Jesus Christ, *a sling*.

Exactly what a government contract killer needs, his left arm wrapped up like a chicken wing. Said nobody ever.

They told me to drink plenty of fluids and to do no heavy lifting until they removed the sling in a couple of weeks. Not that I'd be here then. Later today I'd head back to London.

The nurse left me to rest in a curtained-off cubicle, and I finally had a moment to phone London HQ. I gave my name and LV number, and they put me through to Samuel Dalton's office, the head of the LVs.

I thought I might get his secretary (all men have to sleep after all), but he was still there, working at half one in the morning, and he said, "Steele?"

"Both Carluccis taken care of, sir."

"Good work. You got both of them?"

"Yes. One blown up, the other shot. Dawn should have closed the file."

"You'll get your fee as soon as we have confirmation from the local police."

"Fine." I didn't mention having stolen a purple gym bag containing forty grand or more, which exceeded my fee.

"You on your way back now?"

"Not yet. Later. I'm at the hospital at the moment. Got shot in the arm."

Dalton sucked his teeth. "You're slipping, Steele."

"I was falling, actually."

"What happened?"

Nearly a botched operation, that's what.

*

Friday, 10:09pm. The explosion had sent me temporarily deaf, though I'd known it would. It was still a shock, even though I'd known it was coming. Heat swam over me. I'd turned away before detonating the bomb, throwing myself to the ground, so at least I could still see.

Except for the smoke. I picked myself up after only a second and the smoke was everywhere, shrouding everything.

The Carluccis' guys were yelling, all of them strewn about and off their feet. Panic, confusion. And there I was in the middle of it, my head clear and lucid, my heart steady and strong. The surge of adrenaline made my skin tingle like it always did, but inside I was in control, completely calm like a lighthouse in a storm.

I went for the guy in the leather jacket first, the one with the old Smith and Wesson. I wanted him down and I wanted his gun.

He'd been knocked to his knees by the blast, and before he could gather what was left of his senses I ran up and kicked him in the side of the head. Steel-capped boots. Weapons in themselves. Like kicking a sack of flour. I think something caved in, I'm not sure. He went over anyway, and I relieved him of his gun. Trained it on the other two guys by the door, who were still getting to their feet.

BLAM BLAM. Gunshots like thunder. They went down.

And then the bald guy next to the table, counting the money into the purple gym bag. His revolver was still lying there on the tabletop, ignored, as he stared open-mouthed, his head hunched, a wad of twenties still in one hand. BLAM.

I moved to the table and picked up the revolver. Turned my attention to the other end of the room, which had taken the brunt of the explosion.

Only one guy was trying to scrabble to his feet, and I shot him with the revolver. Two others lay against the walls, burnt beyond recognition. And then there was Big Carlucci, still in one piece, but dead, lying against the filing cabinet with half his face red and smoking like lava. I couldn't tell which bit of twisted, blackened debris was the remains of my briefcase, but the contents - ten thousand pounds-worth of fake, useless paper money - still fluttered on the air and settled like leaves.

And then came movement by the door. I spun and got off a shot, but missed. Oh well. Happens to the best of us. It had been someone running out of the room, not running in. If enemies turn tail and flee I try to let them go. If they're no longer a threat that is. Shooting someone in the back as they run away can't really be considered self-defence. Unless they're running towards a bazooka or something.

Shouting from elsewhere in the drugs den and footsteps running everywhere.

I stuffed the remaining cash bundles from the table into the purple gym bag and zipped it. Finders keepers and all that. The government handed me the contracts and whatever salvage was mine to do with what I liked. I hooked the handles over my arms and wore it like a rucksack, keeping both hands free for my guns.

And then I checked the bodies again. Goddammit. Little Carlucci wasn't one of them. It must have been him escaping. So much for letting him run. I couldn't justify killing him in self-defence, no, but in defence of the innocent? Absolutely. He was part of the contract after all.

So I went after him, leaving the room and the bodies and the smoke behind, just as two more guys rounded the corner. The stair guards. I didn't even need to aim - they just ran right into the middle of my gunfire.

That left one more, the doorman with the ponytail, and then the other Carlucci brother, wherever the hell he was.

I stuck to the wall and crab-walked to the corner, then dropped to a crouch. Corners are for suckers. You walk around one and there's some guy waiting for you with a bullet and a cheeky grin, as the stair guards had found out the hard way. But these guys don't expect you to be two foot tall - they aim at chest height, a good five feet off the ground, and so when I peeped round from my spot on the floor the doorman waiting for me had his gun pointed at a spot high above my head.

I shot him twice, and he shuddered backwards and fell down the stairs.

I followed him down, sticking to the near wall like a shadow, and stepped over his body. That's when I saw the alarm box on the wall, red light flashing. Someone had tripped the alarm, which was hardly surprising. It's what I had expected, and now I had about five minutes to get clear of the building before reinforcements showed up. But Little Carlucci surviving the explosion and running off had not been part of the plan.

One more corner and then the steel fire door to the courtyard. I rounded it, keeping low as before, leading with the revolver and big Smith and Wesson. No one there. The corridor was empty. Little Carlucci must have made a break for freedom and run out into the car park.

I cursed, and ran up to the steel fire door leading outside. I set the Smith and Wesson down, pressed myself into the corner by the hinges and opened the door inward. Three shots echoed out before little Carlucci realized I wasn't standing in the doorway and he had been shooting into empty air. The bullets screamed down the hall past me and made craters in the far wall.

I saw little Carlucci through the crack between the hinges, standing in the middle of the car park aiming at the door, hoping I'd open it and come blundering out like a fool. When I didn't oblige he turned and ran for his car.

I sprinted round the door and went out after him, firing the revolver. He heard me coming and spun round, shooting back at me.

I dived to my right behind some parked cars as bullets sailed past me. I felt one rush over my head. And then one hit my left arm, burnt right through, although pumped up with adrenaline it felt no more than a bee sting.

Goddammit, I'd feel that in the morning.

I tried to fire at him, but the revolver just clicked and clicked. No more bullets. *Fantastic.*

I scrambled along the row of cars and peered out. Little Carlucci sat against the front bumper of his own car, a black four-by-four, cradling one leg. I must have got him after all. He began shooting at the shadows beneath the row of cars I hid behind, presumably mistaking them for me, and he gave a desperate cry as he did so until his gun clicked empty, after which he gave out a series of colourful expletives and began to hunt in his jacket for another magazine.

I left my hiding place and ran over to him, yelling, "Drop the gun!" and brandishing my own in what I hoped was an encouraging manner even though it too was empty.

He pulled himself up using the bonnet, clicked in the magazine, but I reached him before he could aim the gun at me and cracked him in the cheek with the butt of my empty revolver. His finger tensed on the trigger and sent a round into the concrete. He fell against the bonnet and lay sprawled there as if trying to make a snow angel in the dew.

Unconscious.

I threw away the revolver and picked up Carlucci's gun, turned back to the open steel door just in case anyone else should come running out after me. After counting to twenty all remained quiet and I finally exhaled.

I looked down at little Carlucci. Blood came pouring down one side of his face. His eyes were half closed, his breathing thin. I could just shoot him, but I thought about the MDMA lab and my bonus.

So I crossed to my own car, parked only twenty feet away and popped the boot. Returned to Little Carlucci and gave another scope of the area.

Then I put the gun – some sort of Beretta 9mm - in my waistband and lifted the small Italian drug-brother in a fireman's lift over my right shoulder. My left arm still felt heavier, though. Carried him to my opened boot and dumped him in.

I took the purple gym bag from my back and put it on the passenger seat, and then threw the gun and my dummy watch-slash-detonator into the footwell. My left arm felt dead.

No time to hang around. At least the Merc was an automatic.

I used my right hand to put it into reverse and backed up, then put it into drive and got the hell out of there.

Twenty minutes later that cop pulled me over.

*

I gave Dalton an abridged version of what had happened. Little Carlucci had shot me in the arm, so I'd shot him in the leg and knocked him unconscious and put him in my boot.

"Sounds fair."

"I thought so. I hit an artery. He died of blood loss before I could question him."

"Sounds like you've made a right mess of the boot."

"I... it's not my blood."

He wasn't impressed.

"I'll clean it, sir."

"Good. Get your arm fixed and then get down here. And well done, Steele."

"Thank you, sir."

We hung up, and a few minutes later the nurse came back and told me I could go because they needed the bed, and basically, apart from the fact that I'd been shot I was fine.

I put on my jacket over my sling, putting the empty left sleeve in the pocket so it looked like I only had one arm.

And then, when I was out in the corridor, Jeremy came in.

*

He was on a wheely bed, with lots of doctors all around him talking madly to one another. Jeremy was unconscious. He passed me in the corridor and his face was all purple and crusted with blood as if he'd been in a car crash.

But I knew what had happened, and that it was my fault.

How the hell had Brooker found out? I thought I'd been careful.

Mrs Peters sat in the waiting room, wrung the tissue she held in her hands, stared about with bloodshot glassy eyes.

I didn't want her to see me. I didn't want her blaming me, telling me it was my fault.

Even though it was.

I turned round and went out another entrance, managed to reach my car without bumping into her. The medals were in the glove box. I hate to admit it, but I thought about just driving to their house and posting the envelope through the letterbox.

Everyone's a coward in some way or other.

But I couldn't let it lie, not now. So I took the medals back into the hospital. Stood at the door to the waiting room. Mrs Peters had her back to me. I found walking in there harder than I'd found walking into the drugs den a few hours ago. Strange, but there you go.

"Mrs Peters?" I stood in front of her, and her lips drew tight when she saw me. "I... I'm sorry about your husband."

She said nothing for a few seconds, and then, "This is all your fault. Gary knew you dropped Jeremy home."

The blob must have told him.

"He thinks Jeremy sent you after him to get the medals back."

I swallowed. "Mrs Peters, I had no idea this would happen..."

She said nothing.

"Who did it? Was it Gary himself?"

She swallowed, and her eyes seemed to glaze over. "I don't know. I mean, no, it wasn't Gary. He wore a balaclava. And gloves."

"Did you recognise his voice?"

"No."

"Well, was he tall? Short? Fat? Thin?"

"He was... average. He wasn't fat or thin."

Average height, average build. A great help. "Did you see what colour his eyes were?"

"He was wearing a balaclava."

"Balaclavas have eye holes."

"Do they? Oh. I don't know."

I frowned. "What was he wearing?"

"Jeans and a jacket, or something. I can't really remember. And I don't want to talk about it anymore. Please leave. I've already told the police everything I know."

Well at least that was something. I handed her the envelope. "Again, I'm sorry. For everything."

As I was walking away, she turned and said, "You broke Gary's nose. It looked a right mess."

"I know. I hit him hard."

She nodded. "You should have hit him harder."

I wished I had. "He will pay for this. I promise you."

I left the hospital. Put the Merc into drive and steered the wheel with only my right hand.

A couple of hours ago I had been planning to have a few weeks off. The contract was over. I don't make a habit of stirring up trouble.

And I was shot, there was that.

But then Gary Brooker had come along and made it personal.

I knew Mrs Peters had lied to me back at the hospital. Jeremy's attacker had not been a random guy in a balaclava. If he had she'd know that balaclavas had eye holes, and she'd surely be less vague about what he was wearing. But most of all, how did she know what Gary's nose looked like?

She knew exactly who had punched her husband half

to death. Gary might not have done it himself, but he had been there. And then he'd managed to frighten her so badly she'd had to invent this non-descript attacker wearing a balaclava without eye holes.

I pulled into the Travelodge, which had been my home for the last couple of weeks. The guy on the nightshift desk knew my face and we exchanged nods. In my room I slipped out of my jacket and gingerly tested my sling. The pain had dulled a little. I dry swallowed some aspirin but that was all. Then I pushed the chest of drawers across the door using one leg. It's a habit. Much better than a chair under the handle. Worth the extra effort.

Then I called Dalton again. "New plan," I said. "I'll be a couple of days more here."

"I thought the Carluccis were taken care of."

"They are. I have come across another situation that needs dealing with."

"A problem?"

"Only a small one. A loan shark who thinks he's a big fish. Pardon the pun. It won't take long."

"A loan shark? Who cares about a loan shark – let the police deal with it."

"I would, normally, but I'm not sure they can." Plus it was my fault Jeremy was in hospital fighting for his life.

"You shouldn't hang around, Steele. The Carlucci brothers have family…"

"Everyone has family."

"A *dangerous* family. They'll be after you. And it sounds to me like you're going to do something stupid."

"I'm not going to do anything stupid."

"Okay, *illegal*. And I mean illegal even for you. You don't have a contract for this man. I don't want you losing your licence and ending up in jail for murder."

I paused. "That won't happen."

"You shouldn't do it, Steele."

"It'll only take a couple of days. And I'm due a break anyway. My arm's in a sling."

"Then how the hell can…"

"I'll keep you up to date."

"You're not James Bond."

"You're not Judi Dench."

"Cute." He didn't laugh.

"I'll call you." I hung up.

It didn't matter what Dalton said, he couldn't talk me out of it. I was already involved.

I washed and cleaned my teeth. Placed my silenced Glock 17 on the bedside table. Then my wind-down routine. It's kind of like a ritual I do first thing in the morning and last thing at night. Ten minutes of stretching and breathing exercises – basically an athletic warm-down combined with Yoga. Keeps the muscles toned, the core strong and the body in shape. There's nothing more embarrassing than pulling a muscle trying to punch someone. My left arm didn't appreciate the little work out, but I didn't want it seizing up any worse than it was.

Then ten minutes of meditation, sat on the edge of the bed with my back straight and my hands on my knees. I used to have to close my eyes and count breaths, but now I just sit open-eyed and watch my thoughts come and go like leaves on a breeze.

I got into bed and fell asleep in about five minutes.

At half past four I was awoken by the door crashing against the chest of drawers.

*

Most assassins prefer the quickest way into a room. Catch your target unprepared. My door had been kicked in, and it crashed against the drawers loud enough to wake the entire building. I awoke and rolled out of bed in almost the same instant, grabbing my Glock from the table as I went. The man breaking into the room swore, a flapping shadow framed by the light of the corridor. He kicked again and the drawers fell over.

I shot him twice from my spot on the floor. He fell into the open wardrobe and dropped something. A gun.

I reached for the light switch and kept my Glock on the shadow should he move. The light came on and the shadow became a body, all in black. He didn't move.

I shut the door in case any of the guests had been roused from their beds, and shoved the drawers that had saved my life aside.

So the Carluccis had sent a hitman. Not surprising, but how the hell had they found me?

The guy wore a balaclava with eye holes. I pulled it off. Blood dribbled out of his mouth. He looked more like Will Ferrell than Will Smith, to be honest. And the gun. An old Colt, at least fifty years old. I frowned. What was he doing with that antique?

I searched him and discovered his phone. All his texts had been deleted, except for one sent at 3:23am. Just a phone number. No contact name. The message read 'Ginger Scottish. Jon Steel'.

Me, in other words, but with my name spelt wrong.

And then the address of this Travelodge.

I took the phone and put it in my jacket pocket.

The hitman was lousy. Unprofessional. Dirty suit. The Colt was unclean. Cheap. That surprised me. No wallet, but he had a set of car keys, which I took.

I got dressed as quickly as my one-armedness would allow, packed my things away in a heap and left the room.

The night guy was hiding behind his desk, and he poked his head out and gave a little yelp when he saw me.

"There seems to be a dead man in my room," I said.

The guard stammered. "I-I called the police as soon as I could... They'll be here any minute…"

"How did he know which room was mine?"

"He h-had a gun... I'm sorry, but he asked if we had a John Steele staying here and I just… I mean, I couldn't…" He kept looking at my empty sleeve, as if wondering whether in the ruckus the hitman had cut my arm off.

"Don't worry. He didney know what he was doing. Did you mention my name to the police?"

"I... yes – they asked what the gunman was asking and I just..."

"Don't worry. I'm just going to put my bags in my car, okay? Then I'm going to come back in and wait for the police to get here."

It was raining now. I thought I could maybe hear sirens. My left arm was throbbing out across my shoulder and chest. I reached the car park and took out the hitman's car keys. Began to walk along the rows, every few moments pressing the keyfob button to unlock the car remotely. After a few seconds the lights on a maroon Mondeo lit up. I didn't have time to search the car, so I just opened the driver's door and left the keys on the seat for the police when they got here. Then I took a moment to memorise the Mondeo's registration plate.

The police firearms unit arrived a few minutes later. I was sitting in reception with my ID open on the seat beside me and my jacket draped over the back of the chair, so they could see my sling and that I was unarmed, just in case anyone got jumpy and decided to shoot me.

I needn't have worried. The team was led by Sergeant Jane Lane (there was no forgetting a name that rhymed so beautifully with itself), and she had been expecting me.

"I knew you would have something to do with it," she said, crossing her arms.

"Is that because the receptionist gave you my name?"

She didn't respond, nor smile. Just narrowed her eyes and pressed her lips together until they all but disappeared. Her usual expression around me, in other words.

Actually, I thought, she'll probably be pleased if one of her team accidentally shoots me in the face.

Sergeant Jane Lane had helped with my investigation on the Carluccis because she had been working their case for years. Of course, she'd also been *ordered* to help me. I had a feeling she wasn't completely happy about it, given the fact that a large percentage of her career had been devoted to putting the brothers away, and here I was taking over and doing my thing. Basically rendering her years of work meaningless. Or at least, that's how she saw it, and I couldn't really blame her.

"We've literally just come from the Carlucci building you set on fire," she said.

"Everything okay? Area clear?"

"Yes, and the fire's under control." She swallowed. "You got them, then."

I nodded. "You okay about that?"

"What do you care? I've been scooped. Whatever. Now why the hell are we here? I thought we were done with you."

"Sorry. But this guy's inconvenienced my night as well. He's in room 32."

"That was your room?"

"Aye."

"The Carlucci brothers sent him?"

"The Carlucci brothers are both dead."

"You know what I mean. Whoever's in charge over here now. Probably Antonio Carlucci."

"Aye." Antonio was the Carlucci brothers' cousin. "He's probably in charge for the time being. But the hitter they sent won't be winning any awards; he was terrible."

"And he's dead."

"That too."

"Fine. Stay here, will you. I may need you again."

"The guy's car is a maroon Mondeo." I recited the registration. "I left it unlocked and the keys are on the seat. Don't know if you'll find anything useful."

"Right." She led her team to the front desk and then up the corridor. Told some guests to stay in their rooms. Why anyone would decide to venture out after hearing two gunshots was beyond me.

I sat and waited for around half an hour as her team busied themselves around me. And then I heard the low Vvvv Vvvv of a phone on vibrate. It was coming from my jacket, which confused me for one moment because my own phone was in my trouser pocket. Then I realised. It was the dodgy dead hitman's phone. I fished it out of my jacket. Same number as the text had been from. I answered. "Yes?" Dropped the Scottish accent.

"Is he dead?"

"Yes." Because Will Ferrell was definitely dead.

"Good. Did he still have the medals? They were in a brown envelope..."

I froze. Hung up quickly. *Holy shit.*

Not Cousin Antonio after all, nor any other Carlucci for that matter...

It was Brooker.

BROOKER

It hadn't taken as long to find him as I'd thought it might.

Baz hadn't believed it when Jeremy told us the ginger guy was staying in a Travelodge, but I did. It was too specific to be a lie, and by this time I knew Jeremy quite well. I knew how he broke under pressure, and we were pushing him much harder than we'd ever done.

That was a mistake, obviously. But I was pretty sure I'd sorted that. Mrs Peters wasn't going to be shooting her mouth off about what really happened to anyone. She believed I'd do what I said I'd do, and that's the only thing that mattered.

I'd learnt two things from Jeremy about that goddamn ginger Scotsman. One - his name was John Steele, however the hell you spelt it. And two - he was staying in a nearby Travelodge.

So straight after leaving Jeremy's I drove me and Baz back to my house. I cleaned myself up as best I could, but oh Jesus that ginger dickhead would pay for what he'd done to my nose. It almost looked worse with the dried blood washed off – it was purple and swollen and looked like some kind of ugly vegetable, like a – what are they called? An eggplant or something. And I had huge black bruises under my eyes.

Baz had a lump the size of a tennis ball coming up on his head and looked even more like an alien than usual.

I couldn't let the ginger bastard get away with it. That would be no kind of justice.

So.

I keep a few cheap disposable mobile phones in a drawer, because the police can't trace cash-bought, pay-as-you go mobiles. There's nothing to trace.

I called Terry and Jermaine again and told them to come round. Stu's phone was turned off, but that didn't surprise me because I think he worked Saturday mornings. I looked up Johnson and Royce's numbers from my address book - the new guys, the ex-bouncers - but couldn't get through to them either.

Baz said, "I told you, Gary. They're a waste of space."

I ignored him. Pulled up a map of the town on Google Maps. We made a list of three likely Travelodges. Terry would go to one, Jermaine to another, and I'd take Baz to the third.

"Search every car in the car park. He drives a black Mercedes." I gave them the registration number. "Call me if you find it."

We split up. Jermaine in his van, Terry in his car and me and Baz in my Porsche.

Baz kept fidgeting as I drove, wanting to say something but not really sure how. I couldn't bring myself to break the silence. He was a loose cannon, I knew that. Had always known. But he had been with me from the start. We'd get through this.

We'd got through it before.

I swallowed at the memory. Baz kneeling over Catherine Thompson's dead body, his hands still around her neck.

"You wanted it sorted, Gary, and look I've sorted it."

That's not what I'd meant. Oh God that's not what I'd meant.

*

Terry found the ginger guy's black Mercedes.

We drove over there, and there it was in the car park.

Same registration. A couple of marks on the bumper. That made me mad. I wanted to key it, but that wouldn't do. John Steele deserved much more than just a scratched car.

"What are we going to do?" Terry asked, staring at the Travelodge building. "Are we going to go in and get him?"

"No. Leave it to me."

I sent them away, except for Baz. I needed Baz. Then I got back in my Porsche because it'd started raining and the raindrops were stinging my nose.

Baz got in beside me. "Do you want me to get him, Gary?"

"No." As I drove away I thought again about that woman lying dead on the grass, Baz's handprints round her throat. Or rather, I thought about what we'd done afterwards. How we'd got rid of her body. Who we'd had to call. "Baz, I need you to call Will."

Baz frowned at me. "Who?"

"Jesus Christ, Baz. *Will*, the guy who got rid of Catherine Thompson's body for us. The guy who *kills* people."

"Will? Really? But... but I thought you said we *don't* kill people."

And I turned to him and said, "Look at my nose, Baz. Look at my goddamn nose."

*

I'd spoken to Will. Given him the Travelodge's address and John Steele's name. He'd called me just before he'd gone in, said he'd call again as soon as it was done.

But he didn't call, and now half an hour had passed.

Something had gone wrong.

No - there must be a reasonable explanation. Will had got held up, or he had no phone signal, or maybe he just *forgot*, because people forget things, right?

And it wasn't like I'd paid him in advance - I'm not that stupid - so he'd have to call me if he wanted to get paid…

But then what was taking him so long?

The waiting was agony. I couldn't do it any longer, so I phoned him. I had to.

It rang for a long time. Felt like an hour.

And then, "Yes?"

The knot in my stomach loosened a little. "Is he dead?"

"Yes."

It unravelled completely, and it was as if my whole body had been tensed up and now relaxed. "Good. Did he still have the medals? They were in a brown envelope…"

A pause, and then the line went dead.

"H-hello? Will?"

The knot was back and with a vengeance.

Something *was* wrong. There were loads of reasons why he could have been cut off, except...

I replayed that 'Yes' over and over in my head, and the more I replayed it the more certain I became. The man on the other end of the phone wasn't Will.

So I did something stupid. I drove myself over to the Travelodge to see for myself, even though visiting the scene of the crime was the last thing I should have been doing.

This time when I pulled up the police were everywhere, lights flashing blue and red like strobes. That hardly surprised me. One of the guests gets killed and the police are going to turn up.

Except the guest *hadn't* been killed, because the ginger bastard was standing right there in the middle of the goddamn car park, watching a body being loaded onto the back of an ambulance, and even though it was completely covered by a sheet I knew the body was Will. I knew that Will was dead, and instead of sad this made me so unbelievably angry I almost threw up.

I wanted to drive my Porsche over there and run him over, run everyone over, run Steele over twice and make his head burst. But the car park wall and the police cars, the bloody things were in my way and I'd probably just get stuck on the verge and arrested, and he'd be there laughing at my busted nose, pissing himself laughing, pissing on me.

Instead I drove away. And when I reached somewhere quiet I stopped and screamed the inside of my car out, pulled the battery and SIM from my phone and threw them out of the window onto the dark dark road.

STEELE

Brooker. I couldn't believe it. The hitman knew my name, so Brooker must know my name. Had I also told Jeremy I was staying in a Travelodge? I must have. Stupid. I wasn't normally so sloppy.

My satnav found me a Premier Inn close by. I checked in under a pseudonym just in case, paid cash, and once more dropped the Scottish accent. I didn't want another hitman breaking in before dawn and giving me another trashed room to pay for.

No assailant paid me a visit again that night, and I awoke when the sun was up and shining after a few hours undisturbed sleep. My arm hadn't bled any more during the night. I thought about ditching the sling, but decided to stick with it at least for the time being. In movies tough guys sleep off gunshot wounds, but not in real life.

I opened my make-up bag. Keep the comments to yourself - it's as important to me as my weapons haul in the seat locker. And nearly as expensive.

First I dabbed a clear liquid onto my face using a cotton swab. On my forehead, cheeks, round my eyes. My skin first tightened, then puckered. Lines, wrinkles, crows' feet. Ten years in a bottle. Then a little powder to make me more pale. I am supposed to be ginger, and as far as I know gingers don't tan well. The dye in my hair and beard still seemed to be in good shape.

Then the tattoo on my right forearm: a blue snake winding round a sword. A relic from my army days, before I became an LV. It seemed a good idea at the time. The shower had washed away some of the concealer, and parts of the tattoo were becoming visible.

I covered it over in make-up again until it disappeared.

Normally my long-sleeved jacket would cover it, but you can never be too careful. I couldn't have anyone linking John Steele with the real me.

So in ten minutes I was lighter and older, John Steele again. Ready to go to work.

After breakfast I decided I'd better take a look at the Merc. It wasn't mine. It was HQ's, and I was pretty sure they'd want it back in one piece.

So it was a shame about the scratches on the bumper. And the blood in the boot.

Little Carlucci had really made a mess in there. Very inconsiderate.

Luckily, the blood only seemed to be spread out over the plastic boot liner.

I drove into town, parked in the shopping centre and bought a king-sized bed sheet to soak up the blood. It was still early but the car park was beginning to fill up, so I had to check no one was close by before opening the boot and mopping up.

That's when I noticed the guy.

He was sitting on a low wall with his phone in his hand, and he kept looking at it and then staring at me, back and forth, back and forth. He was thin and bearded and wore a beanie hat and joggers and looked a bit like a chicken.

And I recognised him.

Damn it.

I'd seen his face on a print out Sergeant Jane Lane had made when I'd first arrived. A print out of the Carluccis' street dealers.

He was probably meeting a buyer, except the buyer was about to be blown off because Beanie must have recognised me in return.

I shut the bloodied bed sheet in the boot, locked the Merc, and then headed around the back of the shopping centre. Less witnesses.

Beanie put his phone away and began hurrying after me.

I looked back a couple of times, and caught him pull something from his pocket. Probably something small and pointy.

I ran, and he did the only thing that came to his mind: he ran after me. Course he did.

I'm not a great sprinter, I have to admit. Long distance, yes, I'm your man, but when it comes to speed... well, Usain Bolt I'm not. More like Usain Bumble. And my left arm was in a sling. That didn't help.

But I wasn't trying to outrun Beanie.

I turned a corner, stopped and pressed myself against the building, waiting for him to appear. He wouldn't have noticed that my footsteps had stopped - he would only be able to hear his own, and his breathing and maybe the pounding of his heart in his head.

So he raced round the corner expecting to find me off running some distance away. Instead I pounced out of nowhere and hit him high in the chest. His legs went out from under him and up in the air. I think they were still running. He landed hard on his back and lay there like a Beanie Baby doll.

The knife flew out of his hand.

I pulled off his beanie and threw it on the shopping centre roof.

He groaned and felt his head with one hand.

"You need to wash your hair," I told him. No wonder

he wore that beanie.

I pulled his phone from his pocket. Pushed the power and a photo of me appeared on the screen. Probably taken from the drug den's CCTV and text around to all Carlucci associates.

This is why I should have left town.

Except I'd made Mrs Peters a promise, and I intended to keep it.

I left Beanie without his beanie groaning on the ground and headed back to my car. Then I drove to the police station, a large, old, one-storey brick building on the main road near the centre of town. Only a few cop cars parked out front.

I walked in and the woman at the desk paused mid-telephone conversation and stared at me. I didn't need to show my ID; I'm memorable. I showed myself into Andrews's office, and found him in conversation with Sergeant Jane Lane round his desk.

"Aw, Christ," said Andrews.

"Chief Superintendent. Sergeant." I sat down uninvited in the chair next to Lane and opposite Andrews. "Should my ears be burning?"

"Not just your ears," said Jane Lane.

"You said you were done here," Andrews reminded me.

"I thought I was."

"I didn't get home until after midnight, and then when I came in this morning I had Sergeant Lane telling me something about you and a hitman."

"Lucky for me he wasn't a very good hitman."

Lane had folded her arms and leant away from me. "Yes, very lucky."

"He was a small time crook from Northamptonshire,"

Andrews said. "Called Will Pharrell."

"Will Pharrell? You have to be kidding."

"He was already on the database. Spent ten months inside in 2006 for GBH."

"Well that really straightened him out."

"And recently went on disability benefit. Said he couldn't walk very far."

"He can't walk anywhere anymore." I shrugged out of my jacket and hung it over the back of the chair.

Andrews whistled. "Christ, Steele, why is your arm in a sling?"

"Little Carlucci shot me."

"He *shot* you? *You never told me that.* What happened?"

I went through an abridged version of the story I'd told Dalton in the hospital earlier.

"We've identified both Carlucci brothers," Andrews said. "That was your job, right? To kill those men?"

I shrugged. "Aye."

Andrews exchanged glances with Lane, shifted in his chair and made a sound in his throat. "Steele, *is this really legal?*"

"Yes. Brussels wouldn't like it, but what they don't know canny hurt them."

Lane sat up. "Are you saying Europe doesn't even *know?*"

I raised my eyebrows. "You'd have to speak to the Security Service about that, sergeant, all I do is carry out the contracts."

She scoffed. "It'll be easier for you lot when we leave the EU, then."

"*If* we leave. And yeah, sure. Except the economy will be so much in the shitter the government won't be able to afford us anymore."

"Oh no. Whatever will we do." Probably sarcastic.

Andrews fidgeted some more and didn't look at me. "So are you done here now? You kick the hornets' nest and leave us to pick up the pieces."

"I blew it up, technically."

"It won't change anything," Lane said. "What you've done. Antonio Carlucci will take over and they'll just carry on as before."

"Not as before," I said. "They'll have lost their distribution and the confidence of their buyers. Another supplier will try and move in, probably. They may not even be able to get back up and running again."

"But in the meantime we have dozens of angry pushers on the street looking for blood."

"I know. They have my picture." I showed them the phone. "Took it off a dealer by the shopping mall half an hour ago."

"You took it off a dealer?"

"I think his name was Beanie."

Sergeant Lane ignored that. She looked at me. "You know everyone who works for the Carluccis is going to have this picture. You need to leave. Now."

"I can't."

"Why?"

"I have things to do."

"What things?"

"Important things."

Sergeant Lane pressed her lips firmly together. I think I was annoying her. She stood. "So do I," she said. "Excuse me." She left the room.

I turned back to Andrews. He said through gritted teeth, "*What important things?*"

"The Carluccis didn't send that hitman after me."

Andrews blinked. "What do you mean?"

"The hitman was sent by a man called Gary Brooker."

Andrews froze. "*What?*"

Ah, so he knew the guy.

I told him about Jeremy Peters and the medals I'd taken back off Gary and how I'd punched him in the face and ran into his Porsche. As I talked Andrews slowly put his face in his hands.

"Jeremy Peters was badly assaulted last night," he said. "He's in hospital."

"I know. I saw him when I was there."

"His wife came in this morning to make a formal statement, but she couldn't really tell us anything about the guy who did it."

"I know. I asked her last night. She was lying."

Andrews frowned. "Lying?"

"Yes. Brooker definitely had something to do with it. He must have scared her."

"Well that wouldn't surprise me."

"Why, have you had dealings with Gary before?"

Andrews chuckled. "We have a *file* on him and his guys, and he only moved into the area a few years ago."

"You know he lends people money and then extorts them for every penny they have."

"Yes, yes. Using threats and intimidation, and often following up on them. Two of his previous associates are inside at the moment. We've actually arrested Brooker twice before on suspicion of assault and fraud, but didn't have enough evidence to charge him. Nothing'll stick. He's like soap." He began typing away on his computer. "Come round here."

I circled the desk to look over his shoulder, and recognised the photo he brought up to the screen. Gary

Brooker. Age: 38. 5ft 11. Resident at 17 Willow Drive.

"We don't know all his business deals, as he uses cash," Andrew said, "but we know enough." He brought up another window of file notes. "These are just the ones we know of who required hospital treatment. And then there's this woman. Catherine Thompson. She actually got as far as making a statement. Then..."

"He killed her?"

"She disappeared. Never heard from again. No body, no nothing. Unsolved."

"He had a solid alibi, of course."

"He had an alibi, but I still think he had something to do with it."

"Anyone else you know about who might want to talk to me?"

He paused. "T-talk to you?"

"Aye. About Brooker."

Andrews frowned. Made a kind of grimace. "Why?"

"I want to know what I'm dealing with."

"D-dealing with?"

I sighed. Was he going to keep repeating everything I said like a moron? "George, Gary Brooker put someone in the hospital last night, after extorting him for thousands of pounds. You said you think he also had something to do with the disappearance of this Catherine Thompson. He put a *hitman* on me. And if you can't deal with him I'm going to have to."

He went all sour-faced at that. "By deal with him, you mean kill him? Just go up to him and... and... *pop*..." He made a gun with his hand and mimed shooting it.

I frowned. "No, George. I can't just go around killing whoever I like for whatever I like."

"Well that's the way it seems to me."

"Well you're wrong. I have to justify everything I do in relation to my own safety, the safety of the public, the chance of a fair trial and the probability of justice being served, the possibility of reform and the greater good..."

"The greater good? Christ."

"And I don't just go around shooting everyone who gets in my way. I have other means of dealing with people."

He grumbled to himself something about me thinking I was the Terminator.

I almost rolled my eyes. "*George*. Will any of Brooker's victims talk to me?"

"What? Oh, no, I doubt it. We don't know who most of his victims are, of course. They don't make complaints. Of the ones we do know, they tend to move away. Or disappear."

I waited. "No one?"

Andrews sighed. "If you really want to know, there's an old couple who still live round here. Mr and Mrs Chappell. We only know about them because of the hospital visit. They wouldn't talk to us, but hey, if you pull a gun on them maybe they'll answer your questions."

"Oh thanks, George. Thank you very much."

He shrugged, like I deserved it. Then scribbled something on a post-it and shoved it at me. "That's their address."

"Thank you." I took it and headed there.

But nothing prepared me for what I found.

BROOKER

I didn't sleep at all. Just lay in bed and simmered and raged, and thought about what I'd do to John Steele when I finally caught up with him.

It hadn't even registered that the guy who'd killed Will must be dangerous. Because I'd get him, I had to.

I must have dozed on and off because the next thing I knew it was half eight in the morning and the sun was starting to come up and poke me in the eye as I hadn't bothered shutting the curtains.

I showered, and *Jesus Christ my nose*, even the goddamn *shower* hurt it. And it hadn't improved in appearance during the night, I can tell you. I couldn't have people seeing me and thinking I'd been beaten up. I'd have to say I'd been involved in a hit-and-run or something – yes, some arsehole had run me over and driven off. The car had hit me square in the *face*.

I'd told Baz what had happened to Will, I'd had to. He hadn't believed it at first, kept asking the same questions over and over again. None of my other guys even knew I'd got Will involved, and the less they knew about it the better.

I had to use *another* of my spare pay-as-you-go mobiles as a replacement for the one I'd used to call the hit.

I rang Jermaine, then Terry, then Johnson and Royce. Told them I'd had it out with the ginger guy, told them I'd made him squeal like a piggy and then told him to leave town. If he had, all well and good. If they happened to see him they were to call me immediately.

I needed something to keep me busy, so I decided to go and pay Kevin West a visit. I knew it wasn't wise. The weirdo was likely to send me crazy the mood I was in, and the last thing I needed was an actual assault charge. But I had to do something productive.

And Kevin West seriously had it coming. Not only did he obviously have issues and a goddamn rat of a dog I'd have gladly strangled, he'd actually paid me back all the money I had lent him and thought we were quits!

As if that's the way it worked.

As if I wasn't entitled to some interest. As if I lent other people my money for the good of my goddamn *health*.

Kevin was one hell of a wet weekend - I'd have him snivelling like a woman and agreeing to pay me whatever I wanted by the time the morning was out.

The daylight was not kind to the back of my Porsche. It showed everything, and I felt my insides knot, and the only reason I didn't have a meltdown out there on the street was because I didn't want to give the nosy old bitch over the road the satisfaction. She'd be at her net curtains now, revelling in the scratches on my car and my busted nose and giggling with nosy old bitch glee.

I kept meaning to have one of the guys shake her up again, tell her to keep her beak of a nose pointed elsewhere. Perhaps I'd do that today, after I'd dealt with Kevin West.

Not that I'd make a load of profit off the deal - not like the ten grand I'd made off Jeremy.

I gritted my teeth and had to remind myself that I'd *lost* the medals. Or rather, had them *stolen*.

But I showed Jeremy in the end, didn't I. Wonder if he's still laughing his head off at me as he eats through a tube.

That was another thing I'd have to sort today - the alibi.

But anyway, Kevin had only borrowed four thousand (and had already paid it back), so I was looking at getting a grand or two out of him, and maybe one of his computers.

So I drove over to his house, and he opened the door and beamed at me. Not a reaction I usually get.

"Gary! What a lovely surprise!" His voice was thin and squeaky, like one of the goddamn Muppets. "What happened to your nose?"

My insides boiled and my mouth twitched and my busted nose started throbbing. "Just... a little accident, Kevin. Nothing to worry about." I pushed past him into his lounge and straight away his goddamn dog started yapping from the back yard and I swear it made my eyes quiver. It was a small brown ratty thing like a turd. "We need to talk."

"Anytime," said Kevin. "Would you like tea?"

"No. It's about the money I lent you." I looked at him, and he stood there with his moustache and his glasses and his tweed and I just wanted to punch him.

"I'm so grateful, you know. But as I said, I only needed a few days…"

"You still owe me two thousand."

He stood there for a moment not moving or reacting. "No," he said. "I repaid you in full on November the fourth. Four thousand pounds in fifties. I wrote it down."

"It's interest. You know what interest is, Kev?"

"My name is Kevin. Not Kev. And yes, I know what interest is. We did not agree on any interest charges."

"You didn't read the small print."

"There was no small print. There was no contract."

Literal people make my balls ache. His dog just

wouldn't stop barking and was giving me a migraine. "Look, I'll give you a few days," I said, "but you still owe me two grand. That's the deal."

"That is *not* the deal." And then his eyes softened and he reached for his wallet. "If you're hard up at the moment I could lend you fifty pounds." And Christ Almighty he took a fifty out and brandished it at me. "Here. You can pay me back whenever."

I would have been less offended if he'd flipped me the bird. "Two thousand," I growled. And I turned and left him with the fifty still held out and ratdog yapping his ugly goddamn head off.

STEELE

My memories of 2007 are mostly sand and sun. Iraq. The kind of sand that eats at your flesh, and the kind of sun that bakes the life out of you.

I was in the SAS by that time. 22 Special Air Service regiment, 'A' Squadron. In Baghdad with Task Force Black. The Special Boat Service and United States' Delta Force were with us, and as the summer of 2007 rolled on we must have killed three thousand Al Qaeda insurgents in Baghdad alone.

Still. I'd had enough. The sun, the sand, the goddamn Iraqi desert.

The politics.

I'd had enough of it all.

Major Campbell, commander of A Squadron, called me into his office on a night as dry and hot as the inside of a kiln oven. He was a rugged-faced Scotsman, hard as rock and less expressive. "At ease, Kitson," he said. "Take a seat."

"Thank you, Major." I tried to work out from his unreadable expression whether he was pleased or pissed off or somewhere in between.

"Are you doing okay?" he asked eventually.

"I... yes, sir, thank you."

"You are?"

"Yes, I'm doing fine."

He considered me, not saying anything. The silence got awkward.

I cleared my throat. "Er, was that all, Major?"

"Are you thinking of leaving after this tour?"

Goddammit. I knew he'd find out sooner or later. I should never have discussed it with the rest of my troop.

Once the genie's out it's not going back in the bottle. "I... I am considering it, sir, yes."

"Aye," Campbell said, "I thought as much."

"Who told..."

"It doesn't matter where I heard it. We don't have secrets, you should know that. So. Can I ask why? You're the best in your troop. You'll make a damn good Captain one day."

I sighed. "Sir, it's hard to explain..."

"Is it the Yanks?"

"No. It's... I just don't think this is right. For me."

Major Campbell didn't have a clue what I was going on about. "Jesus, Kitson. Not right for you? What does that even mean?"

"It... It means I don't think we should even be out here."

He sat back in his chair and stared at me. "We're not here to *think*, laddie. We're not here to discuss the finer points of British Foreign Policy - it's not our call. We're here to do a *job*."

"I know. That's the problem. I'm frightened we're just making this whole situation worse." I forced myself to hold eye contact, even though I just wanted to look at the floor.

Major Campbell pursed his lips. "We've reduced bombings in Baghdad from a hundred-and-fifty a month to single figures - how is that making it worse?"

"There weren't a hundred-and-fifty bombings a month in Baghdad before we got here."

"So you're saying we should have left Saddam to it?"

"No. I..." I sighed again. "I don't know. But I remember when we were fighting him the last time. My father died in the Gulf War in 91. I was twelve."

Campbell gave a small smile. "I'm sorry."

"That was only a few years after we'd been *helping* Saddam fight the Iranians."

"Aye, well. That's politics for you. This time we had *humanitarian reasons* for removing Saddam Hussein. And we were protecting British interests."

"There were no WMDs, Major. But of course the American oil companies have their oil contracts, so that's something."

Campbell shrugged. "It is what it is."

"I joined because I wanted to *protect* people. In ten years time, Iraq and Afghanistan aren't going to have magically become liberal democracies, leading the way in human rights. This whole region is unstable - we've created a power vacuum and who's going to fill it? Something worse will come along."

And of course it did. Though none of us expected anything as bad as Islamic State, not even me.

The Major considered again, this time for longer, and I just sat there wondering if I'd got myself in trouble. Eventually he said, "I know a guy. Part of the Security Service back home. Undercover operations on UK soil. Highly classified."

I frowned. "Okay..."

"Going after major criminal organizations. I think they could use someone like you. And you'd be doing some real good."

"Is it like police work?"

"No, it's a little more... *covert* than that. MI5 type stuff, I think. Although I don't really know. As I said, highly classified. When the tour is over I could talk to him. If you're interested."

I thought about it. "Thank you, Major. I am."

He set up a meeting a few months later when we were back in the UK. I travelled down to London and waited at the designated meeting place: a park bench by a lake. It was early evening, and no one else was around.

The guy sat down next to me and said, "Don't tell me your name."

I looked at him. "I'm sorry?"

"I don't want to know your name." He didn't look at me as he said it, nor at any other time through our whole conversation as far as I could tell. He just looked over the lake and spoke as if to the geese. "You'll need to make up a false name, but don't tell me that either."

"Er, okay..."

He was obviously ex-forces, he had the look. "No one can know who you really are. The work we do is... *sensitive*. Our agents need to be able to disappear."

"Disappear?"

"They only exist for the extent of their contracts, and then they disappear again. You'll need to become someone else. New name, new history, new identity. New appearance."

"New *appearance*? But how am I..."

"We can help you with that if your application is successful. You'll have to do the best you can until then. Grow a beard. Wear sunglasses. Change your accent, if you can."

I thought of Major Campbell. The Scot. I thought I could probably manage a Scottish accent.

"Pretend to be someone else," the guy said. He pulled a card out of his pocket and held it in my general direction. "There's a number on there. Call it if you're still interested. But for God's sake use a public payphone. Preferably in a big city far away from where you really live. Ask for the 'recruiter', and use your fake name." Then he got up and walked away.

Two days later I got the train to Birmingham. I called the number.

"I would like to speak to the recruiter," I said. I used a Scottish accent. "Aye. My name is John Steele."

*

The Chappell's lived in a small semi-detached that looked in need of some care and attention. I had to watch my feet walking up the drive. The slabs lay broken among the weeds and stuck up like teeth.

Mrs Chappell only invited me in after I'd shown her my ID and assured her everything was off the record, and that she wouldn't need to come to the police station or make a formal statement.

Mr Chappell sat in a wheelchair in the lounge, with the shades drawn and the lights off. He had a blanket across his knees, and the hands atop it shook. He looked like a skeleton, and I thought I might hear his bones rattle. His head turned as I entered, like a skull with a thinning curtain of white hair hanging down the back of his neck. He had an oxygen mask strapped to his face and breathed like Darth Vader.

Mrs Chappell sat next to him and took his hand, but she stared at me. They both did. "Ask your questions, Mr Steele."

She told me how they'd met Gary Brooker, and how he'd persuaded them to sign up to a pyramid scheme. But when they'd tried to pull out he'd... convinced them not to.

"He took all our savings." Mrs Chappell looked at her husband, patted him on the knee.

"What did he do to convince you?"

She swallowed, then looked slowly up at me. "He took a wrench. And smashed my husband's legs."

My stomach flipped.

"He didn't do it himself, of course," Mrs Chappell continued. "He had another man do it. But Gary was there. Gary told him to."

I looked at Mr Chappell. Mr Chappell in his wheelchair with his broken legs covered with a blanket. "The guy who did this, what did he look like?"

"He was bald, I think - but it was a long time ago…"

"Was he white, black, Asian?"

"White."

"Can you describe his build?"

Mrs Chappell frowned, then shook her head. "I… I don't know. It's all a blur."

"That's okay. Don't worry."

A bald white guy. Baldy Baz fitted the bill quite nicely, didn't he? "What did you tell the police?"

"That he'd fallen down the stairs."

I winced. "Jesus. They would never have believed that."

"Of course they didn't. But that was our story and we both stuck to it."

"Because Brooker threatened much worse if you told the truth."

"Exactly." And tears of anger burned in her eyes. "He said if we told anyone what really happened someone would come back. And instead of my legs they'd break my back."

I exhaled slowly, put a fist to my mouth and shook my head. "I'm so sorry."

"So if you need me to make a statement I won't do it."

"You don't need to. I have all I need."

*

I parked up on Willow Drive in the shadow of some trees, about a hundred metres shy of the place my satnav faithfully assured me was my destination.

The difference between this street and the ones on which the Chappells lived was striking. The houses here were big, and some of the drives had gates or Porsches, or both.

The house across the road from me was number 9, so I counted four houses into the distance to locate number 17. I could only see one white wall because of the bend in the road, but thought I could maybe see flashes of Brooker's silver Porsche on the drive behind his neighbours' cars. I wondered if he'd tried to polish out the scratches on his rear bumper.

"Okay," I said aloud, as if giving myself permission. I climbed out and circled around the back of my Merc to the curb-side back door. No one else was on the street, and I was covered from behind by the trees and from any prying eyes in number 9 by the body of my car. I opened the back door and flipped the seat lever. The bench yawned open, revealing my weapons locker.

It was quite a sight. AWC sniper rifle with folding stock as used by the SAS. Colt Canada C8 assault rifle. Police issue Heckler and Koch MP5 submachine gun. Two Sig Saur P226s as used by MOD police, and two Glock 17s, current army issue. Grenades, flares, binoculars, gas mask with built in infra-red goggles. Bulletproof vest, computer hacking hardware, assorted tools, listening bugs, two trackers, and lots of boxes of ammo.

I took out a Glock and managed to fit a silencer to it between my good hand and the one in the sling. I checked and then slotted the magazine.

Good. Ready to go. Boy, would I give Brooker a surprise. He was about to receive one hell of an ultimatum.

But before I could close the seat bench I heard an engine coming from the opposite direction. I looked up in case Brooker was leaving - *escaping* - but what I saw was even more complicated.

A car, some red family-friendly thing, had pulled up in front of his house. I grabbed the binoculars and crouched against my Merc.

Yes, definitely Brooker's house, because he had just come out onto the drive and stood with a hand on his Porsche's roof. It was him - same cropped black hair, same tan – but oh God his nose. It looked like a plum. Despite that, Brooker wore a big, genuine smile.

I trained my binoculars on the car, a Ford Fiesta I now realised, and the woman driving. There was some glare on the windscreen, but she looked attractive - long brown hair, delicate features. Except she didn't smile, hardly looked at Brooker, in fact, and she kept one hand drumming on the wheel.

That's when the kid got out the back.

He yelled, "Dad!" ran briefly into Brooker's arms and then gasped. "What happened to your *nose?*"

"Ha, you should see the other guy."

Ha indeed. Look down the street and there I am.

The boy seemed to accept this, and started jabbing his father like a boxer.

Brooker laughed, made a show of raising his hands and bobbing about, and then grabbed his son over the back of his head and mussed his mop of hair.

The boy, he looked about eight, squawked and bounded up the drive to the house, pulling Brooker by the hand.

The woman in the car - I guessed the boy's mother - didn't get a goodbye or give one. She just bumped off the curb and carried on up the road towards me.

I watched Brooker take his young son indoors, and I thought, *Oh shit.*

*

"You didn't tell me he has a son," I said, once more on the phone to Andrews.

"Does that make a difference?"

"Of course it does." I wove through the traffic to keep the red Fiesta in sight. "He has a *kid*, George."

"You're not... not going to use the boy…"

I flinched. Almost choked on my words. "*What?* Jesus. *Use the boy?* What the hell do you think I am?"

"Well, I..." He stuttered, "I didn't mean... it's just that, with everything you've done..."

"Everything I've done?"

"... I don't know how you work. Or what you're prepared to do."

"Clearly, George, clearly. I mean, bloody hell."

"Okay, fine. Good! You won't hurt the boy."

"Course not. But I need him out of the way. What's his name?"

"Gary."

"Not Gary. The *boy.*"

"Oh. I can't remember, hold on." I heard keys clacking and then, "His name is Alex. He's seven. Says here as far as we can tell his mother looks after him during the week and Brooker has him weekends."

And today was Saturday. "That's just great."

"So what are you going to do?"

"I'm following the mother at the moment. What's her name?"

"Melissa. They're still married, but separated."

"Okay. Look, I've got to go." I hung up. Melissa had pulled into a café car park, and I followed her in and parked in the nearest empty space.

I watched her walk in through the cafe's plate windows. A guy sat alone at one of the tables with a newspaper, and Melissa hurried over to him and said something. He looked straight at my car and said something back, although not being a great lip-reader I couldn't tell what it was. Probably wasn't *I'll buy him a milkshake,* though.

I got out of my Merc and made for the café. The guy got up and came to meet me.

I am paranoid, but not *that* paranoid. He wasn't just going to the gents.

I slowed down so he'd reached the front door first, and he stood there with his arms folded, waiting for me.

I thought he was just a concerned citizen, looking out for a young woman being stalked by a ragged Scottish hobo.

I was going to get my ID out when he said, "I believe Mr Brooker told you to leave town."

I froze, and he laughed at my face.

"Ah, yes. I know all about you. You robbed him with a machete."

I almost laughed back at him. "That's what he told you?"

"And then he found your Travelodge and went in and kicked your arse. Got you to promise to leave town."

"He did, did he."

"Yes. He had you squealing like a piggy."

"A piggy."

"And look, here you are, chasing after his *wife*. You honestly do have a death wish, Ginger. Wait til he catches up with you. This time he won't go so easy on you."

Wow, all Brooker's guys were humungous jerks. Figures. I thought about Jeremy getting beaten to a pulp last night. "Let me see your knuckles."

"Pleasure." And the idiot went to grab me. Even with one arm in a sling, you shouldn't try to grab me. I stepped aside and then I broke his knee. Kicked him from the side, right at the joint, and his leg gave way and made all kinds of wet cracking sounds. A bit over the top, maybe, but remember I only had one arm. Besides, anyone in Brooker's employ would hardly be a saint.

He went down and howled, clutching his knee. His knuckles were unmarked.

I left him there and went into the café.

Melissa was not happy to see me. She stood behind the counter tying on an apron.

I'd been right about her being attractive.

I managed to pull free my wallet and let it fall open. "Police," I said, which wasn't exactly true, but who the hell cared.

She backed against the cabinets behind her and set the coffee cups rattling. "You're a cop?"

"Aye."

"Has something happened to Alex?"

"No, no. Nothing like that."

She exhaled. "Oh, well, I don't want to talk about Gary."

"You don't need to be frightened."

She glared at me, hissed, "What the hell do you know? Where's Terry?"

"Terry?"

"He's the guy Gary sends here to spy on me."

"He's having a lie down. *And spy on you?* I thought he was your bodyguard or something." I tried a grin, which she didn't return.

"Terry's here to stop me doing something stupid - like *talking to the police.* Do you know what Gary will do to you if you've hurt him?"

I raised my eyebrows. "I can take care of myself."

"You have no idea what he's capable of."

That's exactly what he told me after I'd punched his slimy tanned face.

"Please leave," Melissa said. "I've told the police before, I'm not saying anything."

"I only want to ask you about Alex - how long will Gary have him? When will you pick him up?"

"What's that got to do with anything?"

"Humour me."

She whisked a strand of hair from her face. "Am I under arrest?"

"What?"

"Am I under arrest?"

"Of course not." I didn't even have the power to arrest her.

"Then please go away. I don't want to talk to you."

A fat man with a cap - the manager, I assumed (he had a name badge anyway) - came up behind me and said, "I think you should leave, sir."

I thought about showing him my ID, but what would have been the point? Melissa wasn't talking, and I was only going to make things worse.

"Okay, okay," I said, holding up my one hand. "I'm leaving. But I just want you to know, Melissa, you don't have to be scared anymore."

She stared at me with pursed lips. "I'm not scared for me, I'm scared for my son," she said. "Please go away. You're just going to make it all worse."

*

Terry had crawled to the edge of the pavement and sat there cradling his knee. "You better run," he growled as I passed. "I called Brooker. Two guys are coming here right now…"

"You'll need more than two." I didn't look at Terry, just strolled on past, got in my Merc and drove away. Terry threw a pebble at my windscreen, but what the hell was that going to do? The glass was designed to stop a *bullet*.

I circled the café and pulled into a side road, parked between two cars. After spying on Brooker's house I'd left the binoculars on the passenger seat, and I picked them up now and trained them on the café car park and poor Crippled Terry.

He sat there swearing to himself and beating the ground with a stick until a familiar white van pulled up to him five minutes later.

Two men got out. One was the large black guy who'd been at Jeremy's house. The other was Baldy – The guy who'd been with Brooker last night when they'd picked up the medals. He had a huge lump on his head from where I'd kicked him unconscious. I could see it from here.

They helped Crippled Terry up and supported him as

he hopped to the van and fell in the back. I watched them drive away.

And then my phone rang. It was Andrews. "Steele," he said. "I've just heard from the hospital. Jeremy Peters has died of his injuries."

*

My first thought was to go after the white van, to chase it down and make it crash. There was a good possibility one of them was Jeremy's killer. Or they'd at least know who did it.

I thought of Jeremy's wife in the hospital last night. She said she didn't recognise the attacker, but I knew it was one of Brooker's guys, if not Brooker himself.

They'd killed Jeremy but it was my fault.

I drove back to the police station with blood pounding in my ears and what felt like an elephant sitting on my chest. My gunshot wound began to throb and burn like the bullet was still in there doing somersaults. At a red light I dry swallowed more pain killers from the glove box, but they didn't make a bit of difference.

I took a minute and tried to calm myself down, but my headache wouldn't quit and the elephant just sat there and sat there. Killing bad guys doesn't affect me at all, but when innocent people die and it's my fault? Yeah. It's like a part of me breaks.

I headed straight into George Andrews's office. He looked up from his desk.

"It was Brooker or one of his guys," I said. "I know Mrs Peters wouldn't say anything, but I'm sure of it."

He nodded. "I think you're probably right. It's the sort of thing he'd do."

"Can you tell me more about them?"

"I can tell you what we know. Come round and take a look."

I pulled a chair round to his side of the desk and sat. He took six printouts from a brown envelope and spread them over the desktop. "As far as we know, these are Brooker's guys."

"I recognise these three," I said, pointing them out. "Baldy. Crippled Terry, and the blob."

"The blob's name is Jermaine. The bald one is Baz."

"'Baldy' and 'the blob' are more descriptive."

"And... *Crippled* Terry?"

"His knee is broken."

"Aw, Christ, Steele."

"He went for me first. Anyway, he didn't kill Jeremy - his knuckles weren't damaged. Whoever did it punched him to death, and that'll show."

Andrews nodded. He prodded another printout, a muscley guy of about thirty with his middle finger raised at the camera. Where did they get these photos? The information below read 'Stuart Stockson, 31' and gave his address and extensive rap sheet.

"He owns a garage on the outskirts of town," Andrews said.

"He's a bald white guy as well."

"As well?"

"As well as Baldy Baz."

Andrews frowned. "Okay? What's your point? I don't think Brooker hires them because he likes their bald heads."

"Oh, so you do have a sense of humour after all." I studied Stockson's photo more closely. "I went to see the Chappells earlier."

"I wondered if you would. Horrible thing. Horrible."

"I trust you realise he didn't fall down the stairs."

Andrews spread his hands. "*Of course*, Steele, but neither of them would tell us a thing. We had doctors and nurses and cops all trying to persuade them to tell us what had really happened, but they stuck to their story. What could we do? We had nothing else to go on..."

"I realise that, George, I do. But I did get her to talk *off* the record." I pulled forward the printouts of Baldy Baz and Stuart Stockson. "She said Brooker was there, but he didn't actually break her husband's legs himself. She said the guy who did that was a bald white man."

"She did?"

"Aye. That's why I'm looking at these two. And she also said he used a wrench."

Andrews raised his eyebrows. "Christ. A wrench? Christ."

"And Stockson is a mechanic?"

"Yes. It wouldn't exactly be difficult for him to lay his hands on a wrench."

"Or he might have just given it to Baldy Baz to do it."

"True. Also, it happened more than a year ago, I think. Brooker might have had another bald white guy working for him then."

I nodded. "Possible. So, we have Baldy Baz, Jermaine the blob, Crippled Terry, Stuart Stockson the satanic mechanic..."

"Hilarious."

"Now what about these last two - they don't have any information or anything."

The last two printouts were just photos of middle-aged men in suits. One of them was already going grey and the other had hair nearly the colour of straw.

"We haven't identified them yet." Andrews bent

closer to study them. "Only been linked to Brooker in the last few weeks. We don't know who they are or where they come from, or if they're even working for him."

"I havney seen them about." They would henceforth be known as Mr Blonde and Mr Grey. "Anyway," and I pushed their printouts aside, "going back to who beat Jeremy Peters to death. My money's still on one of these guys. Baldy or the blob. They were both out and about last night, working with Brooker."

"Baz has been inside twice before. ABH both times."

"I'll start with him, then." I pulled out a post-it and jotted down Baldy Baz's address, and then Jermaine the blob's under that. "Leave it to me." And then I got up and walked out before Andrews could stop me.

BROOKER

I was halfway to the café when Baz phoned me.

"He'd already left when we got there, Gary," he said.

I swore. Alex looked up from his Nintendo 3DS and laughed beside me, and then repeated the word with gusto.

He waited for me to laugh, and usually I would have. The only thing funnier than old people falling over is little kids swearing. But just then I wasn't in the mood. "Where are you now?" I asked.

"We're going to the hospital."

"Why?"

"Terry's leg, it's... like, hanging off the wrong way. The ginger guy kicked him for no reason."

I could feel myself going red, and I clenched the phone a little too hard so the shell creaked. My nose still felt twice its normal size. I remembered Baz getting knocked out. And now Terry. Terry wouldn't be working for months if it was as bad as they said.

"Gary? You there?"

"Yeah."

"What... what should we do now?"

I had no idea. "Just drop Terry off, and... I don't know. Go home and wait for me to think of something. I'll call you." I hung up. I couldn't listen to Baz anymore. Even the beeps and whizzes coming from Alex's DS were driving me mad.

I pulled up in front of the cafe. "Stay in the car and play your game. I need to talk to your mother."

Alex didn't complain. Just sat there with his seatbelt still on and his eyes fixed on the screen.

I crossed the car park, threw open the door, and

Melissa paused midway through pouring coffee and stared at me. She turned away. Handed over the coffee cup to a fat pigman customer and tried a smile on him. Like she was flirting with him in front of me, trying to get me jealous, like *she* controlled *me*, and the only thing that stopped me punching the fat pigman customer was that he just took his cup and left - *as if she wasn't good enough for him!* - and this suddenly made me much madder until I realized the pigman was probably a goddamn faggot, he looked the type.

I strode up to Melissa. The bitch wouldn't even look at me. Just wiped the counter.

"Gary, I'm working."

"That guy was in here," I growled, low, so no one else would hear.

"What guy?"

"*The ginger guy, you dumb bitch*. The one who did *this* to my nose."

She looked at me then, at my nose, and for one moment I thought I caught her mouth twitch, but she wouldn't, she wouldn't *dare*...

"Does it hurt?" she asked.

"*Does it look like it hurts?* What did you say to him?"

"*Nothing*." She stared me out, eyes blazing and her mouth all screwed up tight like she thought she could defy me. "He asked me about you but I didn't tell him anything, alright?"

"He broke Terry's leg."

"And that's my fault?"

I grabbed her wrist and squeezed. She *dared* talk to me like that, with less respect than she'd show a goddamn homeless guy. And I thought maybe if I squeezed hard enough she might apologise and I might even see some tears, but instead she just glared at me, the bitch just stood there and glared at me.

"Let go of me, Gary."

And my God, she actually grabbed my hand and dug her nails into the back of it like some common street whore, staring me out the whole time, until she managed to pull free, leaving me bent over the counter with great wheals on the back of my hand.

The fat manager was coming over.

"You're going to take a five minute break and come outside with me," I said to her.

And she said, "No."

I don't enjoy hurting women, but my God was she asking for it. I said very quietly, "If you don't come out right now…"

"Go away, Gary. You're not *my* boss."

The fat manager had arrived. "Is there a problem?" He was so nervous he was sweating.

"No problem," Melissa said. "Gary's just leaving. Aren't you, Gary?"

The bitch stitched me up good and proper. There was nothing else I could do, and she knew it. But she'd pay for making me lose face in front of her sweaty manager and the gay pigman and all the other customers. I could feel them watching me. As I turned and walked back to the door I could feel their laughing eyes - *Oh look, that Gary Brooker can't even control his wife!* - and oh God she'd pay for that.

I got back in my Porsche and slammed the door. I felt like my skin was boiling in an oven.

Alex looked up from his DS and said, "Dad, are you OK?"

Anyone else and I'd have gone apeshit - *Do I goddamn*

look okay? _What part of my face looks goddamn okay?_ - but for Alex I managed a smile, I actually managed a smile despite everything, and perhaps that's because he's the only person in my life capable of making me smile without offering something in return.

I mussed his hair. "I'm fine, son."

"You sure? You look mad."

"Nothing for you to worry about." My thoughts turned to Kevin West, who still owed me two grand but was having a hard time getting it through his thick head.

So I called Jermaine.

"Boss? You found the ginger guy?"

"No, not yet. Did you leave Terry at A and E?"

"Yes, boss - I've just got home…"

"I need you to do something for me. I need you to go and give Kevin West a message."

"No problem. I'll head over there now."

"I suppose you dropped Baz back at his place."

"Yes boss. But I can go back and get him if you want the two of us."

"Good. I do."

STEELE

I was driving to Baldy Baz's address when the Carluccis showed up again.

They were in a black Land Rover coming the other way and must have recognised the front of my car, or maybe they got a glimpse of the registration. Even though I tried not to look at them as they passed they damn well looked at me.

I watched them in my rear-view mirror as they screeched a one-eighty, drawing a horn blast from another driver, and began to follow me.

"Shit."

I sped up, weaving through the traffic, putting more cars between me and the Land Rover. I turned left, jumped a red light and got a horn blast of my own.

Luckily, they must have been caught at the lights and I managed to lose them by taking a few turnings and doubling back on myself. In a few minutes I'd put a couple of miles between us and even managed to lose myself.

You should not still be here, Steele.

But I had a promise to keep. And those medals. Taking the medals had really pissed me off.

And they'd killed Jeremy Peters.

I hadn't exactly forgotten the hitman, either.

The reasons were stacking up.

Fifteen minutes of aimless driving later, and still no sign of the Carluccis.

I found Baz's address and parked a little way down the street. His house was a narrow old terrace, and I made sure I didn't have to walk past his front window to get to his door.

I didn't knock, I just tried the handle as quietly as I could. The door clicked open. It's amazing how many people don't bother to lock themselves in. I'm not advocating a chest of drawers in front of the door, not for the ordinary person, but geeze.

The TV blared from the front room. I stopped with the door ajar and listened for movement. I think Baldy was watching *Soccer Saturday*. I heard him laugh.

I shut the front door as quietly as I could with one hand and then strolled into the lounge.

He'd heard my footsteps, but only had time to mute the sound before I wandered in.

"What the..." He stopped when he recognised me. "*You...*"

"Don't get up," I said. "I'm not an old guy on the bus." I looked at his hands, which he'd clenched on the arms of his chair. Knuckles red and raw.

"You broke Terry's leg…" Baldy said. He stood up. "You robbed Gary with a machete and kicked me in the head!"

"You killed Jeremy Peters."

Baldy faltered.

"He died this morning. Of the injuries *you* gave him."

Baz swallowed. "You... you can't prove anything."

"Your knuckles for one."

"Don't mean a thing."

"Where were you last night? After I'd taken the medals from Brooker, I mean. Where did you go?"

"You know where." He smiled a cold, humourless smile. "I went and taught that ratting son-of-a-bitch liar a lesson. He deserved it."

"He didney even know I'd got the medals back off you."

"Don't matter. What's that matter? He was a lyin' bastard, and I gave him what he deserved. But you'll never be able to prove it. Gary told the woman we'd go down and kill her grandkids if she told, so she ain't gonna. You can't do anything to me." He began laughing, and so I took my silenced Glock 17 out of my jacket and shot him between the eyes.

He stopped laughing.

He went down face first.

I can do *that*, buddy.

I called Andrews. "I was right. Baldy killed Jeremy Peters."

"Do you have proof?"

"His own admission. Brooker told Mrs Peters if she testified someone would go and kill her grandchildren."

"What, her *grandchildren*? But... but Steele, Baz isn't going to confess in court..."

"Course not. So I shot him."

There was a pause. "You..."

"Shot him in the head. Aye. He's dead."

"Christ, Steele, you have to be joking…"

"I don't joke about things like this."

Andrews fell silent.

I said, "You don't approve. That's fine, I'm okay with that. I don't need you to approve. It's done, and I'm glad. Don't tell me he was going to give away all his possessions to charity and devote the rest of his life to helping others."

"Would it have made a difference if he had?"

"Of course it would. This wasn't about Baz killing Jeremy. I shot him to stop him hurting anybody else. And only because you didney have enough evidence to put him away."

Andrews muttered, "We would have got him eventually."

"Probably. But how many more innocent people would have died? Anyway. I need you to send someone over here. The gun had a suppressor, but you know how those things work – just tones it down from 'deafening' to 'extremely loud'."

"But... but..."

"Hold on..." I looked out the window. "I have to go." I hung up, peered through the shades.

A white van had pulled up outside.

*

I hit the standby button on the TV remote and dragged Baldy behind the sofa. He slid across the bare floorboards with little effort.

The van door slammed shut outside. I ran down the hall and, not finding the front door key handy, I grabbed the handle with my right hand and held it still just in case the van man tried to open it.

There was a peep hole in the door. Jermaine the blob came waddling up the drive.

Oh, just perfect.

He rang the bell and waited. His face ballooned in the peephole lens and looked even more inflated, like a black Mr Mackey off *South Park*. Obviously, Baldy didn't answer, and so he rang the bell again.

"Baz, come on man, we got an errand to run for Mr Brooker!"

An errand? I didn't like the sound of that. It probably involved killing someone.

"I'll go without you!" said Jermaine, and then he tried the handle. I saw him reaching for it, and I braced myself against the door and held it fast. The handle wiggled in my hand a couple of times, until the blob swore and gave up. He turned and waddled back to his van, opened the door and with considerable effort pulled himself in.

I let him drive well out of sight before I opened the front door and peered down the street. The van sat at a junction. I watched it turn left in a break in the traffic, and then I sprinted to my Merc.

Baldy Baz might not be available for Mr Brooker's 'errand', but I'm in. Just try and stop me.

*

I followed the white van, just like I had last night. It was light now, so I stayed a few cars back.

Eventually it pulled into a quiet terraced street, and then outside one of the houses. There was a fairly new blue Peugeot on the drive, but the curtains in the living room window were flowery and faded like at an old people's home.

I hung back and watched Jermaine the blob decamp and slog up to the front door. He knocked, and a dog started barking from within.

I'm not a huge fan of dogs. I got bitten by a Rottweiler a few years ago. This dog had the high-pitched yip of a terrier or something.

A man opened the door, and I knew at once that this was another of Brooker's victims. Thin, small, reedy. A boyish faced with a ridiculous fluff-tuft of a moustache and hair already thinning. No wonder Brooker had decided he could pick on him.

"Yes?"

Oh God, his voice. Like a child's cartoon character.

"Kevin West?" said the blob.

"Yes," said the man who must have been Kevin West. "Can I help you?"

The dog still yipping from somewhere near the back of the house. There was a flat cap hanging on the coat stand by the door.

"I'm a friend of Gary Brooker's. Can I come in?"

Kevin's face seemed to light up. "Gary? Yes, of course." He stepped back and allowed Jermaine in. "How is Gary? He was here only..."

There was a yelp.

The door drifted closed.

I fumbled with my seatbelt. "*Shit*..." I hadn't been able to stop Jeremy's beating, but I could stop this.

The front door stood ajar just a crack. I drove closer, pulled up, climbed from my car, slammed the door, locked it with my keyfob and hurried up the drive and into the hall.

They were both in the kitchen now. I heard Jermaine say, "This is from Mr Brooker," and then a *thwack*, and then a cry of pain. The dog was chained up in the back yard, yipping and yipping.

"Please stop... I don't understand... what have I done to offend Gary?"

Oh foolish, naive child-like Kevin.

"You owe him money."

"No I don't! No I don't! I paid it all back! I have it written down!" Another cry of pain.

"You owe him money, and this is a gentle reminder to pay up."

I reached the kitchen doorway. The blob stood over Kevin, who lay against the washing machine with his hands in the air and blood dripping down his chin. He reminded me how Brooker himself had looked, lying in the road against his Porsche with his own streaming nose.

I said, "Hold it there, blob." I had my right hand around the gun in my pocket, but I wasn't going to shoot him. He deserved to get his arse kicked, but I couldn't say he deserved to die. Not yet, anyway.

The blob looked around. "Ginger!"

Ginger? I guess that was fair. I had just called him 'blob'.

"Mr Brooker told you to leave town!"

I rolled my eyes. "No he didn't, that never happened. I suppose he also told you I'd robbed him with a machete?"

"You should bugger off back to Scotland."

"Don't be racist."

He glowered at me. "You tryin' to be funny?"

I thought it was pretty funny myself. "Why are you attacking this man?"

He didn't have chance to answer, because Kevin grabbed something from the draining board, I think it was a wok, and smashed it with all his might into Jermaine's balls.

Jermaine fell to his knees, clutching at his crotch, his eyes bulging and a thin reedy sound coming out of his mouth. Kevin smacked him again over the back of his domed head, and Jermaine went sprawling across the kitchen lino and then curled up like a hedgehog.

"Yeah, how does that feel, you fat bastard!"

He was going to hit him again, possibly keep on hitting, so I hissed, "*Kevin*," and he stopped and stared at me.

"Who are you?"

"My name is John Steele. I'm with the Security Service."

"I haven't done anything wrong. You can check, you won't find anything."

I shook my head. "No, no. That's not why I'm here. I'm here to protect you from Gary Brooker."

"I don't need protecting." He raised the wok again over Jermaine's head.

"Woah..." I raised my hands. "I think he might have learnt his lesson."

The blob lay moaning and dribbling, trying to crawl for the door.

"He punched me in the face!"

"I think you've got your own back. And if you knock him unconscious we'll never be able to drag him out of here."

"I wasn't going to knock him unconscious, I was going to kill him."

He said it matter-of-factly, without a hint of anger, and I tell you it sent a chill down my spine. I shook it off. Left the gun in my jacket. I thought the blob was probably taken care of.

"Do you only have one arm?"

"No. My other's in a sling."

The blob had managed to crawl to the door and I kicked it wider so he could reach the hall. I pressed him against the jamb with one leg and fished in his pocket for his phone. He whimpered as I frisked him.

"I don't understand." Kevin dropped the wok on the floor and began to dab his nose with a hanky. "I paid Gary back everything I owed him. We had an agreement. I told him I only needed a few days until I got paid."

The dog kept on yipping and yipping.

I took out the battery from Jermaine's phone and stashed both pieces in an inside pocket. "Gary Brooker is an arsehole," I said. "As you are finding out."

"I thought Gary was my *friend*. He lent me four thousand pounds even though we hardly knew each other. And I have no one else. My mother and father died in a fire when I was young, and my brother's in a mental hospital."

I looked up from the blob's sprawled out, slug-like body. "Oh. I'm... sorry to hear that..."

"Without Gary I'd have never been able to pay off my credit card." Kevin turned to the window and yelled at the dog to be quiet, not that it did any good.

"Look, if you bare with me for just a second I'll call the police and..."

"No!" His face lit up. "I can handle this myself."

I looked at weedy Kevin in his cords and tweed and almost laughed. I doubted he could handle a toddler's tantrum. "I... don't think that's a good idea. Gary will..."

"Oh, I'm not scared of Gary," and he actually grinned. "He should be scared of *me*. He's picked on the wrong gentleman."

*

It took ten minutes to help Jermaine into his van. There was no way I was getting him up in the passenger seat, so I guided him to the back and pushed him down flat onto the van bed. He had a concussion, flailed his arms a bit and then threw up on himself.

I didn't feel sorry for him.

"I'll get a taxi back here to pick up my car," I told Kevin, as he waited in the doorway with his hanky held to his nose. He just gave me a single nod. The far-off look in his eyes - the thousand-yard stare - it worried me a little. "You're not going to do anything stupid, are you?"

"No. I never act rashly."

I shouldn't have left him there, I know that now. But I didn't know what he'd do, alright? Or how things would escalate.

I drove the white van with Jermaine lying in the back and parked it at the row of shops outside Brooker's office. I tried the office door, but of course it was locked; Brooker was at home with his kid. Then I checked on Jermaine to make sure he was still breathing and wasn't going to choke on his own sick. He'd live. There was a possibility that he wouldn't have any kids, but that was probably a good thing.

I returned to the office door. No pane of glass, so I couldn't see anything inside. But I remembered last night Brooker setting an alarm before he left. Motion sensor, no big deal. Sends a radio frequency signal to the control system whenever the door is opened. Easy enough to jam the signal with a burst of radio noise. No signal, no alarm.

Unless of course the system wasn't wireless, in which case I'd have to get a little smash-happy with the alarm box.

Still, no biggie. I only wanted a look round and that wouldn't take long.

So I got out my phone. I can do more with it than make a phone call or take a selfie. The camera can record in infra-red. I can connect to military satellites and encrypted frequencies. I can hack software and passwords. I can jam radio signals.

So that's what I did, standing outside the office door.

Problem two: obviously, the door was locked. I did have a bump key somewhere, which would have allowed me to bump up the pins in the lock with the key's specially designed teeth, but I think it was back in my car. No matter. I had a pair of lock picks slotted into the face of my watch, and I'm quite good with them.

The white van hid me from the rest of the road whilst I worked.

The door opened. The alarm remained silent.

I climbed the stairs into Brooker's office space.

What a dump.

Dark and dingy, with one small window overlooking the street and a desk in one corner. Nothing in the other three corners except mothballs.

A computer monitor and telephone on the desk. I circled round and sat in the chair, looking out at the rest of the room like Brooker must have done so often. There was a cupboard and two drawers in the desk, and the computer tower beside them. I turned the computer on and opened the cupboard whilst it was booting up.

Hidden inside was a safe. Small and square and aluminium, with an old-fashioned number dial that went *ticker ticker ticker* when I spun it. No way I could open the safe without the passcode or a powertool, so I closed the cupboard door and looked through the drawers.

Nothing in the bottom drawer except some pens, scraps of paper and an old calendar open on July 2012. In the top drawer I found a pink pay-as-you-go mobile phone and a large black logbook. I left the phone but took the logbook out and opened it on the tabletop.

Bingo.

Brooker had listed all his business dealings going back

to January 2008. Dates, names, amounts. The last entry was *14th November 2014, Jeremy Peters, repayment of goods (medals) to the value of £13,000 approx.* COMPLETED.

I sighed, because of what had happened, because of what I'd done.

You were just trying to do the right thing, I told myself, but it didn't help.

I flipped to the back of the logbook and found some names and addresses. The most recent was Kevin West's. Brooker's victims, then. But just as I was going to snap it closed the names on the adjoining page caught my eye.

Baz. Jermaine. Stu. Terry. And then also a Royce and Johnson. They must be the new guys, Mr Blonde and Mr Grey. Although of course I didn't know which was which. Written underneath each name was an address and mobile phone number.

I looked again at the phone on the desk and thought how hilarious it would be if I called one of them from Brooker's office phone. Couldn't call Brooker himself, which would have been even better, because I'd stolen his mobile last night and I didn't know his landline number. But one of the others, sure.

Baz was dead. Terry was in hospital. Jermaine was lying unconscious in his van outside. So either Stu, Royce or Johnson.

I called Royce, mainly because it made me think of Rolls and I was getting hungry.

"Hi boss," said Royce.

Even better. Brooker's office number must have been programmed into his phone.

I said, "Hi Royce."

A pause. "Boss?"

"No. Does your boss have a Scottish accent?"

Royce thought for a moment. Didn't get it. "Er, no... I'm sorry, who is this?"

"Didn't Gary Brooker tell you about me? The ginger Scotsman who robbed him with a machete?"

He thought again. Finally it clicked. "You're the guy."

"I think you might have finally got it."

"You robbed Mr Brooker with a machete?"

"Apparently."

"You coward."

I chuckled. "I'm phoning from inside *his office* and you're calling me a coward?"

Another pause. "How did you get in?"

"I flew through the window, how do you think? Now listen. Jermaine the blob is unconscious in the back of his van just outside. He might appreciate it if someone came and checked on him."

"He's... but..."

"Okay Royce, nice talking to you."

"Don't..."

"Bye." I put the phone down.

Damn, I should have asked him if he was Mr Blonde or Mr Grey.

The computer had opened on a password screen, so I just shut it down again. I didn't have a USB cable to connect it to my phone and hack my way in, nor the time to do it. So I got up and left, taking Brooker's logbook with me.

*

There was a Tesco at the other end of the row of shops, so I bought myself some lunch and then headed over to the toys aisle on the off-chance they might still have one of those golden Robotik bunnies. It was the must-have gift for Christmas, and although it was only November I couldn't find one anywhere. As a special edition they were only available in-store, so that ruled Amazon out. And I'd only seen one on Ebay, but I'd been outbid at the last moment.

I found the shelf of little Robotik animals. They had dogs, cats, and little robotic bunnies in black and white, but none in gold. I sighed, but it was hardly a surprise.

I ate my sandwich on the low wall outside Tesco as I waited for Royce to arrive. He did so ten minutes later.

I had a great view up the street and of the back of the white van. They wouldn't see me because I was half hidden by the trolley stand, and lots of Saturday shoppers were milling about, walking this way and that.

Royce arrived in a blue saloon, parked on the other side of the van from me and so disappeared from view for a few seconds. And then Royce himself appeared on the pavement and hurried to the van's rear doors.

It was Mr Blonde. In real life his hair almost made me wince.

I'd left the van's rear doors unlocked, and Royce opened them and found Jermaine lying there. He climbed in and bent over Jermaine and shook him, presumably checking he was still alive. I imagined his huge gut wobbling.

Then Royce jumped from the van, threw open the office door and went haring inside.

Twenty seconds later he reappeared. Presumably he hadn't found me.

Jermaine had managed to sit himself up. They talked briefly, and then Mr Blonde helped him scoot to the open doors and climb out onto the road. Jermaine patted at his pockets and then grabbed his balls again. Kevin smacking them with a wok must have really hurt.

Royce found the keys I'd left lying on the van bed and handed them over. Jermaine slammed the rear doors, locked them, and limped back to his cabin. Royce returned to his car and they both drove away.

Show's over.

I finished my lunch and called a taxi, having to find a number off the Internet.

A couple of minutes later a red Ferrarri pulled into the car park. It idled slowly past me, as if showing itself off, and then parked in a free bay.

A man got out and glowered at me. Began to walk over.

Perhaps I had not admired his car to his satisfaction.

Or, more likely, he was pissed at me for another reason. Maybe because I'd just killed his cousins, because I was pretty sure this man was Antonio Carlucci.

I reached into my jacket pocket and put my hand around the Glock.

I could shoot him. I mean, it would be *legal* for me to shoot him. I could kill this man and justify it for a hundred reasons. Firstly, I doubted he was striding up to me to discuss the weather. If his hands went anywhere near his jacket I was going to put him down no matter what. He was a drug manufacturer, dealer and a killer, and the police couldn't touch him. I tallied up the probability of him seeing the error of his ways and volunteering at a local homeless shelter and decided it was pretty low.

Everyone would be better off without him. He was a leech and a drain on society, and if you subtract a negative you get a positive, every secondary-schooler knows that.

But still. I couldn't shoot him. Not unless I absolutely *had* to.

There were families everywhere, milling about, walking to their cars, pushing trollies.

Did I really want a car park full of people, many of them kids, seeing me shoot a man dead in front of them?

No.

I just hoped he wouldn't make me do it.

"You." Cousin Antonio stopped in front of me, his hands clenched into fists by his sides. "*You*. I know you."

"Hello, Cousin Antonio," I said.

He bared his teeth and hissed, "You killed my cousins."

"Sorry." I wasn't sorry.

"You will die for what you did."

"Okay."

"Get in the car."

I raised my eyebrows. "Why?"

"*Get in the car.*"

I smiled at him. "Or what?"

"Or I kill you." And he opened his jacket a little to reveal the butt of a gun protruding from his waistband.

"That's a very nice butt."

He didn't laugh. "*I will give you to the count of three...*"

"You're not going to shoot me," I interrupted. "For the same reason I'm not going to shoot you. Look around. How many more witnesses do you want? And you'll be on CCTV. You wouldn't see the outside of a prison again, and you don't want that."

He didn't say anything, just stood with his chest rising

and falling and his hands clenching and unclenching and his mouth curled into a sickle.

"And by the way," I said, "I'm already pointing a gun at you. Glock 17 in my jacket pocket. I could empty the magazine before you got your gun out your pants. So how about you drive on out of here and be thankful you did *not* find me in a deserted alley, because if you had... well. I don't think it would have gone well for you."

He stood there for a couple of seconds more. "There will be nowhere you can hide. We will catch up with you." And stalked off back to his Ferrari.

"Antonio."

He turned.

"Nice car," I said.

He didn't appreciate the compliment. He just got in his nice car and roared on out of the car park.

I released my grip on the Glock in my pocket and exhaled.

First the dealer with my picture and then the Land Rover tailing me and now Cousin Antonio trying to lure me into his car.

The Carluccis were not happy with me at all.

You should go, I told myself. Forget Brooker and get out of there.

But then I thought about Jeremy Peters and The Chappells and Catherine Thompson and Will the hitman Pharrell.

And Kevin West.

Poor prematurely-aged Kevin West, he of the dead parents and the house fire and the lunatic brother. He of the wok-beating incident.

The taxi arrived a few minutes later and when I got back to Kevin's house his blue Peugeot was gone.

BROOKER

After McDonald's, I'd taken Alex to the park and he'd crashed his toy helicopter into a tree. One of the rotor blades came off and for a horrible moment I thought he might cry.

"Don't you dare," I warned him.

"But... but it's broken..."

"And I'll fix it when we get home. But not if you start bawling like a little girl."

He bit his lip hard and nodded.

"That's my boy. Now go and play."

He ran off towards a group of other boys, and before long they were playing out some kind of epic gun battle. They ran around the playground and through the woods shooting at each other with their fingers. One of the smallest boys got pushed over and ran away crying. I thought maybe Alex had done it, which pleased me. If you can't take the heat stay out of the kitchen and all that.

It had been nearly an hour and a half since I'd sent Jermaine and Baz round to Kevin West's. I thought they'd have rung by now to fill me in on what the blithering idiot had said. I'd tried calling them earlier, but for some reason Jermaine's phone was off and Baz wasn't answering.

I tried Jermaine again. *Connection failed.* I tried Baz, and it just rung through to voicemail. I never leave voicemails. You never know who might pick them up. I haven't stayed out of prison this long by leaving traceable incriminating messages.

So where were those guys?

Not long after my own phone rang, but it was neither

Jermaine or Baz. It was Royce. The new guy. The ex-bouncer with hair like Boris Johnson. I answered. "Yes?"

"I've got some bad news, Mr Brooker. It's Jermaine. His van was parked outside your office and he was lying in the back. He wouldn't tell me what happened, but I think the ginger guy beat him up."

My stomach burned like acid and I stomped both my feet on the grass. "*For Christ's sake!*"

"Also, Jermaine said that he'd lost his phone, but I think it was stolen."

That's why I couldn't get through. "Where is he now?"

"I think he went home. But that's not all. The ginger guy, John Steele, he... he..."

"What?"

"Well Mr Brooker, you're not going to be happy about this, but, well I mean…"

"Just goddamn tell me, Royce!"

"He... he broke into your office."

My blood ran cold. That couldn't be. It made no sense. "He what…"

"He broke into your office. I don't know if he took anything…"

"I'm on my way." I hung up, my heart thudding and cold angry sweat breaking out on my brow. "Alex!"

Alex and the other boys were playing football with a ball they'd borrowed off some other kid. "What?"

"We have to go. *Now.*"

He must have seen the look on my face because he came without a fuss.

I carried his broken toy helicopter home because he had worn himself out, and he said his arms were dead. He may have been winding me up, but I didn't care. I had more important things to worry about.

"Dad, what's the matter?"

"I'm fine," I lied. "I just need to check something. Can you keep up?"

I needed to get home, get my car and get out to my office, but the walk seemed to take forever. Alex regained some of his energy as we turned up Willow Drive, because he ran on ahead and started calling for ice cream.

He stopped outside the house, stock-still, and then screamed, "*Dad!*"

"What?" But then I saw. And I dropped the toy helicopter. And my stomach flipped, and I felt as though I'd been punched in the chest.

My Porsche…

My Porsche looked like it had been in an accident. The windows were smashed, the doors and bodywork were dented and bent, the rear bumper hung off and glass and chips of plastic peppered the driveway.

*

It must have being John Steele. Who else was crazy enough? First he'd broken into my office and then he'd driven over to my house and trashed my car. But how the hell had he found out where I lived?

I'll kill that ginger son-of-a-bitch.

I grabbed Alex, who had started to cry. "Dad... what..."

"Stay here."

Steele could be hiding nearby, waiting to attack me where my back was turned. That was the sort of thing he'd do.

I checked round the corner of the house and then the

side gate to make sure it was still locked. Then I opened the front door and the burglar alarm started beeping.

"Come on, Alex, it's okay. There's no one here."

He gave my battered Porsche a wide berth and joined me in the hall as I punched in the code and shut off the alarm.

"Are you going to call the police, dad?"

"No. What have I told you about the police?"

"D-don't trust them."

"And?"

"They're not our friend."

"Good." I checked every room, even though I knew he couldn't really have got in without tripping the alarm. He wasn't a ghost. "It's okay, we're safe here," I told Alex, sitting him down in the front room. I tried calling Baz again, but still couldn't get through. *Goddamn, where is he?* No point calling Terry or Jermaine, so I tried Stuart Stockson. "Stu, where are you?"

"I'm still at the garage, Mr Brooker. I'll be finished at 6 – you got a job for me?"

"That Scottish ginger guy's smashed my car."

Stu paused. "You mean..."

"Looks like he took a baseball bat to it. The windows, the bodywork, he knocked off the bumper..."

"Bloody hell, man, what a dick..."

"I want him found, Stu. *I want him found.*"

"Yes, Mr Brooker. As I said, I got things to finish off here and then..."

But I'd already hung up, and straight away I called Johnson. Told him what had happened, and he assured me the ginger bastard would be his first priority.

Then I called Royce. "When did John Steele break into my office, do you know?"

"Er, I think... about half an hour ago, Mr Brooker."

I considered. In the middle of the day it took maybe fifteen minutes to get from my office to my house, so he had enough time. I'd probably only just missed him. "Half an hour. Are you sure?"

"I think so. You see... well, the thing is, he actually called me."

I frowned. "He called you? John Steele called you?"

"Yes. About half an hour ago. F-from your office."

I thought I'd misheard. "He what?"

"H-he actually called me... from the telephone in your office."

That goddamn cheeky bastard. "*Why are you only telling me this now?*"

"I wasn't sure what to do, Mr Brooker – you were out with your son, and he told me Jermaine was parked outside in his van and I needed to come and see to him, and I didn't know what he was planning so I thought I'd go over there first but he'd already left..."

"You need to tell me *everything*, Royce, hear? Every goddamn thing, especially when it comes to *him*. He went straight from the office and smashed up my car!"

"He smashed up your car?"

"Yes! I want him found, goddammit!"

"U-understood, Mr Brooker, I'll..."

"And have you seen Baz?"

"Er, no. Is he not at home?"

"I don't know. He's not answering his mobile."

"Do you want me to..."

"No, leave him. I need you to go and talk to my wife. The ginger guy was there earlier but she wouldn't tell me what they talked about." I eyed Alex and lowered my voice. "Perhaps you could be more... persuasive. I wouldn't be surprised if she has something to do with this. You should have seen the way she talked to me earlier."

"You can't have that, Mr Brooker. Consider it done."

We rung off. I felt pumped and furious all at the same time.

"Dad," Alex said, "is mom in trouble?"

And I gave him a small smile. "She might be, son. Now, put your coat back on. I just need to go and check on my office." And I wasn't going to leave my son home alone whilst I did it, not with that ginger maniac on the loose.

"But your car..."

"I'll get the BMW out of the garage. Now come on."

I think the tax had run out on the BMW, but at that moment I didn't give a damn. We drove across town and parked up outside the launderette.

"Stay here," I told Alex.

The office door looked in one piece. I was half expecting it to be standing open. I had the only key, but somehow John Steele had managed to unlock it himself. God knows how. I mean, who the hell was this guy?

I went inside. The alarm was off or wasn't working. And I was *positive* I'd set it last night. "Hello?"

No reply. I couldn't hear any movement from above, but I still wished I'd brought a weapon of some sort.

I crept up the stairs. Released the breath I'd been holding.

No one there, and everything looked untouched.

The computer was off, the telephone in its cradle. I opened the cupboard door, suddenly convinced the safe would be standing open and empty, but of course it was still locked up. I put in the code and opened it anyway, just to check, but nothing had been taken.

If he'd got into my safe I would most probably have self-combusted.

I checked the bottom drawer. Nothing missing. Then the top drawer.

"Oh goddamn."

My logbook was gone.

STEELE

I got back in my Merc and chomped some more pain killers from the glove box because my gunshot wound had begun biting again. Exceeding the recommended dose, not that I gave a damn. Threw the silenced Glock 17 into the glove box with the pills.

I thought about going over to Brooker's house again, but what was the point? Andrews had said Alex would be with him all weekend, and I wasn't going to deliver my ultimatum with the kid there. I could have gone back to Baldy Baz's to clean up, but Andrews had probably already sent a team round, and I didn't fancy trying to explain to them that I was the killer but that was alright as I had a licence.

The fact I'd hardly got any sleep last night, *and* being shot, *and* had a hitman sent after me decided it. I drove back to my hotel, making sure I wasn't followed. Managed an hour's sleep before my phone woke me. Better that than a hitman breaking down the door.

"Steele," I said.

"Steele, it's Dalton."

I sat up, fully awake. "Hello sir."

"You said you'd be done by now," my boss said. "Is he taken care of, your loan shark?"

"Not yet… there have been complications."

"Steele, you need to finish this, and quickly. Pappa Carlucci is not happy with what you did to his sons."

"I didn't expect him to be."

"He's booked on a flight over here from Italy - he's probably in the air now."

"Thanks for the head's up. I'll be careful."

"Hurry it up and get back here. There aren't many

ginger Scottish assassins about and he'll find you sooner or later."

"I need to be back by Wednesday anyway - I have a party to go to."

"This is serious."

"I know, sir. I'll handle it." I thought of how Kevin had said *I'll handle it* and how he had almost beaten Jermaine to death with a wok. "Just one more thing - could you put me through to Dawn? I have some more file notes to give her." I didn't really have any file notes to give her - I just didn't think Dalton would approve of what I really wanted.

"Okay, I'll put you through. And Steele? I expect the Merc back in one piece this time."

"Sure." I didn't mention shunting Brooker's Porsche. Or the blood in the boot.

The line beeped a couple of times and then Dawn said, "Steele, I thought we were done. I'm just looking back through the file – after I have your written report I can close it."

"Good, thank you. And I am nearly done here, I'd just like you to run a background check on someone."

"Okay, no problem. Who?"

"His name is Kevin West." I gave her his current address. "Something's not right - he said his parents died in a fire and his brother's in a mental hospital."

"Sounds like he should be on Jeremy Kyle."

"Aye, I know. But I don't know why he'd lie."

"I'll check him out now and send the information to your tablet."

"Thanks." I hung up. My tablet computer lay at the bottom of my overnight bag, and I fished it out, opened it up, turned on data roaming and set it on the bed. I cleaned my teeth and picked at my bandage while I waited. Thought about Pappa Carlucci landing, probably at Heathrow, and having a limo drive him up here. It was half 3. Wouldn't take him more than two hours.

I went out to my car, checking the car park for idling Land Rovers. There were none. I flipped the back seats and took out the bulletproof vest.

Not paranoid, I told myself. *Sensible.*

The purple gym bag was still hidden under the passenger seat. I pulled it free, zipped it open and dumped twin waist holsters, the two Glock 17s and a box of 9mm magazines into it on top of the cash.

Just a precaution.

I zipped up the bag and returned to my room.

Dawn had done her job. There was an email waiting for me on my tablet.

It didn't take me long to read and didn't make me feel any better. Just more confused if anything.

When he was twelve, Kevin's parents died in a house fire. It had been started by Kevin's own brother, Lee, which is why I guess he ended up in a mental home. Either that or prison. Lee was a few years older than Kevin, and had a history of violence. Arrested for assault, burglary, possession of class A drugs.

And arson.

He'd set a car on fire when he was fifteen.

After the house burnt down, their neighbours had told police stories about how Lee would continually bully Kevin and argue with their parents. They said they were frightened of Lee, said it would only be a matter of time before he killed someone.

He'd killed *two* someones. Mr and Mrs West, nineteen years ago.

Lee never admitted it, but an empty jerry can was found in his car. It was an open and shut case.

He was diagnosed with psychopathy and admitted into Saint Mary's mental hospital, and has been there ever since.

Kevin moved from foster home to foster home until he turned eighteen, when he received his parents' will, to the tune of ninety-eight thousand pounds.

According to the file, he'd never been employed and had always lived alone. But he'd said to me *I told him I only needed a few days until I got paid.*

So what exactly did he do?

BROOKER

When I got back home I noticed the curtain's twitch in the nosy old bitch's house across the street.

When me and Alex were both inside I said to him, "Now look, I'm just going across the road to ask Mrs Avery what she saw."

He looked panicked. "Don't leave me alone…"

"I'll be two minutes. And I'll only be there-" I pointed at Mrs Avery's front door. "Out on the step. I'll be able to watch the house the whole time. Okay?"

I could see Alex wasn't happy, but he sucked it up and nodded.

"That's my boy. I won't be long."

I hammered on Mrs Avery's front door for what felt like five minutes before the nosy old bitch opened it.

"When did it happen?" I stuck my foot in the door just in case she decided to terminate the conversation prematurely. Mrs Avery didn't need to ask what I meant. I knew the beak-nosed old bitch would have been at her window, egging the ginger bastard on and laughing and rubbing her hands together.

"I don't know. Maybe an hour ago," she said. And then, "He has gone to town on it, hasn't he."

She was almost smirking, the bitch. I thought about grabbing her wrist but she was half hiding behind the door. "You're loving this, aren't you."

"What would you have liked me to do?" she asked insolently. "You've already made it clear as far as the police are concerned…"

"You better not have called them."

"Of course not. And the man had a cricket bat. Would you have liked me to fight him off? Perhaps with my walking stick?"

My hands clenched into fists. I looked back at my Porsche and growled, "That goddamn ginger son-of-a-bitch..."

And she said, "He wasn't ginger."

I stared at her. "What?"

"He wasn't ginger, Gary. He had dark hair, from what I could see under his tweed cap."

It was as if she'd shot me. "Tweed cap?"

"Yes, he was an odd-looking fellow. Drove a blue Peugeot."

And I thought, *Goddamn.*

STEELE

I exercised my sling arm with a couple of circles and chicken flaps. Damn thing had begun to stiffen up. I stretched it as far as I could without tearing something, and then began the slow, laborious task of fitting the twin holster belt round my waist. I cinched it tight and high so that my jacket would hide the holster. And the guns.

The vest next. I put it on over my top and spent the next ten minutes buttoning a shirt over the top of it. Casual, and loose enough to hide the shape of the vest. I tucked it in to my trousers though, obviously, or drawing a gun would be a nightmare.

I put the Glocks in each holster, although having to reach across and draw with my right would be a pain. Just hoped I wouldn't need to do any drawing at all.

And then my jacket over the top. I left it unzipped.

Half past 5. Dinner time, right? So I drove to the café.

I saw Melissa waiting tables as I walked in. The place wasn't busy, and she looked up as the door clanged. Probably habit.

Her face dropped. I have that effect on lots of people. She hurried behind the counter, heading for the manager, the guy who'd asked me to leave earlier.

I sat down at a table in the middle of the room, facing the door. Picked up the menu, flicked through.

The manager came over. "She still doesn't want to talk to you."

"I'm just after some food," I said innocently. "The scampi please. And do you do J2O?"

"No."

"Just a coke then. Scampi and a coke."

He thought about it. Noticed my sling, but didn't comment. Probably wondered how I'd eat with just one hand. Sighed. Then, "Okay."

Melissa watched, but I deliberately didn't look at her. I scanned the room instead, looking for any likely hardmen, anyone who might be Brooker's.

No likely suspects. The diners consisted of two elderly couples, a young man on a date with his girlfriend, a group of teenage girls drinking milkshakes and a family of four eating pizza.

And I'd walked in wearing two handguns and a bulletproof vest.

Melissa avoided even walking too close to my table, giving me little glances which I returned, trying to look as friendly as possible and less like an armed killer.

When my scampi came she stared openly as I ate, probably because I did so using only my fork and didn't (couldn't) cut anything up.

The family of four finished, and on passing me the youngest - a little girl of five or six - said, "That man's only got one arm!"

Oh, the bluntness of kids. I almost choked on my scampi. The mom went all red and started blustering admonitions and apologies, trying to pull her daughter as fast as she could past the table.

I raised my hand - my one hand - laughing out, "It's fine, honestly." And then to the girl: "Look, my other arm's in a sling."

The girl said, "Ah. Did you breaked it?"

I didn't think *no, I got shot* would go down too well, so I said, "Aye, lassie, I did. I had to go to the hospital."

"Why do you talk all funny?"

"Okay, Maisy, let's leave the poor man to his dinner,

shall we?" The mom gave me an embarrassed look and pulled her daughter away.

I laughed it off, turned back to my food, and saw Melissa hovering by my table. "Mrs Brooker." I blinked.

She swallowed. "You should go."

"I haven't finished my scampi. I might want a pudding."

"This isn't a joke." She bit her lip and sat at my table. She looked even more lovely close up. I felt self-conscious eating like a pig in front of her. "Gary is *really* mad at you."

"I imagine he is."

"He wants you *dead*."

He can join the queue. "He doesn't scare me." I saw the bruises on her wrist. "Who gave you those?"

"Gary did it himself. For talking to you earlier."

"You never said anything to me earlier."

"He didn't know that. All he knows is that Terry said you'd been following me, and then you broke his knee when he tried to stop you coming in here."

"I guess Gary told you to call him the minute I show my face again."

"Yes."

"Have you?"

"No."

"Why?"

"Because screw him, that's why."

I smiled to myself. Studied her. She just stared right back. "I'm sorry he hurt you," I said. But hey, at least I didn't get you beaten to death like Jeremy Peters.

Melissa sighed. "It's not your fault any more than it's mine. But you've really pissed him off, putting Terry in hospital like that."

You haven't heard the half of it. I robbed him, shunted his Porsche, punched him in the face and shot Baldy Baz.

She looked at my sling. "Did one of Gary's guys do that? Were you getting your own back on Terry?"

"No," I said. "I don't do what I do for revenge."

"And what is it you do, exactly?"

I kept my eyes on hers, didn't blink. "I stop bad people."

She raised her eyebrows. "You stop bad people."

"I stop bad people from hurting innocent people. That's why I broke Terry's knee." I added, "And also because he tried to grab me. I don't like bad people hurting *me*, either."

She studied me, trying to work me out. "You're not really a policeman, are you."

"Technically, no. Although I am with the government. The police have to work for me."

"Really."

"Aye."

She scoffed. "What, are you Interpol or something?"

"No." I fished out my wallet and flipped it open on the table, my ID face up.

"John Steele," she read. "Security Service. Who's Jacqui Smith? I recognise the name."

"She was Home Secretary a few years back."

"What's an LV Number? Is that something to do with the army?"

"Sort of. I used to be in the army. It's the reason you should trust me, at least. It means I'm one of the good guys."

"The good guys. Well there's certainly been a shortage of them in my life."

"I need to ask you about Alex."

Her expression hardened. "What about him?"

"Gary's not exactly the best role model."

"What can I do?" she asked, defensive. "I mean, do you really think Gary would let me stop Alex from seeing him?"

"I'm not judging you, Melissa. It looks like Gary has a habit of getting what he wants. Using any means necessary."

"Yeah, well. I've been married to him for five years. When we separated he said he'd kill me if I tried to take Alex off him. And he meant it."

And given Brooker's record, he probably did. "I'm going to sort this," I said. "Trust me."

She stared at me for a moment and then nodded. "Okay."

And that's when the familiar white van pulled into the car park.

*

It didn't stop out the front. There were no spaces, so it headed off round the side of the building.

Melissa saw me looking and turned. "White van?"

"Aye."

"I didn't call them."

"I believe you."

"They come in here often anyway."

"Melissa, I believe you. Now go back to the bar. I don't want them to see you with me."

She thought for a moment, sighed, then headed to the counter. Picked up a cloth and began absently skimming it over the surface. Her lips had drawn tight.

Three of them came in. I recognised them all. Royce

and Johnson. Mr Blonde and Mr Grey. The other was Jermaine the blob. That surprised me. He'd been dribbling and vomiting all over himself with a concussion a few hours ago. At least he'd changed his shirt. As they walked in I noticed him limping, and couldn't help but smile.

Mr Blonde was in the middle of a story when Jermaine spotted me. He clapped a hand on Royce's shoulder, making him wince.

"It's him," Jermaine said, looking like he'd seen a ghost, which of course is what I am.

The others didn't ask who, just turned and stared at me.

I sipped my coke as they approached my table. Mr Grey turned to Melissa and snapped, "How long has he been here?"

She jumped, stuttered, "Er... I..."

"I told her not to call you," I said, trying to save her another bruise. "I was very... insistent."

"Get off on threatening women, do you?"

"Do you get off on threatening men?"

They were all around my table now. The other diners had stopped to watch. The group of milkshake girls got up and left quickly.

"Mr Brooker's not answering his phone," said Mr Grey, returning his own mobile to his pocket.

"Please boys, I don't want any trouble," said the manager, although he went very quiet when Mr Blonde put one finger to his lips.

"You shouldn't have messed up Brooker's car," Mr Blonde said. "That was an extremely stupid thing to do."

"It was only a scratch on the bumper."

"You put in the windows. Cracked the windscreen.

Took a baseball bat to the bodywork, it looked like."

I fought my first instinct, which was to frown. Kept a poker face instead. "What makes you think it was me?"

"Who else would it be?" Jermaine said, his voice thick as if the wok had knocked something loose. "You robbed Mr Brooker, broke Terry's knee..."

Shot Baldy Baz, I added in my mind. I didn't say it though. I didn't want them to know I was armed.

So who'd trashed Brooker's car? Except, of course the answer was obvious. That idiot is going to get himself killed.

"You're coming with us," said Mr Blonde. "We can either do this the easy way or the hard way."

"I haven't finished my drink," I said.

"How about I *smash it in your face?*" said Jermaine.

"How about I smash your balls with a wok?" I said.

He didn't like that. Stood there glowering at me.

I picked up my fork, held it upside down in my fist, like I might stab the prongs into the tabletop. Or alternatively into someone's face. I saw Melissa on the phone out of the corner of my eye - pretty sure it wasn't a social call. Pretty sure she was calling the police.

Gary Brooker would not be happy with that.

"Who's first then?" I said. "I may have one arm in a sling, but I warn you that in the other I have a *fork*."

But no one had a chance to go first. Because Gary Brooker himself rushed in at that moment with Alex trailing after him.

*

"Melissa!" Gary called. "You need to have Alex for a while. Give him an ice cream or something."

Melissa looked like she wanted to protest, but

obviously didn't say one word. I dropped the fork and my hand crept to my waist, and the holster, and I could feel the bulge of the gun. I hadn't been planning on killing him, but there it was. Not that I'd have shot him there in front of everyone, even if I had wanted to.

Alex stomped off and said, "I don't *want* to stay here."

Gary ignored him, but he saw his guys. "You three come with me. I know who trashed my car - I went and spoke to that old bitch who lives across the street and she saw him do it."

"We already found him, boss," said Jermaine, and stepped aside so Brooker was looking straight at me.

His face pinched up. His eyes grew wide, his mouth into a grimace. "*You...*"

"Gary. Nice to see you again."

Alex saw my sling and said, "Look, that man's a cripple." He laughed. Already one half an arsehole.

"It wasn't him," Gary said. "It was Kevin West."

"*What?*" Jermaine screwed up his face.

"You guys stay with him," Gary said, stabbing a finger at me. "Take him for a ride in your van, Jay, and wait for my call. I've got to deal with Kevin West first. I'll see to *him* later." He turned and hurried out.

I wondered what he was driving. One thing I was sure of: Kevin was going to get himself killed.

"I don't *want* to stay here!" Alex actually stamped his foot. Melissa grabbed his hand and led him away from my table to the other side of the room, whispering in his ear no doubt promises of as much ice cream as he wanted.

Jermaine glowered down at me with a flabby, furrowed brow. "So you *didn't* trash his car?"

"I think you owe me an apology."

"You'll be the one grovelling soon enough, mate."

Mr Blonde said, "Come on then, Van Gogh. Time to go."

"Hilarious." I do look a bit like Van Gogh if his self portrait is anything to go by.

"And keep your hand where I can see it."

"And again. You're on fire." I stood, using my elbow to clamp my jacket closed to stop my gun flashing. Mr Grey moved behind me.

"Don't even think about the fork," Mr Blonde said, moving aside and gesturing to the door.

I didn't. Funnily enough, my hope was with my gun.

"After you." Mr Blonde gestured for me to move again.

"What a gentleman."

"Don't try anything stupid, okay mate? And don't try to run."

"Hadn't even crossed my mind."

I went first, presumably to stop me sucker-punching anyone in front of me with their back turned. They crowded in quite close, though that was okay. I felt like I had three bodyguards, except they weren't there to protect me. Quite the opposite.

I pushed the door open and ducked my head against the breeze. And slid my right hand around the butt of the Glock.

Mr Blonde came next. Poor old Royce. I could see him out of the corner of my eye, just over my left shoulder. He had drawn the short straw.

We were now walking down the side of the cafe, out of view of the windows and the street. I could see the white van parked just a few feet away. So I drew.

Glock from holster, spun to my right, cracked Mr

Blonde in the jaw with my right elbow before levelling the gun at the rest of them.

They stopped short, except Mr Blonde who crumpled against the wall and swore.

"Don't move," I said, but they weren't moving.

The tables had turned so quickly, Jermaine the blob didn't even look like he knew what was happening, but maybe that was the concussion.

Eyes went wide, mouths open, hands up.

"Woah, man," and "Easy," and "We wasn't gonna hurt you."

"Get up, Mr Blonde." I actually called him that.

He did so, without any help. They weren't moving, remember.

"We were only gonna frighten you," said Jermaine.

I told him to shut the hell up. "Take out your phones and throw them on the ground."

Mr Blonde and Mr Grey did so. Jermaine began bumbling about how I'd taken his phone off him back at Kevin's and he didn't have one anymore. I got him to turn out his pockets just to make sure.

"Okay. Are those the keys for the van?"

"Y-yes..." gulped Jermaine.

"Huh. You let this guy drive? He threw up all over himself a few hours ago after being hit with a wok. How are your balls?"

"Still hurt."

"Good. Move to the van and open the back door. *Slowly.*"

Jermaine did so. His hands shook in the lock, but he got it open.

I slowly held out my sling arm and left hand. "Give me the keys. Notice the gun I'm pointing at your fat head."

Jermaine handed over the keys and stepped back again. "All of you in the back."

They looked at each other. Mr Grey said, "Where are you taking us?"

"Nowhere, you idiot. I'm going to lock you in to keep you out of the way. Or I can just shoot you."

They got in the van. I slammed the door and managed to turn the key in the lock with my left hand. "Good."

Holstered the Glock, transferred the keys to my right hand, picked up the two mobiles and ran back to the café.

Melissa was pacing as the manager looked on. Alex sat at a table, playing with a Gameboy or DS or something.

"John..." She put a hand to her mouth. "You're okay, thank *God*..."

"They're locked in the back of the white van round back," I said and handed her the keys. "Give these to the cops when they arrive - I'm going to call CSI Andrews and get him to take them in."

"W-wait a minute - where are you going?"

"To save Kevin West."

BROOKER

Alex was not happy when I told him I was dropping him back with his mother, so he gave me the silent treatment as we drove to the cafe, just sat and played on his 3DS and that suited me just fine. Perhaps he could tell I was ready to explode, because he kept giving me furtive glances, and that pissed the hell out of me and I just wanted to tell him to *goddamn stop it* because he was putting my nerves on edge.

I gripped the steering wheel so hard my knuckles turned white, and I thought of how that was poetic because in ten minutes they'd be red with blood.

And I led Alex into the café and my guys had only gone and caught the Ginger. I stared at him as Melissa hurried Alex away, stared at his small smile and his goddamn ginger hair and his goddamn ginger beard, and for one long moment I completely forgot about Kevin West.

This ginger Scot had robbed me, punched me, tried to take my woman (because look where he was, *again*, turning up to fawn over my wife) and here he sat, surrounded, at my mercy.

But then I remembered. Not Kevin exactly, but his tweed cap, and I could hear my Porsche screaming as he went at it again and again with his cricket bat, smashing the windows, smashing plastic, smashing metal, smashing, smashing.

And I knew I'd kill them both, somehow, but I'd have to go and get Kevin now before he escaped. So I got the guys to hold the Ginger until I was ready for him. They'd take him on a drive, and then when I'd dealt with Kevin we'd take him deep into the forest chase and kill him. And that would be the end of the ginger ninja.

But Kevin first. I drove to his house feeling on steroids, like my blood was electric, and everything looked red and I could taste something acidic.

Oh dear Christ I felt *glorious*.

I parked outside his house and sprang up the drive feeling both heavy and light with my heart *bumbumbumming* and I slammed my fist against his door *bangbangbang*, "*Open this door you son-of-a-bitch!*"

And oh Jesus my heart! Banging away as if egging me on, *kill the bastard kill the bastard*, and I swear I saw a curtain twitch from upstairs. He was home and he was up there and laughing at me. I could almost hear him, laughing at me and touching himself and laughing with tears streaming down his cheeks.

He would not come to the door, despite my screaming, despite my banging, the yellow-bellied tweed coward stayed locked up in his castle congratulating himself on getting the better of me.

But he hadn't. He couldn't. I looked at his car, his tweed-mobile, and I took a flying kick and knocked off one wing mirror. And then I saw a hunk of broken brick lying in the weeds by the garden wall and lifted it, ready to put it through the windscreen.

And then I had an epiphany. It wasn't just my heart I could hear, wasn't just the sound of my blood rushing around my head, wasn't just my ragged breathing.

I turned to the side gate. Locked. I reached over and slid the top bolt free. Tried the latch. Opened the gate. Walked along the side of the house holding the lump of brick, my head full of that dreadful noise.

Yap yap yap.

I stepped into the back yard and ratdog strained his

lead to get at me, bouncing and yapping, bouncing and yapping. And I was completely calm as I approached him, my mind had emptied completely and even ratdog's yaps tuned out until all I could hear was ringing in my ears.

I knelt down just out of reach of his pitiful pussycat jaws. And I cocked my head.

And I hit him with the brick.

Once. Twice. I don't know how many times. Until my arm ached and I looked down to find the brick dark with blood and ratdog lying there yapping no more.

STEELE

"Steele, Christ, what's happening? We just had a call come in... Mrs Brooker said that you'd..."

"Don't worry about it, George, I'm fine."

Andrews snorted.

"Brooker's hardmen tried to get me at the café Melissa works at, so I locked them in the back of their van."

"How many?"

"Three."

"Three?"

"Yes, but I did have a gun, and that did most of the persuading. Melissa has the keys. I need you to tell your boys to arrest them. They attacked me."

"Are you hurt?"

"No, they didn't 'attack me' attack me, just said some nasty things about how they were going to. I just need them out of the way for a few hours whilst I deal with Brooker."

"What about his kid?"

"Melissa has him. I'm going to find Brooker now. Hopefully I'll get to him before he kills Kevin West."

"Remind me - Kevin West is?"

"Brooker's newest victim. He, er, didn't appreciate Gary's intimidation techniques and took a baseball bat to his car."

"He *what?*"

"He's a nutjob. I'm on my way to his house now. Hopefully it won't be too late." I hung up using the button on my steering wheel. It was full dark now so I had to concentrate on the road.

I'd thrown Mr Grey's and Mr Blonde's phones on the passenger seat and they skitted around. Turning corners at high speed with only one hand isn't the best idea. I drove to Kevin West's like an Italian taxi driver.

As I pulled into his road I saw a ten-year-old black BMW heading off into the distance.

I knew it was Brooker. He'd already been and gone.

Kevin's blue Peugeot sat on the drive, so presumably he was home. I just hoped he wasn't dead.

I pulled up, got out, and stopped before going to the front door. The side gate to the back garden stood open, and everything was deadly, unusually quiet. I went to the gate and down the side of the house, my heart thudding faster and thrumming in my ears, my hands (both of them) clenching and unclenching, because the silence said everything, didn't it, everything I needed to know. I knew just what Brooker had done because the dog wasn't barking, and as I turned the corner I heard the most God-awful wail, a scream to chill your insides, a sound of pure primeval misery.

Kevin. He knelt in the middle of the yard and wailed. Knelt and cradled his dog's body, which was still chained to its kennel.

Brooker had smashed its head in.

"I'll *end him*," Kevin spat. He turned to me, and his face looked like nothing human, all red and twisted, and his *eyes*, oh Jesus, his eyes... "What had Percival ever done, eh?"

"Tell me what happened, Kevin. Was it Brooker?"

"He... he came round here because of what I did to his car. But I wouldn't answer the door." Kevin sniffed, wiped away a glob of snot with his bloody hands. "He could hear Percival barking, so he... he..." Kevin went all rigid, all clenched up. He wailed again, and then buried his face close to the dog's body. "I will get him for this, boy," he whispered to it. "I will totally *destroy him*..."

I'd turned away, my own muscles clenching, unclenching, grinding my teeth, my heart hammering away *boom boom boom* in my head. "Kevin, don't be stupid. You'll get yourself killed, or locked up."

And he said, "No. I know what to do."

BROOKER

Time went all spongy. I only vaguely recalled hurrying back to my car and fleeing Kevin's as though in a dream.

I found myself some time later pulled over in a random street, half on the pavement with my engine grumbling. For some reason I'd brought the lump of brick with me. It sat on the passenger seat, stained, staring at me, accusing.

It was only a dog, I told myself. I'd got off lucky, because if Kevin *had* answered the door there'd have been a good chance I'd have killed *him* instead.

And be sitting here now contemplating murder and life in prison. And anyway, Kevin *had* killed my Porsche. Me killing ratdog was only fair. Justice.

We were even now.

I nodded to myself. Blew air through my mouth.

Okay. Did I need an alibi? Would Kevin even risk going to the police? I mean, he was hardly the innocent party, was he? First degree vandalism - he was probably looking at a stretch inside longer than I was, because my Porsche cost thirty grand and ratdog must have cost, what, three hundred quid at most. At most. Which was like, a hundred times less than my Porsche, so do the maths - what he'd done was a hundred times worse *at least*.

And ratdog was probably a rescue dog and didn't they give them out for free? So in reality he was probably worth not a goddamn thing.

That made me feel better.

My anger was spent and I hadn't really done anything too terrible.

I doubted an alibi would have worked anyway - there

must have been a couple of his neighbours at least attracted to their windows, watching me hammer on his door.

But he had asked for it, right? No one could deny that.

I rubbed my face. Okay, what was next? Fetch Alex and give Melissa a talking to. A stronger talking to, this time.

And so I got my bearings and drove to the café. Except I pulled into a nearby side street without actually getting there. And stared. And I felt myself growing hotter and my skin start to prickle and my heart begin to *bumbumbum* again because the café car park was awash with blue and red flashing lights.

"Melissa, *you little bitch...*"

She'd called the police. I *knew* it. After everything we'd been through she'd called the cops because her goddamn ginger boyfriend had been kidnapped by my guys, and I found myself clenching the steering wheel and imagining it as her neck and, "*Jesus Christ, Melissa!*"

I wanted to get out and go in there and teach her a lesson, but the car park was dotted with cops including a goddamn *policewoman* - I mean what the hell's with *that?* - and giving a woman power is the worst thing because I knew she'd arrest me just for looking at her funny because power goes to their heads.

And then, *wham* like my heart had exploded, I saw my three guys being led from the back of the cafe. Royce clutching his head, Johnson looking at his feet, and Jermaine for some reason holding his balls. All in handcuffs. Escorted by a group of cops all with smugged-up grins and rosy cheeks and noses like snouts.

And I put my fist in my mouth and screamed.

STEELE

My satnav told me it should have taken nineteen minutes to get to Brooker's house. I did it in ten. I admit I used my left hand now and then to help with the corners. My gunshot wound burned. I could feel my heart beat there, *thrum thrum thrum*, as if the bullet had planted an alien life form now digging its way out.

I pulled up. It was the first time I'd seen Gary's Porsche since the incident, and Kevin had really gone to town on it, Jesus. But no black BMW. The bastard hadn't come home.

I pressed my hands-free button and said, "Call Andrews."

It rang. Andrews answered. "Did you get him?"

"No. I got there just as he left."

"Christ. Is Kevin dead?"

"No, but his dog is."

"His *dog*?"

"Yes. Look, Brooker's not at his house, and I'm worried he might have gone to the café after Melissa."

"Well he hasn't yet, but I warned them about him. And he'll get himself nicked if he does. He may think he's untouchable, and maybe he's been clever til now, but killing a dog *is* an offence."

"I'm going to head back over there. Although I doubt he'll turn up with the cops outside." I sighed. "He's probably running."

"Yes. Knows that he's messed up, that we have something to pin on him."

"But I have this feeling he means to teach Melissa a lesson. She called the police on his boys."

"You're sweet on her, aren't you."

"Goodbye, George." I hung up, turned around and drove back to the café. There were three police cars parked in front of the windows, their blue lights flashing and reflected in the glass. Two cops stood by the doors.

I parked up and approached them with my ID already out. One of them was the guy who had pulled me over last night, and when he saw me he swallowed and stepped back, should I opt to take out my crazy justice on him.

"I left three guys locked in the back of a van…"

"Already on their way to the station," he said. "Just like you asked. Sir."

"Good. And the van?"

"We, er, well, the recovery truck hasn't come yet so..."

"That's fine, thank you." I went inside. A policewoman stood talking to the manager and Melissa. Alex sat at the closest table finishing off an ice cream sundae, an ugly sulk on his face.

Melissa noticed me and took a step forward. "John..." She said to the policewoman, "This is the man we were talking about."

"I couldn't find him," I said. "He wasn't at home. Melissa, do you know where else he could be?"

"I never knew where he was even when we were living together. He'd always go out and come back at strange times, often at night."

"I'm going to try his office now, although I don't hold much hope." He'd know that I'd broken in earlier so the chance he'd go there was next to nil, but where else could I try? "Are you and Alex going to be okay at home?"

"Yes, we'll be fine."

"Okay, call me if you need anything." I left again, sat

in my car for a few moments and thought about Brooker's office. Actually, I was thinking about how it was by that big Tesco, and wondering if they'd had another delivery of that bloody Robotik golden bunny I had three days left to find.

And then I heard buzzing from inside the car. Definitely a phone on silent, ringing. Vvvv. Vvvv. Not my phone, because my phone connected automatically to my Merc's bluetooth and would jingle away through the speakers when it rang.

I looked at the passenger seat, at the two phones I'd taken from Brooker's guys. One of them vibrated and lit up and Vvvvd like an intermittent vacuum cleaner.

I picked up the culprit. 'Gary' said the screen. Vvvv Vvvv in my hand.

I remembered him saying back in the café when those three punks had me surrounded - "Take him for a ride in your van and wait for my call."

I guess this was the call. But whose phone? Mr Blonde's or Mr Grey's? It didn't really matter. They sounded pretty much the same to me anyway.

I answered. Dropped the Scottish accent. Made my voice a little deeper. "Yes?"

BROOKER

I'd been about to drive away and out of town when would you believe it the ginger ninja himself pulled into the cafe car park. I watched him go in and talk to my wife and I knew then they were lovers, I could see the way she looked at him and it wired me right up. I had no idea how he'd escaped from my guys, though I was pretty sure Melissa had had something to do with it. Probably got in their way. Locked them inside or something, that was the sort of thing she'd do.

And then I had a thought. Hadn't the ginger taken Will Pharrell's phone earlier? I'd set the hitman on him during the night, and somehow Steele had survived and taken his phone - and then *pretended to be him when I'd called*. And back in the café hadn't I said I'd call the guys after Kevin was dealt with?

Perhaps he had taken the phones off my guys to stop them phoning for help, and was now waiting for my call. Maybe he just collected goddamn phones, I don't know.

But I watched him leave and head back to his car, and I grabbed for my phone and dialled the last number I'd called, just in case he *had* got Royce's phone.

Steele sat in his Merc and the cabin light came on and lit him up like a Christmas tree.

Royce's phone was ringing my end.

Steele looked at the passenger seat and I knew I had him. He'd somehow overpowered my guys and then stolen their phones. The bastard.

He didn't answer for a long time. I watched him just sitting there, thinking.

"*Pick up*," I growled.

And then he did. He said, "Yes?"

The dumb son-of-a-bitch didn't sound anything like Royce! I said, "Come to Stuart Stockson's garage." And then, because I was pretty sure Steele didn't know where it was, "It's on Lower Mill Street near the chase."

I waited for him to try another Royce impression, but all I got was, "Okay," and then he hung up.

The dumb, dumb bastard.

I needed to beat him there, so I pulled away and dialled Stu whilst I drove.

"I'm just done, boss," he said. "Just locking up..."

And I said, "No Stu. Stay there. We have a job to do."

STEELE

I wondered briefly why Brooker had needed to give out the address of Stockson's garage, but then I remembered that Mr Blonde and Mr Grey were new and maybe didn't know where it was.

Boy would I give Brooker a surprise, showing up alone with a gun in my hand instead of half-unconscious in the arms of three of his guys.

The satnav loaded and I pulled away into the darkness, driving away from town towards the chase, a sprawling patch of woodland I guessed Brooker planned to bury me in.

He'd be lucky.

It took fifteen minutes to reach Lower Mill Street. Spitting distance to the place I'd brought Little Carlucci last night. Where I'd nearly run over Jeremy Peters.

If I'd managed to blow both brothers up in their den last night I'd be home now, and would never even have heard of Gary Brooker or Kevin West. And Jeremy Peters would probably still be alive.

I saw the sign *Stocksons Garage* by the light of the sodium street lamps. No apostrophe in *Stocksons*.

Not particularly surprising.

The roller doors were open. The lights were on.

Time to say hello.

I got out and hurried to the shadows of the neighbouring building. A wood merchant's. Slipped the Glock out of the right holster and held it at my side. There would be no messing around this time. I'd go in, tell Brooker what was going to happen, what he was going to do, and then tell him what would happen if he didn't do what I said.

Simple. Quick. Straightforward.

I crept along the side of the building to the garage. A sign on the wall said *All major credit cards excepted.*

Oh Stu, you're killing me.

I peered up the ramp. Empty. The main garage opened out through a doorway on the left, so I hurried up the ramp and peered through.

A car jacked up in the air. Shelves of tools and tyres and God knows what else.

I went in, and that's when Stuart Stockson himself jumped out at me from the darkness and smacked me with a wrench.

*

It happened so fast that the best I could do was get my head out of the way. The wrench cracked me in the chest and knocked me off balance.

Thank God for my bulletproof vest.

I dropped the gun and it skitted under the jacked-up car. Stockson was winding up for another swing, but that's the problem with blunt weapons - they're ungainly. Leave you vulnerable after each swing. Stabbing weapons are better, and shooting ones better still.

Pity I'd dropped mine.

The vest might have stopped my heart being pulverised, but it's not like I didn't feel it. It felt like I'd been hit by a car.

I managed to dodge his next swing and dance away.

And that's when I saw Brooker.

The three of us stood in a triangle around the jacked-up car, both of them staring at me.

"You brought a gun," Brooker said, and looked at the place where it had fallen. "That's not fair."

I tried to speak, but couldn't get enough breath. I clutched my chest instead and inhaled what felt like fire. That wrench hurt. One could do a lot of damage with that. Like break an old man's bones. I looked at Stockson. Managed to gasp out, "You smashed Mr Chappell's legs."

"Scared are you, Ginger?" He tried to do a Scottish accent and failed miserably.

Having said that, I obviously hadn't done the greatest impression of whoever's phone it was.

Brooker went for the gun. Obvious he would. I sprang after him and delivered a meaty kick to his side as he bent to retrieve it, knocking him over. Stockson appeared an instant later, and I dodged his swing and fell against the bonnet of the jacked-up car. He bought the wrench down like a hammer, and I rolled out of the way as it crashed down on the metal and dented it, and then he smashed it inches from my head and broke one headlight.

The car's owner would not be using *Stocksons Garage* again.

I landed on my arse, striking the back of my head on the bumper as Brooker crawled for the gun again. I grabbed him by the neck before he reached it, hauling him between me and Stockson who was gearing up for another swing and stood there snarling with the wrench held above his head, trying to find a bit of me to smash.

Brooker grabbed my arms when he should have been punching my face. I bent my legs under him and shoved, and he went sprawling into Stockson and toppled over like a drunk marionette.

It put Stockson off his stride, too.

I reached for my fallen Glock, brought it up and shot

the wrench-weilding maniac mechanic through the chest.

He toppled over backwards against the tower of tyres and knocked some down. The wrench fell and dinged on the concrete floor.

"*Jesus Christ...*" Brooker scrabbled backwards across the floor on his butt, trying to get away from Stockson's body, trying to get away from me. His back met the wall and he stalled there, apparently without noticing, because he kept pumping his legs as though he thought he could push himself through the mortar. "Oh Jesus Christ don't shoot me."

I climbed to my feet, pointing the gun at him and leaning on the jacked-up car for support. "Don't move." It hurt to speak. It hurt to breathe. It hurt to hold the Glock steady.

"Okay..." Brooker managed, raising an arm. "You win. What do you want? You can have the medals. Keep them…"

"I gave them back to Jeremy's wife."

He nodded his head, his eyes wide and goggly. "You did? That's... that's great..."

"*Be quiet.*"

"Okay... okay. Look, please don't kill me. I... I have money..."

I almost shot him then. There are only two instances when it is acceptable to kill and this wasn't one of them, but I almost did it anyway. "You just don't get it, do you?"

"I... I..."

"I know how you make your money. That's *exactly* why we have a problem."

"I'll stop... I swear I will."

I shook my head and gave a small smile. "I'm sorry

Gary, but I don't believe you. I don't think you can."

He started crying. His face went all red and screwed up and he began burbling nonsense. And that was just fine. "P-please... *Please don't kill me...*"

And I said, "I'm not going to kill you."

It seemed to take him a while to understand what I'd just said. "You... you're not?"

"No. Not if you do exactly what I say."

He sat up a bit straighter and wiped his face with his hands. "Anything, just..."

"You're going to go to prison," I said. "It's over, Gary. You have no one left. I had the police pick up the guys you left me with at the café. Jermaine is loyal, I know that. But Royce? Or Johnson? One of those guys will roll. They'll talk. They'll rat you out. Terry's still in the hospital. Stockson's dead. Baz's dead."

Brooker looked up from Stockson's body. "B-Baz is dead?"

"Aye."

He dropped his head and stared into his lap for a few seconds. "When he wasn't answering I did think... but, Baz... I mean, we went to school together..."

"How proud your teachers must be." I transferred the Glock into my left hand, though I had no chance of holding it steady. Not that it really mattered. Brooker wasn't going anywhere. I took out my phone with my right and called Andrews.

He picked up immediately. "Steele? Have you got him?"

"Aye, George, I've got him."

"Alive?"

"Yes, alive. Although I had to shoot Stuart Stockson. Self-defence. He tried to beat me to death with a wrench."

"I don't blame him."

"Hilarious. Anyway, I've made Brooker a deal. He admits what he's done and goes to prison or I come back and kill him."

"You think he'll accept that?"

"Oh he'll accept it." And I met Brooker's eyes and held them. "He knows I mean it. He knows I'll find him no matter where he runs. And he knows no one can stop me."

All the colour drained from Brooker's face. He swallowed and dropped his head again and looked just about ready to fill his pants.

"We're at Stockson's garage," I told Andrews. "You can send a detective inspector round - someone who's been working Brooker's case. *Someone who'll make the handcuffs extra tight.*" I hung up and put the phone back in my pocket. Stared at Brooker. "I mean it," I assured him. "I find out you've made a break for freedom then I come after you. I will find you and I will kill you." I've always wanted to use that line. "Do you believe me?"

"Yes." And he did, for now. Whether he still would when he had his lawyer whispering in his ear, assuring him everything would be alright, there was no evidence, that he had nothing to worry about... well. I'd just have to wait and see.

"That was the police?" Brooker asked.

I nodded. "Chief Superintendent Andrews. Why?"

"You ordered him about."

I shrugged. "So?"

"Who gets to order about the police?" He looked at Stockson's body. "You have a gun on you. This isn't America. We're not *allowed* guns."

"I am." You should see the inside of my seat locker.

"I saw you show something to the cops at the café, some ID or something. They just let you come and go as you pleased." He thought it over as he went. "You... you work for the *government*."

I didn't say anything.

"You're an MI5 agent or something? Undercover?"

I didn't say anything.

"A spy? Like James Bond?"

I sighed. "No, not like James Bond."

"But some kind of spy, right?" He climbed warily to his feet.

I raised the Glock. "Don't come any closer."

"I'm not coming any closer, okay? I'm standing right here."

I lowered the gun again, so my arm was resting on the bonnet of the jacked-up car. How long before the police got here? My arm was killing, my chest felt like it had been squashed in a vice. Stuart Stockson had a more serious chest wound, given the fact that it had killed him, but still.

"Can I see your ID?" Brooker asked.

"What?"

"The ID you showed the cops at the café. Your spy ID."

"No."

"Is your name even John Steele?"

"Of course it is, what do you mean?"

"Well, it's not a very Scottish name, is it? Steele?"

I paused. He had me there. "Not all Scots are called McDonald."

"I know, but…"

"Be quiet, Gary." And I looked away from him. It was

only for a second. I was just looking towards the door, wondering where the hell the cops were. I don't know what he pressed - just some button on the wall. But he knew what it did. I guess he'd been in here often enough.

The jacked-up car dropped from beneath me, crashed to the concrete, and I lost my balance and fell down with it, over the bonnet, the bumper, until I found myself flat on my back, and Brooker was running, heading for the door.

I swore, scooped up the Glock. Pointed it at his back as he ran.

Oh Jesus. I couldn't shoot him, not in the back as he ran away. He wasn't running towards a bazooka. He was running for his car.

I jumped up and went after him, but by the time I reached the doorway he was already at the bottom of the ramp and turning the corner.

I hurried after him, my chest feeling strapped up by a red hot belt. I reached the pavement just as his car door slammed and the engine roared.

The BMW screeched away. I aimed the gun and pulled the trigger, but instead of blowing out the tyre I'd been aiming for I made only a bright silver dink in one rear wing.

Jesus Jesus Christ.

I ran back to my Merc, cursing, transferring the Glock to my left hand and pulling free the keys with my right. Got in, threw the Glock onto the passenger seat, started the engine and pulled away before closing my door.

He'd reached the bend in the road and turned onto the narrow woodland rutted track. I roared after him.

"Turn around when possible," said my satnav, whom I

told to piss off, although its twisty road map was a great help to tackling the corners. I had to use my left hand on the wheel, and my shoulder started to scream.

His BMW skidded through the fallen leaves ahead of me, slewing now and again, reaching branches drumming against his windows. I tried to gain on him, pushing the accelerator to the floor. I was going too fast. I knew it, but I couldn't let him escape, not now.

I took the next corner, then the next.

And then I came off the road.

*

It happened fast. One moment I was on the road, the next I was up the bank and in the bushes, and I felt a tremendous *thump*, which could have been the wheels or the car's underbelly or the bonnet or the windscreen, I don't know, but suddenly there were branches beating at the windows and the front grille was pointing at the sky.

I hadn't put my seatbelt on in the rush to chase Brooker, and head butted the windscreen. My chest smacked into the steering wheel on the way down, and I ended up crumpled in my seat feeling like I'd fallen down a mountain, curled up like a prawn and swearing like a genuine Scot.

"Jesus Mary goat shit!"

The bloody wipers came on for some reason. Twigs skittered off the glass and I saw that the front end of the Merc had ploughed right through the hedge into the farmer's field beyond. Hay bales and a tractor and about a dozen cows stood there wondering what the hell I was doing.

I tried to reverse out of the hedge but went nowhere, the wheels spinning and spinning and spitting up clods of soil. I stamped on the accelerator, making the engine scream and screaming along with it as if that might help, pulling at the steering wheel.

I got nowhere. And Brooker was now long gone. I couldn't even hear his BMW anymore, only the mooing of the cows in the field. The fat bastards had ventured closer to get a better look at me.

I left the handbrake off and opened my door. Had to force it open against the hedge, which conspired to keep me locked in.

"*Let me _out_, you bastard.*"

I won the fight with the hedge and finally made it round the bonnet into the farmer's field.

The cows stopped and swished their tails and chewed vacantly at me.

"Come any closer Daisy and I will shoot you in the face and eat you for dinner." I'd slipped out of my Scottish accent, which was never a good sign. Luckily, the cows didn't seem to notice.

The Merc was stuck on a ridge, its front wheels in the air. I threw all my weight against the bonnet and eventually the car shifted backwards, succumbed to gravity, and drifted back onto the road.

It had only taken five minutes, but Brooker would now be miles away.

I got back behind the wheel and retrieved the Glock, which had flown off the passenger seat into the footwell. Then I carried on driving. Brooker was long gone, I knew that, but what else could I do? Give up?

My phone rang over the hands-free. CSI Andrews. I sighed. "Hello George."

"Steele, I thought you said you had Brooker at the garage? My DI found Stuart Stockson's body but he said there was no sign of you."

"Aye. Brooker escaped."

Silence. That made me feel even worse.

"*Escaped?*" Andrews said. "Christ. You let him *escape?*"

"I didney *let* him escape…"

"I thought you had a gun."

"What, you'd have liked me to shoot him in the back as he ran away?"

"Well no, although I'm surprised you didn't."

That annoyed me even more. For a moment I sat and ground my teeth, wondering whether to point out that he knew nothing about me, about my methods, about what I was or was not prepared to do. And besides, I was only there because he couldn't do his own bleeding job properly. How much more evidence of ruined lives did he need?

"Look *George*," I said, "I'm handling it. Tell your boys to be on the lookout for his black BMW. Call me if you get anything."

I hung up and exhaled through my nose. Turned on the CD player. Something by Debussy. Soothing and peaceful like the sky at midnight. That's more like it. Calmed me right down.

Pop and rock music has never had the same effect. Too safe, too cliched. Too much use of the one-five-six-four chord progression.

And if I hear any more power ballads by pop princesses I will scream.

I came to a junction and took the left fork. Fifty-fifty chance of guessing right. A mile ahead I came to another. Took the left fork again. Now only one in four chance of being right, of being on Brooker's tail. Seventy five percent chance of being wrong.

Not good odds.

I had to work out where he was *going*, not how he was getting there.

I found out a minute later when George Andrews phoned again.

"We've just had a phone call from Melissa Brooker," he said. "Gary has kidnapped Alex."

BROOKER

I was going to prison this time, for sure. There would be no coming back from this, not after what I'd just done.

I locked my office door behind me and ran up the stairs. It was dark, but I couldn't turn on the lights. Anyone on the street outside would see my office lit up a mile away and I didn't want to draw unnecessary attention.

Besides, I knew what I needed.

I knelt down behind my desk and opened the cupboard door and fumbled in the combination. *Click click click* went the wheel and the safe drifted open.

A red rucksack. One of Alex's.

I put it on. Probably looked goddamn ridiculous in it, not that I cared. Closed the safe again, then the cupboard.

I had to leave. Had to get away from this goddamn town as quickly as possible.

Had to get away from the police.

Had to get away from John Steele.

STEELE

Andrews gave me Melissa's address and I put it into my satnav.

Jesus, this was all my fault. Andrews was right: I *had* let Brooker escape. I was the one with the gun after all. Yes, everything I'd been through in the last twenty-four hours was beginning to show, to wear me down. But still. He should never have got away.

First I screw up and get Jeremy killed, and then I screw up and get a little boy kidnapped by his deranged maniac father.

My stomach felt full of helium, like it might rise up out of my throat.

All I'd done was make things worse. It was Iraq all over again.

It took me over twenty minutes to get to Melissa's. Brooker had managed it in less than ten. I'd obviously picked wrong at the junctions and gone off in the opposite direction. Not surprising. Seventy-five percent chance of getting it wrong. And he must have driven faster than I could, what with my busted arm and burning chest and banged head.

Melissa rented a two-bed semi on the outskirts of town. She stood on the drive with her coat wrapped around her, talking to two WPCs. Two more police officers spoke with the neighbour across the street. An ambulance was parked between the two police cars, and all had their lights still flashing in the early evening darkness.

"Melissa, are you alright?" Stupid question. I flashed my ID at the cops, who exchanged glances. One of them took a step back.

"Gary's taken Alex…" Melissa said, in case I didn't know. "And I don't… I don't know what to do…"

"Tell me what happened."

"I'd just got back from the café with Alex - I opened the front door and he must have followed me in…" She couldn't keep her hands still. They kept going to her face. "H-he smacked me over the back of the head with something, something hard…"

"Are you hurt?"

She shook her head. "No, I'm okay. They said I won't need stitches, but they still want me to go to the hospital to check I don't have concussion."

"Did you black out?"

"Only for a couple of minutes. But I can't go anywhere, *not until I know Alex is safe*…" She wiped at her eyes with hands that shook, and then clutched at her throat. "You hear stories," she whispered. "When marriages break down - fathers who go crazy and kill their kids and themselves…"

"Melissa…"

"You don't think Gary would-"

"*No.*" But I couldn't be sure. No one can ever be sure. "We'll find him."

I approached the two policemen talking to the neighbour. They thanked her for her time and she turned and began trudging back to her house.

"None of the neighbours saw anything," one of the cops said as I reached them. "It's dark. They had their curtains closed."

I nodded. It was pretty obvious what had happened here. I'd frightened Brooker - told him if he didn't go to prison I'd kill him - and then I'd let him escape. He'd driven straight here for his son. Why?

Obvious.

He was running away.

And I'd told him what would happen if he tried *that*.

I was heading back to my car when a call came over the police radio. I couldn't hear exactly what was said through the static, but the officers were suddenly animated.

"It's Brooker," one of them told me. "His car's been sighted!"

I stopped. "Where?"

"Parked around the corner from an office premises he rents."

The safe.

He was going for his money. The bastard just couldn't leave it behind.

I ran back to my car and pulled away without another word. The police would need to wait for a warrant to enter the premises, but that wouldn't stop me.

I'd told him. Nothing would stop me.

Especially now, after what he'd done. I doubted he'd actually *hurt* Alex, but then again I'd been wrong about what Brooker was capable of from the start.

I needed to find him and stop him before anyone else got hurt.

I'd only been on the road a couple of minutes when I heard a buzzing sound coming from the passenger footwell.

Holy Christ.

Mr Blonde's phone had flown off the seat when I hit the hedge, and there it lay, buzzing and flashing. I picked it up without slowing.

No name. Just a number. Could have been anyone.

Except.

Except for the fact that Brooker and his boys were very careful about their phones. They used untraceable pay-as-you-go models to communicate for obvious reasons, just like this one.

So it couldn't have been *anyone*, because only Brooker and his boys had the number.

Baz and Stockson were dead. Jermaine, Royce and Johnson were in custody, without their phones because I had them.

That left Terry and Gary Brooker himself.

Terry was in hospital.

And Brooker knew I had this phone. He'd called me once on it already, only an hour ago.

So why the hell was he phoning me?

I answered. "Gary. *Stay where you are.*"

He replied, all croaked up and sounding out of his mind, "S-Steele... I'm in big trouble..."

You got that right: I'm coming for you. I said, "Don't make this any worse for yourself."

"I know you're some kind of secret agent or something…"

"Gary..."

"*Well you gotta help me.*" His voice had become a frantic whisper. "I'm at my office. There are police outside... I don't think they know for sure I'm here. You gotta get me out of this. You have to get me past them."

I clenched my jaw. "Now why the hell would I do that?"

And he said, "Because if you don't Alex will die."

BROOKER

My voice shook as I said it, but it was the truth.

I hung up and pressed my eyes shut and the pink pay-as-you-go mobile against my mouth and hoped to God Steele would come.

Everything had fallen apart in a matter of moments.

Two minutes ago I'd received a call.

"Get out of there, Gary," the caller had said.

I'd paused. "What?"

"The police are coming. I heard them on the radio. They found your car near your office."

The cold had come and still not left me. My stomach had clenched into a ball and remained so.

I'd thought, No... Not now, it's not fair...

And outside the window, yes, there was the police car on the street.

"*Goddamn it...*"

"Quickly, Gary."

"Why are you helping me?" I'd run to the stairs.

"Because I don't want them to catch you."

"Even after what I did?"

"We shall talk about that later. Have they seen you inside?"

"No, I don't think so..." I'd paused halfway down the stairs. Sank onto them, staring at the door. "*Oh shit...*"

The handle wiggled. Someone knocked. "Police, open up!"

"They just tried to open the door," I whispered, feeling the strength drain from my body. "I'm trapped."

"Well you better find a way out of there, Gary. I mean it."

I crawled back up the stairs and sat against the wall.

"I... I can't..."

"You have to. This isn't just about you killing a poor defenceless dog. They think you've kidnapped Alex."

I gripped the phone tighter. "They what? Why? Alex is with his mother."

A laugh in response. "No, Gary, he's not." And Kevin West, the flat-capped, tweed-wearing old sap had said, "I've got him. I've got your son."

*

It was like his words were physical, like they were made of ice, like they got inside me and ripped me open and crushed my heart.

"W-what..." I couldn't breathe.

"I have Alex," Kevin said, "and if you ever want to see him again you will do exactly as I say. Do you understand?"

"P-please..."

"*Do you understand?*"

No I don't understand I don't understand at all I think my mind is broke

"*Gary?* Are you there?"

No I'm afraid Gary isn't here right now would you like to leave a message?

"Gary, I will *kill* him. I will kill him if you don't do what I say. Do. You. Understand?"

Kevin's voice came from a long way off, maybe the moon. "Y-yes..." I managed. And then, "I understand."

"Good. You've got to lose the police. I don't think they know you're in there for definite - they're waiting for a warrant, and you need to be out of there before they get it."

"H-how do you..."

"Because I'm listening to their radios. And Gary, I've tapped your phone. If you make a phone call I will know, and I will be able to listen to the conversation."

I pressed my eyes together. This couldn't be happening. Not Kevin…

Not Alex…

"If you try to warn anybody," Kevin continued, "I will kill your son. If you try and tell the police what's really going on, I will kill your son. I will kill your son like you killed my dog. Do I make myself clear?"

I opened my eyes. At some point I'd clenched my jaw. I said through gritted teeth, "*Yes.*"

"Good. Now get out of there and call me when you're free. Do I need to tell you what will happen if the police catch you?"

"No."

"I need them to believe you have kidnapped Alex. If you give them reason for doubting that then I will…"

"I know," I said, baring my teeth. "You will kill my son."

"Good. Phone me when you've got away from the police." And he hung up.

I did too.

The police had stopped knocking on the door. I imagined them sat outside, waiting for me to go out or the call to say that they could go in.

I was trapped. They were waiting outside the only door and below the only window.

I had to call for help. Kevin had said he had tapped my phone, and maybe that was true - he *had* known about the police showing up.

But this wasn't my only phone.

I crawled to my desk, dumped the rucksack on it and

opened the top drawer. No logbook, but the pink pay-as-you go mobile was still there.

Could Kevin know about it?

I thought hard. No. I'd never used it before - it still had all its £10 credit. No one had the number. And I'd paid cash. No way to trace it to me. I was always careful about that.

No way Kevin could know I had it.

I didn't have any guys left. They were either dead, in hospital or in custody.

There was only one person I could think of who might be able to help.

STEELE

"Kevin West has kidnapped my son," Brooker said again, and again I could only sit there squeezing the steering wheel with one hand and Mr Blonde's phone with the other, gobbling air like a fish.

Kevin West kidnap Alex Brooker? In what way did that make sense?

"Steele, are you there? *Steele?*"

"You've got some balls, Gary," I said, "I'll give you that."

"It's true, I swear... He said if I don't do exactly what he says he'll… he'll k-kill him..."

I gritted my teeth. "Melissa says you hit her over the head when she arrived home. You knocked her out cold."

"She's lying, Steele! I didn't do it - I don't know why Melissa would say I did!"

I thought back to what Melissa had said.

I'd just got back from the café with Alex - I opened the front door and he must have followed me in... H-he smacked me over the back of the head with something, something hard…

And I realised. Melissa hadn't actually seen who had attacked her. He had been behind her the whole time, following her into the hall and smacking her over the back of the head without her seeing who he was.

She had just assumed it was Gary because, well, it was the sort of thing he would do.

"Where did you go after you left Stockson's garage?" I asked.

"I came straight here!"

"Your office?"

"Yes! I didn't have time to go anywhere else."

And that was probably true too. Getting from Stockson's garage to Melissa's house in ten minutes would have been easy on a straight road doing fifty, but on a twisty country lane? Doubtful. And I'd only been at Melissa's house a few minutes before the call came in that Brooker's car had been sighted near his office.

All pointing to the conclusion that Brooker could *not* have kidnapped his own son after all. I should have seen it earlier.

But Kevin West?

The guy was a weirdo, sure, but so were lots of people. It didn't make them kidnappers.

But then I remembered what he'd done to Brooker's Porsche, and how he'd nearly beaten Jermaine to death with that wok.

How his eyes had looked.

"If this is another little ploy, Gary - if you're trying to lure me there to kill me like before I promise you I will shoot you in the face."

"I'm not, I swear," he assured me. "Please, you have to help…"

"What did Kevin say to you?"

"He says he was listening to the police radio - he knew they were outside before I did. He said he can listen to them, the police, I don't know how. He also says he's tapped my phone, which is why I'm calling you on this…"

I frowned. "I'm pretty sure Kevin can't tap mobile phones, Gary."

"But that's what he said! He said if I called anyone or tried to tell the police what was happening he'd know. And he'd kill my son."

I almost said *he's bluffing. He's just trying to scare you.* But then I remembered that I'd said exactly the same thing to Jeremy last night, and look how that had turned out.

I'd been wrong and someone had ended up dead.

I didn't want that to happen again.

Brooker continued, "And he knew about the police, Steele... He obviously found out somehow..."

"Aye, okay," I said. "Look, I'm almost there. Sit tight and don't call anyone else."

"Okay."

"Do the police definitely know you're in there?"

"No, I don't think so."

"Good. Make sure it stays that way. I'll be there in five." I hung up and put Mr Blonde's phone in a pocket in case I needed it again.

I doubted this would be over quickly.

I was right about that.

There were three police cars parked around Brooker's office when I got there, all with their lights flashing, blocking most of the road.

I double parked, got out, and one of the policemen said, "You can't park here, sir."

Chevrons above his shoulder number. A sergeant.

I showed him my ID, and his eyes widened for a second. Even though Andrews had told them all about me, most seemed to doubt I was real.

"Sergeant, I understand Gary Brooker's car has been found parked nearby," I said.

"Er, yes. I mean, yes sir." He pointed at the dark window over the launderette. "That's his office, and we believe he could be in there."

"You don't know for certain?"

The sergeant swallowed. "Well, no. We're still waiting for the search warrant..."

"I don't need a warrant." I walked up to the office door and picked the lock, a little quicker than I had done just hours before.

The sergeant exchanged glances with his other officers.

I said, "Wait here," and drew my Glock and slipped inside.

*

I went up the stairs backwards, pointing my gun at the upstairs railings in case Brooker should appear and try to drop the safe on my head.

He didn't try anything. I found him sitting against his desk next to a red rucksack. A red rucksack that must have been Alex's.

"You lying bastard..." I whispered. "You *do* have him..."

He looked down at the rucksack then back up to me. "What, *no*. This is... one of his old ones. Kevin's got him. He said... he..." Brooker's head dropped. Even in the darkness I could see from his face that something inside him had broken.

Either he was an Oscar-worthy actor or he was telling the truth.

I doubted Daniel Day Lewis had anything to worry about.

I holstered the Glock.

"You came," he said. "Are you going to kill me?"

I shook my head, but he made no reaction, as if at this point he didn't care whether he lived or died.

"You say Kevin phoned you with these demands?" I asked.

Brooker nodded.

"Then I want you to phone him back. I want to hear it for myself, because a part of me still thinks *you've* got Alex somewhere, and this whole thing is an elaborate plan now you're cornered to avoid being arrested."

Again, no reaction. But he got out his mobile, presumably the one Kevin had called. "What do you want me to say?"

"Say you want to hear Alex's voice. Say you won't do anything until you know he's okay."

Brooker grimaced. "He won't like that. He won't like that at all."

"It'll be okay. Call him. Put it on speaker so I can hear."

He did so and it rang out, once, twice.

And then: "Have you got away from the police yet?"

My fingers went numb, my spine tingled, and for a moment my brain stalled. It was Kevin alright. Cold, hard, reedy-voiced Kevin. Like an evil Kermit the Frog.

Oh my God.

"I- I want to speak to Alex," Brooker stammered.

"I beg your pardon?"

"A-Alex... I want to know he's okay..." Brooker looked at me and I nodded. "I... I won't do anything for you until I've heard from him."

There was silence for a moment, and then Kevin said, "You think I'm bluffing. You still think you're in charge."

"N-no..."

"*Well you're not.* You do as *I* say, understand? You think I've never killed before?"

I felt my knees go weak. Brooker stared at me, his eyes getting wider and wider until I thought they might pop out.

"You better not mess with me, Gary Brooker," Kevin continued, "I mean it. Alex!" There was a scuffle, a burst of static, and then: "Speak to your father."

A little voice said, "D-dad?"

It was like an arrow to my heart.

"*Alex...*" Brooker gasped. "Alex... are you okay? Has he hurt you?"

"Dad I'm scared..." But that was all we heard, because Kevin came back on the line.

"*Satisfied?*"

"Wait..."

"The police are still camped outside your office, Gary, I've been listening to them. And if you don't find a way out of there in two minutes your son will end up buried in the countryside, and the police will never find him and they'll never find me, you can be sure of that."

The line went dead.

Brooker started hyperventilating, and he clasped a hand over his mouth as if to stop his head exploding. Or to stifle a scream.

I turned on my heel and ran back downstairs, slowing up as I opened the door and stepping out onto the pavement like nothing was wrong.

The sergeant and other police officers turned expectantly to me.

"Brooker's not in there," I said, and they all groaned. "He must know everyone is looking for his car, so he abandoned it. He's probably got a taxi or a bus or something."

"We should check the taxi rank," said one of the cops.

I nodded. "The taxi rank, the bus station, the train station... We need to clear the area and get back on the road. Radio it in, okay?"

They began heading back to their cars, except the sergeant, who just stood there with a frown on his face. "Someone should stay by his car in case he comes back for it."

"I will," I said. "Now you need to head off, Sergeant. He's still out there and..."

"You were up there a long time," he interrupted, tilting his head and pausing. "What were you doing?"

I narrowed my eyes and clenched my sling-hand into a fist. Two of the police cars left, so it was only him. "I was being *thorough*, Sergeant. Now perhaps you should do as your superior officer tells you and *go back to the station and follow up on what I suggested.*"

"Superior officer? With respect, *sir*, I'm not sure you have authority over..."

I pulled my gun on him. Did it in a flash, pointed it in his face. "Want to question my authority again, eh, laddie?" I went very Scottish. I probably overdosed on the Scottish, but that was okay. He got the message.

The frown melted off his face remarkably quickly. He began stammering and walked backwards towards his car. Stumbled down the curb and almost fell over. Got in and drove away with the siren going.

I ran back up to the office, just in time to hear Brooker's phone go again.

"*Speaker...*" I hissed.

He did so. Answered. "H-hello?"

"Very good, Gary," Kevin said. "I heard the police radio - they said you're not in there. What did you do, hide?"

"I er..."

"Listen, I have my first job for you. I want you to call Melissa. I want you to tell her you have Alex. Tell her the current arrangement is not working out. Say you won't let her take him off you. Do you understand?"

"I don't... why..."

"*Because I said so.* Stop questioning me, Gary, I am *not* in the mood to be questioned. You think she's trying to take Alex off you for good and you can't have that. Do you understand what you have to say?"

"Y-yes..."

"Good. Phone her now. And Gary? I will know if you don't. I will hear exactly what you say to her. If you try to warn her, or tell her what's really going on, I will kill your son. Do you understand?"

Brooker closed his eyes. "Yes."

"Good. Do it now." And Kevin hung up.

Brooker looked at me, holding his phone out like he didn't know what it was. "I... I think I have to do it, Steele," he said. "I don't want to, but... but he *did* listen to the police. If he can listen in on my phonecalls..."

Again, I thought it highly unlikely. But what the hell did I know. I shrugged.

Brooker called.

"*Gary?*" Melissa answered. "Gary, where are you? *Where is my son?*"

And Brooker garbled out, "I've got him, Melissa... This isn't working, I can't take it anymore. I know you're trying to take him off me, to stop me seeing him... I... I'm not having it!" He added, "Bitch!" and hung up. Began panting again.

Ten seconds later, Kevin called back. "I'm impressed," he said. "I thought calling her a bitch was an especially nice touch."

Jesus. Kevin *could* listen in on Gary's phonecalls. I took it like a punch to the gut. Thank God Gary had been cautious enough to call me on a different mobile.

"I have a couple of errands to run," Kevin continued. "I need you to lie low for an hour or so. Can you do that, without getting caught by the police?"

"Y-yes," Brooker said.

"Good. Now listen, you will *not* be able to use your own car. The police will most certainly be watching it. You need to steal a vehicle, and you need to do so without breaking a window. Do you understand?"

Brooker looked at me. "Yes."

"Good. Don't go to your house, for God's sake, or your wife's house, or do anything else stupid. I'll call you again when I've prepared everything. Then we can begin."

And I thought *begin?* Begin what?

*

Brooker seemed to consider taking the red rucksack with him, but in the end he just hid it under his desk.

"Kevin's right," I said, "we're going to have to leave your car here. Every police officer in town is out looking for you, and if they see your car driving down the road they're going to pull you over and report it."

"And Kevin will find out."

I gave a small nod. "Aye. Certainly seems that way."

"Are we going to have to steal one, then?"

"Hopefully not. You're going to come with me for the time being. You sit there and be quiet and let me do my job, understand?"

He nodded.

"Good. Come on." I led him down the stairs. A small part of me still thought he might try to push me down them, but he didn't. "Wait here, I'm just going to check that the police have gone."

No flashing lights outside. No police cars, no cops standing about. Just the dark street and the wind.

"It's clear."

Brooker locked the office door and followed me to my Merc. Got in the passenger seat beside me. Looked at the one remaining phone in the footwell. Mr Blonde's phone was still in my pocket, so that one was Mr Grey's. I don't know if he recognised it. He didn't comment if he did.

I drove away, saying, "Call Dawn Gainsborough," to the Merc's hands-free. Whilst it rang I told Brooker to find out Kevin West's mobile number.

Dawn answered. "Steele, I hope that's you saying you're on your way back here. Dalton's asked me twice when you're coming back."

"Soon, I hope. But not yet. Remember running a background check on a Kevin West?"

"The one whose parents died in a house fire?"

"Aye. Well he's kidnapped a child."

Dawn gasped. "You're joking..."

"I need you to set up a phone trace. He's supposed to ring us in an hour or so, and I want to be able to find out where he is."

"Of course, do you have his number?"

Brooker had brought it up on his phone and I recited it.

"I'll get right on it," Dawn said. "As soon as he makes a call we'll have him."

"Thank you." I hung up.

Brooker was looking at me funny. A mixture of awe, respect and trepidation. Not only had he picked on a psychopathic kidnapper, he'd also picked on me, a highly-trained, highly-resourced government assassin.

He'd have to pick his targets more carefully.

"Where are we going?" he asked.

And I said, "The police station."

"Very funny."

"I'm not joking. I'm going to tell Chief Superintendent Andrews exactly what's going on. I was going to do it over the phone, but as it looks like Kevin has some kind of happy hacking skills I'll have to do it in person. Don't worry," I added at the look on his face, "you can wait in the car."

"But... but they'll *see* me!"

"They won't. It's dark - they won't even know you're in here. And it's *my* car, so they'll leave it alone."

I parked in the road as far away from a streetlight as I could.

"What if Kevin calls?" Brooker asked as I opened my door.

I shrugged. "Answer it."

Cops stared at me like they always do as I walked through the police station to George Andrews's office. He was still there, and when I walked in he just stared at me from behind his desk.

"You really ballsed this up, Steele."

I closed the door behind me. Stayed standing. "George, you have no idea what's really going on."

"I have a pretty good idea. You decided to get involved with Gary Brooker even though you had nothing to do with the case - you just decided to waltz in here and take over. And look what's happened. You let Gary Brooker escape, and he goes round and knocks out his ex-wife and kidnaps his son. That about the size of it?"

"No, George. Not at all."

"Wait, why are you even here - didn't you say you'd watch his BMW? What happens if he goes back for it?"

"He won't."

"How the hell do you know?"

"Because he's in my car."

Andrews was all geared up to shout at me some more, but that stopped him. That stopped him good. "What are you talking about?"

I told him everything. About how Kevin was the real kidnapper, how he was listening to the police radios and somehow Brooker's phone. I told him how he was framing Brooker for the kidnapping, getting him to confess to Melissa, setting him up. "And George, most importantly, you must keep this to yourself."

Andrews lowered his hands from his mouth. "What do you mean? My men are out there looking for the wrong guy..."

"And that's how it must stay. If Kevin finds out that the police know about him he said he'll kill Alex and disappear."

"But..."

"No buts, George. You are not to inform *anyone* about this. Your men will continue searching for Gary Brooker, who will remain the prime suspect."

Andrews stood up. "Now wait a minute for Christ's sake... I don't have to..."

"I'm only telling you what's really going on out of professional courtesy."

"Professional courtesy my arse."

"This is an *order*, George."

He just stared at me, dumbstruck, his face getting redder and redder like a beetroot. "You can't..."

"I can. And you *will* obey me. Or perhaps you need reminding who it is you're dealing with?"

Andrews blustered some more. "Are you *threatening* me, Steele?"

"I really hope it doesn't need to come to that."

"How *dare* you come in here and... This is my office! This is my town!"

And I shook my head. "No, George. I'm here. Which means at the moment it's *my* town. You're in my world now." I turned and made for the door.

"Steele?"

I looked back.

"Don't you ever pull a gun on one of my officers again."

I paused, then nodded. "Make sure they let me do my job and I won't have to."

*

Brooker needn't have worried about being spotted. As I walked back to my car I couldn't see a thing through the windscreen, and it was only when I got right up to the driver's door window that I could make out any kind of shape at all.

"Did he believe you?" he asked as I got back in.

"Aye." Although we didn't leave the best of friends. "He's not going to tell the rest of the police. I was adamant about that. They'll keep looking for you and Kevin won't know anything's wrong."

"Where are we going now?"

I smiled, pulled away and joined the traffic. "We're going to Kevin West's house."

Brooker squirmed. "*What?* Why? He won't be there..."

"I know he won't - that's the point. I'm going to have a look round, try and get in his head."

Kevin's blue Peugeot wasn't on the drive when we arrived, of course, and when we got out no little dog yipped its head off at us.

Brooker looked about ready to throw up. He'd gone a pasty porridge colour. "He's not here."

"No. Still. Got to be careful. Let's go round back."

The dog still lay in the yard with his head caved in. Brooker swore, made a gurgle from the back of his throat. I said nothing, because I knew I could never have said anything helpful. I crossed to the back door and tried the handle. Locked, as I'd thought.

I could have shot out the lock, but I wasn't going to fire my gun out in the open, in the middle of a neighbourhood unless I absolutely had to. The Glock 17 had a suppressor, but they don't exactly work like they do in the movies. Suppressors are useful in that they make it harder for an enemy to locate your position, but they're hardly silent.

So instead I fumbled inside my sling with my right hand to get at my watch. Used my nail to pry free the lock pick hidden in the face. Took about twenty seconds to crack the lock. "There we go."

"Is that how you got into my office?"

Yes, on both occasions. But I didn't answer him. Slotted the lock pick back inside my watch and pushed the back door open. No alarm.

The kitchen looked different in the dark, sterile. The wok that Kevin had used to pulverise Jermaine the blob's balls still lay on the floor. I kicked it aside.

"No lights," I said, as Brooker made a move to the

switch.

"I can't see."

"You don't need to see."

We moved through the rest of the house. I didn't much like Brooker following me on my blind side, but I figured he needed me because he didn't have a clue what to do.

The rest of the house reminded me of Kevin in little ways. It looked like it was owned by an old couple. Neat and tidy. The decor and furniture in the lounge/diner and bedroom upstairs was tired, 1950s-style floral. The wardrobe looked like something from World War II. There pervaded a mothy, musty smell all around the house, as if I'd gone back in time a few decades. Everywhere, that is, except for the small study of the back of the house.

Kevin West had one hell of a computer system. Towers and monitors and hard drives and God-knows what covered the tables along three walls. The main computer - that is, the one with the biggest flatscreen monitor and the one the wheely chair faced - took up most of the back wall, obscuring the small window, which was curtained-off.

"Goddamn," said Brooker. "He *is* a hacker."

"Seems so." Kevin West was definitely a computer expert. Maybe he'd started off twenty years ago as an analyst or something, before realising he could make more money as a hacker. Working freelance, not paying any tax.

The flatcap, tweed-wearing middle-aged granddad was a computer geek.

"Maybe this is how he found my address," Brooker said, mainly to himself. "He - he hacked the phone company database or something…"

I turned the main computer on, and it booted up in less than ten seconds. Asked for a password.

"I'm just going to get something from my car," I said.

"What?"

"A way into his system. Maybe find some clues. Just stay here and for God's sake don't touch anything."

"What if my phone goes?"

"Then run down after me as fast as you can." I left him, headed down the stairs (noticing the flatcap was absent from the coat stand), went out into the back yard through the kitchen and circled round to my car.

In the weapons locker was a small briefcase from which I could do some hacking of my own. Well, the analysts at HQ could do it for me. I returned to Kevin's study.

Brooker sat in the wheely chair, spinning himself round and round and looking positively demented.

"Out of the way." I encouraged him out of the chair and sat in it myself, opening the briefcase on my lap.

"What's that?"

"Mobile uplink." I attached the cable of the little black box into one of the main computer tower's USB ports. I could have tried to do it myself using the software on my phone, but I thought it probably needed something more sophisticated. "It's so my guys can get in."

"You have guys?"

"Yes. And they're better than yours."

I called Dawn Gainsborough again at HQ, who answered with, "West still hasn't made a phone call."

"Don't worry – he will."

"I'm ready when he does. I'll know his position in about five seconds."

"Good. Look, I er... need another favour."

Dawn sighed.

"I'm at Kevin's house. I've plugged an uplink into his computer and I need you to access the system for me."

"Bloody hell."

"I know. Sorry."

"You're not even on contract anymore."

"Please, Dawn. There's a child's life on the line here."

She sighed again. "You don't need to dress it up, John, I'm doing it. There. I've got your uplink. A personal computer, password-protected. Okay. The programme tries like… thirty billion different passwords every second. It shouldn't take long."

"Thank you."

A few seconds later Kevin's computer logged itself on as if by magic.

"There you go."

"Dawn, I also need you to flag up his finances, track his credit cards, his car as well as his phone."

"Okay, no problem." She paused. "There is one other thing. When I heard about him kidnapping the boy I did some more digging. Specifically about his parents."

"Okay, what?"

"I... think it'd be better if I showed you."

*

Dawn sent a video to my in-car computer. Brooker had come down with me and sat in the passenger seat. I didn't want him alone up there in the study in case his phone rang or he had some kind of breakdown and smashed all of Kevin's computers with a brick.

The screen was about the size of a DVD case. Not great for watching Blu-rays, but good enough for what I needed it for. Touchscreen too, of course. And it still worked after my foray into some bushes.

I accessed my emails and downloaded the video Dawn had sent. It took a minute or so. We sat there in silence. Awkward.

The video started, and things began to fall into place.

Two men sat at opposite ends of a table, facing each other. The feed was grey and fuzzy. Subtitles in blocky white letters at the bottom of the screen said: 'West, Lee. 17/02/1998.'

An interview then, with Kevin's crazy brother. Probably at the mental hospital. Lee looked young, agitated. He kept fussing with his hands. The other man, the doctor, wore a lab coat and looked in his fifties, although I couldn't really see his face very well.

"Why don't we go through this one more time…"

"We've been through it a million times!" Lee clapped his hands to his head. "I didn't do it - it was Kevin!"

The doctor looked unmoved. "Your brother nearly died in the fire, Lee."

"He *framed* me - waited for me to go out and then started it straight after to make it look like I'd done it and then run off!"

"The firemen had to rescue him from his window."

"That was just to make it look realistic - he wouldn't have let himself burn, he'd have jumped down from the roof if he'd had to…"

"He's only ten years old."

"I know how old he is! Look, doctor, you have to believe me. Kevin locked my parents in their bedroom and filled the lock with superglue…"

"How would he have done that?"

"The house is old, and my parents' bedroom door had

a lock on it."

"Not a bolt, you mean the kind with a key and a keyhole."

"Yes. My parents hardly ever locked it, only when we were going on holiday or something. But Kevin knew where the key was, and he stole it and waited for them to go to bed. Then he locked them inside their bedroom and filled the keyhole with superglue from the garage."

"And then he planted the glue and the key in your room?"

"Yes!" Lee put his face in his hands. "Do you think if I'd really done it I'd have left them lying around?"

"But what about the vodka and the cigarettes? How did he know about them?"

"I don't know! He must have searched my room when I was out or something. They were only under my bed, it's not like I had them in a safe or anything."

"So what, he splashed the vodka around, lit one of your cigarettes and threw it at your parents door?"

"Yes!"

"Having waited until you'd had a very public row with your parents, shouting how you were going to kill them?"

Lee went limp as a puppet. He spoke to the tabletop. "I didn't mean it. They just pissed me off. And I was angry. I didn't do it. It was Kevin."

"But Lee, why on earth would Kevin do such a thing?"

"To get back at me. I use to pick on him. Bully him, I guess, because he's really weird. So he did this to get back at me."

"He killed your parents - *his* parents - to get back at you?"

"Yes. Look, I know it sounds crazy, but he *is* crazy…"

"You already had convictions for arson. And assault. Where do you think your feelings…"

"I didn't do it! It was Kevin! He's mad, hear me? He's a psychopath!"

*

Lee West had obviously got himself into trouble with the law on numerous occasions, but I believed him. I believed that Kevin, at just ten years old, had got so fed up with his older brother's bullying he'd got his own back. Not by killing Lee, but by killing his own parents and getting Lee convicted of their murder.

Of course, on the face of it, someone killing their own parents to 'get back' at a bullying sibling seems ridiculous. Unbelievable. Unthinkable.

But Kevin had said it himself back when Brooker and I were up in the office.

You think I've never killed before?

And I had seen Kevin's eyes. Lee was right. He was a psychopath. Perhaps there'd been other killings in the intervening years, following Kevin as he toured the country like a bad smell. And it made me fear for the safety of little Alex Brooker even more.

We returned to Kevin's study. Brooker just sat in the wheely chair and spun, spun, looking into his lap.

I left him and did a more thorough search of the rest of the house. Kevin had an old record player, with a turntable and a shelf of old vinyls. In his bedroom I found a ukulele or a banjo or something - a tiny guitar, anyway - and I imagined him standing in front of the mirror and singing *When I'm Cleaning Windows* like George Formby.

His clothes looked like they had come from 1945.

Maybe he'd got them from a fancy dress shop. They were arranged by colour – grey, grey-green, grey-blue and brown. I was pretty sure Kevin had OCD. He had three pairs of shoes lined up at the bottom of the wardrobe, and in a drawer was a thick brown envelope.

I withdrew it, popped the flap, which was unsealed. A wad of cash, maybe three inches thick, wrapped tight with an elastic band. The payoff for one of his freelance hacking jobs, I guessed.

Kevin could have paid Brooker off three times over.

I took the money. Put the envelope in my jacket. Does that make me a thief? Possibly. Who cares? I'd give it to HQ so they could repair the Merc. I had promised to get it back to them in one piece, and it had got scuffed about a bit.

In the top drawer of Kevin's bureau I found multiple printouts, all about Gary and Melissa and Alex. Melissa's Facebook page, photos printed out with IP information, her address. Alex's school reports. Gary's business information, his bank accounts, his car details, which included his address. I assumed that's what Kevin had started with - Brooker's number plate, or maybe his business address. And it had all gone from there. I put the papers back.

Brooker had really picked on the wrong guy.

I returned to the study to find him still spinning in his chair like a moron.

"It's strange," he said without looking at me. "I've been wondering. Why do you dress like a tramp?"

"I'm sorry?"

"Look at you. You look like a Scottish hobo, and yet you drive a Mercedes."

"The Merc's not mine."

"Did you steal it?"

"What, like I stole your medals?"

Brooker looked away. "Jeremy Peters owed me. Those medals were mine to sell by right."

"No, they weren't. He'd already paid you back more than he borrowed. He did not owe you fourteen grand. And those medals were all he had left of his father."

"He owed me. That's not my fault. He should never have borrowed the money if he couldn't pay it back."

I clenched my fists and had to turn away to stop me punching him.

"You really gave the medals back?" he asked.

I gritted my teeth. Looked at him. "I gave them back to his wife. At the hospital. After Baz had put him in a coma."

Brooker looked at the floor. "Jeremy was never meant to die."

"Oh, that makes it all okay then."

"No, I'm just saying. I never meant for it to happen. Baz never meant for it to happen. He just had... problems. With his temper."

"He didn't look particularly sorry when I caught up with him."

Brooker glowered at me. "How the hell would you know how he felt? You didn't know a goddamn thing about him."

"He said that you'd told Mrs Peters that you'd kill her grandchildren if she went to the police. Her *grandchildren*."

"Oh, people say lots of things, I'd never have done it, Jesus. I just had to have something to say, something to make sure she'd keep quiet."

I pursed my lips and then shook my head at him.

"You're a sick son-of-a-bitch, you know that?"

"You don't know the first thing about me. Or Baz, whatever you think. He's not... I mean, he didn't deserve it."

"He didn't deserve me killing him?"

"No."

I shrugged. "It's not about whether he deserved it or not. I'm not a judge, or a jury."

He paused a moment, and then nodded. "You're an executioner."

I frowned. "*No*. I didn't kill him as a *punishment*, Brooker. This wasn't about justice. It was about stopping him from killing anyone else. That's all."

"He wouldn't have..."

"Oh don't give me that. It would have happened again, and you know it. So I had to kill him. As I said, this isn't about justice. This is about prevention. There are criminals who the police can't touch, and *I* have to deal with them."

He shook his head. "What about Stockson?"

"Self-defence."

"And Terry? You broke Terry's knee for no reason."

"I had a reason. And he'll recover. Eventually."

"So that makes it okay?"

I shrugged.

"Did you kill Will too?"

"Aye. He was a terrible, *terrible* hitman, Gary. How much did you have to pay him?"

"I didn't have to pay him anything because he never completed the contract."

"Well, he won't be taking out any more of your... clients."

"I'd never used him before."

"What about the woman who disappeared? Catherine Thompson? You saying her disappearance had nothing to do with you?"

He dropped his eyes again. "It's complicated."

"Oh, I'm sure."

"She wasn't meant to die."

"Just like Jeremy wasn't meant to die? Funny, you don't seem to be very good at not killing people."

"It was Baz."

I stopped. Frowned. "Baz killed Catherine Thompson as well?"

Brooker wouldn't look at me. He put his hands to his temples and stared at his feet. "I didn't mean it to happen. I never told him too. I never wanted anyone killed."

"You wanted me killed."

He looked up at me then. "That was different. You crashed into my Porsche. *You punched me in the nose for no reason.*"

"Again, I think I had a good reason."

"*Look at it,*" and he pointed his nose out to me just in case I missed it. "My whole face hurts."

"You deserved it."

"Then you carried on kicking me whilst I was on the ground. You stole my wallet and phone. Then you stole my medals…"

"They were not *your* medals…"

"They were my medals! Mine by right! Why can't you see that? Peters agreed to give them to me."

"Only because you threatened him and his wife. What did you do to him at Stockson's garage last night, eh? I presume that's where you had him."

Brooker looked back at his feet. "We didn't do

anything to him. Just… just held him there for a little while."

"He could barely walk. He fell in front of my car and I nearly ran him over."

"Is that really how you met him?"

"Aye. I gave him a lift home and saw that fat arsehole waiting outside his house. His wife told me all about you. How Jeremy was giving you his father's medals. I couldn't have that."

"It was none of your business."

"I disagree."

"Jeremy Peters owed me."

I sighed. He kept holding onto that – *Jeremy Peters owed me* – as if it excused everything he'd done. "So I took the medals back off you. And you go round and kill Jeremy."

"I didn't kill…"

"You got Baz to kill Jeremy."

"No!" Brooker put his face in his hands. "I already told you - I didn't want Baz to kill Jeremy, I just wanted information about *you*. Baz just… lost it."

"Like he did with Catherine Thompson."

Brooker sighed. "That was different. He… Oh Jesus. Okay, look. I lent Catherine Thompson money. I can't exactly remember how much…"

"Three thousand eight hundred," I said. He looked at me confused, so I added, "It was in your logbook."

His mouth twitched. "Okay. Three thousand eight hundred. She was divorced, bitter, desperate. She had drunk herself into debt, and that's not my fault, is it?"

Nothing was ever his bloody fault.

"She came to me," he continued, "and I lent her the money. That was a generous thing to do, don't you think?"

Oh Jesus Christ. I said nothing. Just stared at him.

"Anyway," he continued, "she wouldn't pay me back. I think in the end I got back about two grand, but that was it. She kept stalling on the rest. This went on for months, Steele - or whatever your goddamn name is. You must understand, I was pissed off. But I hadn't pushed her very much - a few threats, I think someone climbed into her back garden and killed all her plants. Hardly the crime of the century. But she didn't care. She just kept drinking, and that's why she couldn't pay me back, because she kept drinking it away. So me and Baz went round there. Just to talk to her. She was drunk again, and it made me so mad. She had a brown Labrador, and Baz shut it in the kitchen."

"And then he killed her."

"*No*, then we talked to her. Okay, it got heated, but you should have seen her. She was disgusting. She spat her wine all over me, so I hit her with the bottle. Not hard, but the end smashed against the wall and some of the glass cut her neck. Something like that, anyway, it all happened so fast. She was bleeding, but I think most of the blood was actually red wine. She began screaming and lunged at me. Baz pushed her away and she fell and hit her head on something. She was okay, though. Apart from being a mad drunk."

"Did she call the police?"

"Not that night, no. We convinced her not to. But she went to the hospital and they must have persuaded her to report it, because the next day she went to the police. She said we'd tried to kill her. Tried to cut her throat, which was *bullshit*. But they would have done us both. We'd have ended up inside on an attempted murder charge."

"So you decided to *actually* kill her."

"No, *not me*. I've already told you. Baz thought it was the only way, though. He told me about a guy he knew. A guy who… who killed people for money."

"Will Pharell? The guy you set on me?"

"Yes. But I told him no," Brooker said. "I said to him, Baz, we don't do that. We can handle it ourselves. Even though I didn't have a goddamn clue what to do. But Baz must have misunderstood. He thought I meant we didn't need a hitman, that we could do it ourselves. So he followed her into the woods when she was walking her dog. He phoned me to say he was doing it, that he was going to sort it, but he hung up before I could tell him not to and wouldn't answer his phone again. I drove straight there, but it was too late. He'd… he'd strangled her. She was dead. I hadn't meant that." Brooker shook his head. "I hadn't meant that."

"Then what, you covered it up?"

"I had to, Steele. I… I couldn't go to *jail*. So in the end we did call Will after all, and he sorted it. He buried the body. God knows where. He went back to her house and got rid of any evidence. And somehow, *somehow* we got away with it."

"Well lucky, lucky you."

"Steele, I didn't do it… I'm not…"

"I don't want your excuses."

Brooker glared at me. "Well look at you! You're sitting there judging me, when by the looks of it you kill people for a living!"

I glared back. "I am *nothing* like you."

"Yeah, just keep telling yourself that."

"I only kill people who are a harm to society."

"What, like Baz?"

"You've just admitted he killed two people. And he would have killed others, as I'm sure you know."

"And Stu?"

"That was self-defence. He was going to beat me to death. I don't kill people just because they *owe me money*."

There was silence for a little while. Brooker licked his lips. "So did MI5 put you on to me?"

"No. You were an accident. I was here on another contract."

"Is that how you broke your arm?"

"It isn't broken. I got shot."

"You got... *Jesus*... How? What were you doing?"

"My targets were two drug dealers. I had to go into their drugs den and kill them."

"Did you get them?"

"Yes."

"What, on your own?"

"Yes."

"You fought your way into a drugs den on your own?"

"No. I fought my way *out* of it afterwards. I *walked* in. I walked in completely unarmed."

*

Friday night, 10pm.

24-27 Tower Road was an old two storey building with a large gravel car park out front. The Carluccis' drugs den was in a secluded area of an industrial park, completely empty at this late hour.

The neighbouring buildings were derelict, all dark and closed up. The only light came from the Carluccis' building.

I parked in the car park, trying to avoid the huge pot holes, and got out with the briefcase.

I wore suit trousers, a black open-necked shirt, and my jacket. No bulletproof vest, no guns or other weapons of any kind. I'd be going in unarmed.

I'd be lying if I said I wasn't nervous, but I had it under control. Focus on breathing, slow the heart, relax the muscles. Calm, like the light of the moon.

I recognized the guy in the leather jacket at the door. He had set up the meeting two days earlier. I approached him, breathing evenly. He didn't crack his face, just watched me come with his arms folded.

As I neared him he rapped on the front door with his fist and said, "He's here."

A big guy with a ponytail came outside and told me to put my arms out. I did so, still holding the briefcase, and he frisked me thoroughly. Patted both legs, my waist, my chest, my arms, and as he did so the other guy held a gun on me. It was huge. An old Smith and Wesson.

I wanted that gun.

After, the doorman opened the briefcase. I held my breath. The bomb was compact, hidden by the bundles of cash, but if he decided to rifle through it I was in trouble. He didn't. Just looked at the money and then shut it again and handed it back.

I exhaled slowly.

"Okay," said the guy in the leathers, "follow me."

We left the doorman and headed into the building, up a narrow hall and round a corner.

There were two more guys at the foot of a staircase, both with their guns out.

They summed me up as I walk between them up the stairs. Round a couple of corners, and then into the den itself. Seven men, all armed, all staring at me. I soaked it all up as quickly as I could.

To my right, a bald guy with an open purple gym bag on a table in front of him. Money in the bag, money on the table. He had stopped whatever he was doing and picked up a revolver and now just stood there, staring.

Three more guys to my left, standing against the walls, between me and the Carlucci Brothers.

Big Carlucci sat on another table, his arms folded. Little Carlucci stood next to him and was just about as tall. Both wore matching Italian suits, finely tailored. Except Little Carlucci's was about half the size of his brother's.

"This is him, sir," said the guy in the leather jacket who'd let me in.

Big Carlucci did the speaking. "I understand you're interested in our product."

"My boss is. He's going to be away on a six day business trip, and his clients and friends expect certain… entertainments."

"What exactly does your boss do?"

"He's a banker and property tycoon."

"And E is his drug of choice?"

"He's thirty-eight. He likes the London nightlife."

"So his business trip is really an excuse to get high."

"Aye."

Big Carlucci sniffed. "Let me see the money."

One of the guards came over and took the briefcase from me. Took it to the table. Little Carlucci moved aside as the guard set it down and opened it. Big Carlucci peered in as the guard reached inside.

Now. I turned aside, pushing down on the face of my watch and holding it in as I dropped to the ground. My watch gave a *blip*.

The briefcase exploded. I didn't see it because I'd turned away, but I felt the air rush over me and catch my hair. The room quaked, and then the roaring started in my ears. And then the shouts, and the smoke, and I hauled myself to my feet and kicked the leather jacket guy in the head. Felt his skull cave in. I got his Smith and Wesson. And I got the hell out of there.

*

Brooker didn't interrupt once. I don't really know why I told him.

"So you got involved with me entirely by accident?"

"Lucky I did, or else what the hell would you be doing now, with your kid kidnapped? You wouldn't have a clue."

Brooker looked at me, and I could see what he was thinking. *Do you have a clue, Steele? My son's been kidnapped by a psycho and you're the self-proclaimed good guy in all of this so you have to try something, but do you really know what you're doing?*

No. I didn't have a clue either. What the hell did I know about rescuing kidnapped kids - I'm a hitman for God's sake.

"Do you have any children?" Brooker asked me.

"No."

"So you don't know what it's like."

I paused. "No."

Brooker looked at his clenched hands. "Alex kind of saved my life, you know. I was in a dark place before he came along. I was married before Melissa. Married young, when I was twenty-two. Sarah, my ex-wife, found it difficult to conceive. We tried for nearly ten years, and when she finally got pregnant it was... hard on her. But we'd been waiting for a baby for so long, you know? I bought loads of baby things, and decorated the nursery when we found out the baby was a girl. Sarah didn't want me to. Said I might jinx it or something. And she was right. The baby was premature. She died when she was only a few days old."

"I'm sorry."

He shook his head. "Shit happens, right? Well anyway, our marriage didn't survive and we got divorced."

At least he hadn't killed her.

"A year or so later I met Melissa and in a few weeks she was pregnant. We got married. Her father liked me, but her mother never did. She thought I had a temper."

"I wonder why."

"She even tried to stop the wedding. Did you know, 'mother-in-law' is an anagram of 'woman Hitler'?"

I frowned. "Is it?"

"Yes, and it's true. My mother-in-law even had a moustache. That's something to be aware of, by the way, for the future."

"What is?"

"Melissa's mom had a moustache, which means Melissa will probably end up with one too. Just in case you two were thinking of getting together after this."

Oh boy. "What exactly makes you think we'd get together?"

"I've seen you two together. I've seen her flirt with you."

"Brooker, I really don't..."

He raised a hand. "Hey, she's an attractive woman."

"Yes, she is." I wondered how she'd ended up with you, even before your nose went all Rudolph.

"So I'm just saying, you have my blessing."

"I have your *blessing*?"

"Not saying you need it," he said quickly. "I know you're gonna bang her no matter what I say."

I didn't answer that. I didn't know what the hell to say.

"But I'll warn you, she isn't all that," Brooker continued. "You'll see. Anyway, the wedding still went ahead despite Melissa's mother. We got married and Melissa had Alex. I'd been secretly hoping for a boy. It was like my prayers were starting to be answered. I had a good job, a nice house, a lovely wife and kid, and that's when the recession hit and the banks went bust and I was laid off."

"Unfortunate." The recession hadn't affected me. There's always going to be people the government needed killing. But I'd seen the effects. "What job did you do exactly?"

"Construction," he said. "It was hit hard. I worked as a bailiff for a while - the money wasn't as good, but..."

"You realised you could get money out of people by intimidating them."

He squirmed. "I lend people money. It's not really intimidation..."

"Except you kill people who can't pay you back."

"Goddamn it, Steele, I already told you - I don't kill my..."

"I'm not saying you do it yourself. I'm pretty sure *you personally* haven't killed anyone. You don't have the stomach."

And he looked at me with his eyes burning and he said, "My father. I killed my father."

BROOKER

My dad liked his drink. He liked his drink more than he liked me and my mom and my two older brothers. I was the runt of the litter. By the time I was twelve both of my siblings had flown the nest - or as I thought of it, *escaped* - into the army and RAF. It was just me and my mom then.

And my dad and his beer and his belt.

I don't know how many times I got thrashed. Thousands. Always by him, never by her. My mom was a slight, long-necked slip of a thing, with dark hair and eyes and I always wondered what a beautiful woman like her was doing with a man like my father.

And how did he treat his trophy wife? The same way he treated me. Not that I saw him do it very often. He was very careful about that. Although I often heard the sharp *crack* from behind a closed door. My mother rarely cried out, and I loved her even more for that because I bawled like a baby almost every time he thrashed me, and that seemed to make him madder.

I hated my father but I loved him too, in a weird masochistic way, and even now I don't know how that bastard inspired love in anyone.

I use to get up early before he went to work, because that was the only time I saw him sober (the pub just happened to be on his way home, wouldn't you know), and there were mornings when I fancied we were a normal loving family. He'd talk to me without his breath stinking of beer and cook me breakfast sometimes. But then at 7pm a different man would come home, a large lumbering stinking fool of a man bellowing for his dinner.

I was in my second year of the local comprehensive, a slightly skinny twelve-year-old, under-washed, under-fed, dressed in a fading grey uniform that reminded me of coal dust and soot. I got home early from school and caught my mother screwing the milkman - the actual goddamn milkman - on the living room carpet.

Their faces when they saw me.

And the milkman said as he buttoned up his trousers, "At least it wasn't your husband." Because we all knew what my father would have done if he'd caught them.

My mother begged me not to say anything - *"He'd kill me, Gaz..."* - and I thought she was probably right.

She promised not to see the milkman again and I promised not to tell, but things were never the same from then on.

My mother was a whore and a liar, and I fancied perhaps she actually *deserved* my father's beatings after all. Perhaps I was the only injured party in this.

And then, a few months later, I went into the living room where my parents were watching TV in silence and asked, "Could one of you sign my form for the school trip?"

"Ask your mother," my father said.

So I turned to her with the form held out and said, "Would you be able to…"

"No," she said, "you're not going."

I blinked. Thought I must have somehow misheard. "But mama…"

"Your grades aren't good enough."

I looked at my father, who shrugged and went back to the TV. "But... but mama…"

"I'm not changing my mind, Gareth. I told you, you need to work harder."

And I couldn't believe what my goddamn whore of a mother was saying. So I said, "Dad, she's been screwing the milkman," and walked out.

I hadn't really meant to say it. It just slipped out. But it was done, and I stood and listened at the door as my father exploded and my whore-mother pleaded and begged and finally cried out.

He was using his fists. I could hear the difference. My whore-mother was getting her comeuppance, that was for sure. Her cries got weaker and then stopped altogether. I thought maybe she'd had enough, she'd had her punishment, so I pushed open the door.

My mother lay on the rug in roughly the same position she had when I'd found her with the milkman. There was some irony there, somewhere. Except this time her face was all bloody. My father straddled her with his knees and had his hands around her throat.

He was squeezing. Hard. My mother's eyes bulged. She tried to breathe and made a dry hissing sound.

"Dad, that's enough!" I ran over, and he swatted me aside when I grabbed for his arms. And went on squeezing, squeezing. My mother's faced went redder, redder. Her eyes rolled back. And so I grabbed the first thing I could get my hands on - my father's darts trophy from the mantelpiece.

I meant to hit him on the head, but missed. I cracked him on the back of his neck instead, and broke it. The police said he died instantly.

He slumped on top of my mother (exactly like the milkman!) and released her throat and she sucked in a wheeze like a zombie.

I stood over them still holding the trophy, all the strength going from my knees. "Mama?" I dropped the trophy. My knees shook, and I collapsed.

My mother managed to wriggle out from underneath her husband, who we left lying face down with his elbows pointing out.

He never took the belt to me again.

STEELE

"My mother said *she* hit him," Brooker said. "Said she managed to kick him off her and reach the trophy. She was worried I'd end up in prison if we told the truth. But you should have seen the state of her face and neck - it was obviously self-defence. We never talked about that night again."

I listened without comment. If Brooker was expecting me to feel sorry for him he was going to be disappointed. What he'd been through was no doubt terrible, but it was no excuse for the things that he'd done.

We had been at Kevin's house about half an hour when Brooker's phone rang. We looked at each other for a long moment.

"It's him," he said.

I nodded. "Speaker, remember."

"You're going to try and trace it, right?"

"My operations manager is."

"Do I need to keep him on the phone for as long as possible?"

"No. We'll pretty much know where he is immediately. Now go on, answer it."

Brooker swallowed, then did so. "Hello?"

"I've decided what I want you to do," Kevin said. "Have you got yourself a vehicle yet?"

I nodded, and Brooker said, "Yes."

"Do you have a pen?"

"Er..." We both began scanning Kevin's desks.

"If you don't I can text it through."

Brooker found one by the computer and I handed him a pad of post-its. "No, I've found one."

It happens to be yours because we're at your house.

"Write down this address," Kevin said. "23 Westerly Road." And he gave the postcode.

"Okay - is Alex there?"

"Come and see. Call me when you get there for further instructions. Oh, and Mr Brooker? Bring your wallet."

"My wallet?"

But Kevin had already hung up.

Brooker put his phone away. "I *knew* it. He wants money. He wants a ransom."

But I wasn't so sure. Not everyone cared about money as much as Gary Brooker did. I had a feeling getting Alex back wouldn't be so simple.

Dawn Gainsborough called me then. "Kevin West just made a phone call - was it to you?"

"Aye, it was to us."

"I traced his phone, but he was on the move the whole while. His position kept changing. He was driving up Main Street."

"Not Westerly Road?"

"No, why?"

"He told Brooker to go to an address on Westerly Road. Doesn't look like Kevin's going to be there himself."

"Unless he's driving there now. I lost the trace as soon as he hung up so he could be going anywhere."

"Okay, Dawn, thanks."

We left Kevin's house with the post-it and I programmed the address into my Merc's satnav.

As I drove, Brooker sat beside me wringing his hands and taking in big gulps of air. "Why did he want me to bring my wallet if he's not going to be there to take the money? How much does he even want?"

"I don't know. We'll have to wait until we get there."

It was past 7pm when the satnav informed us we'd reached our destination. Pitch black. A quiet road, poor street lighting.

I looked for Kevin's blue Peugeot but couldn't see it anywhere. If he was here he was hiding himself well.

"Can you see him?" Brooker said, twisting round in his seat to look out the rear window.

"No. Doesn't look like he's here." I coasted up the road just to make sure. It wouldn't do for Kevin to see Brooker being chauffeured around in an eighty grand Merc.

"Which one is number 23?"

I turned the car around and drove back up Westerly Road. Pulled in to the kerb at the place flagged by the satnav. Looked at the building I'd parked in front of.

"You have to be goddamn joking." Brooker had seen it too.

PRIVATE stamped on the ghosted out window.

ADULT STORE written over the door.

Kevin West had brought us to a sex shop.

"T-this isn't it, is it?" Brooker started searching for a more appropriate premises. "He wouldn't have meant *here...*"

"I think he did. It's number 23, anyway. Look, above the door."

Brooker saw that I was right. He put his head in his hands. "Why the hell..."

"Ask him," I said. "Kevin told you to call when you arrived."

Brooker nodded. "Too right. I'll ask him, the dirty bastard. Thinks he can piss about with me?" He got out his phone and called.

"Gary!" Kevin answered.

"Why the hell have you brought me to a sex shop you pervert?"

Kevin laughed. "I thought you might react this way."

"Where's Alex?"

"He's safe. Now are you ready to run your little errand?"

"What little errand, what are you talking about?"

"I need you to buy a few things."

Brooker looked at me, horrified. "F-from the sex shop?"

"Yes."

"But... but *what?*"

"Handcuffs. And a whip. I've seen your Internet history, I know you're into that."

Brooker squirmed. "How... I mean, what..."

"Oh stop the dramatics, I haven't got time. Listen, I need you to buy them on your Santander credit card. That's the only one I could find the password for. I'm logged into your Internet banking, so I'll know when you've done it."

"You... you're logged into my Internet banking?"

"You really shouldn't write your passwords down and leave them lying around, Gary. Now go on. Handcuffs and a whip. I'll phone you again when the purchase appears on your account."

"Wait... Why do I need..."

But Kevin had already hung up. Brooker bellowed at his phone and proceeded to hit it against the window.

"Jesus, Gary, stop it," I told him. "You damage anything you're paying."

He snapped his head round, his lip curled into a snarl and his nose looking like a red onion. "He's just trying to humiliate me. That dirty *bastard*. He wants everyone to think I'm some kind of... *sexual deviant* or something..." And then he gripped my arm. "Will you go instead?"

"What?"

"Please. You buy them - nobody knows you. I'll give you my card..."

"No, Gary. You got yourself into this mess, so you can go and buy the whip and chains."

"He said whip and handcuffs!"

Dawn called. Kevin had been driving again during the last phone conversation, this time coming back down Main Street. "I'm sorry, Steele," she said. "It's no use until he stops and calls from somewhere. Somewhere stationary."

"Okay, Dawn, thanks." I turned to Brooker. "Still no joy pinning him down. You're going to have to go in and buy them."

He grumbled to himself a moment more. "You think he was telling the truth about being logged into my bank?"

I thought about the computer systems at his house, and how he'd listened in on Brooker's conversation with Melissa. "Aye, I do."

"So do I. But how could he track my credit card from his car?"

"Logged in on his phone? Or he might have a laptop with him."

Brooker thought about it, then nodded. Then he checked the street was clear, got out and ran into the shop.

Less than five minutes later he stuck his head out the door, checked the street, and ran back to the car with a dark blue carrier bag. The Merc locks itself automatically for security reasons however, and so he couldn't open the passenger door and just stood there pulling at the handle, checking the street should someone see him and swearing at me.

I let him in, and he called me a bastard and slammed the passenger door. "That wasn't funny."

"I didney do it on purpose, the car locks itself."

"Just drive!" He'd gone all red and out of breath as if he'd run a marathon.

I smiled to myself and pulled away with no destination in mind.

"I saw my postman in there," Brooker said after a moment.

"Your postman?" That must have been fun for both of you. "Did you say hello?"

"*No, I didn't say hello, Jesus Christ...*"

I had to swallow back a laugh. "Well did you get the stuff?"

Brooker sighed. "Yes. I've never been so embarrassed my entire life." He pulled the whip halfway out the bag, and then did the same with the handcuffs.

"At least they're not pink and fluffy."

"Oh shut up, Steele, you dick."

Kevin phoned again a few moments later. "The money has been charged to your account, Gary, congratulations."

Brooker set his jaw, his nostrils flaring. His free hand had made a claw on his thigh. "*What now?*"

"Now I want you to buy a vacuum cleaner."

A vacuum cleaner? I thought.

"A vacuum cleaner?" Brooker said.

"Yes. The Homebase on Main Street is open til 8 - I've checked. You should go there."

Brooker looked exactly how I felt: totally confused. "What kind of vacuum cleaner? A... a Dyson?"

"I don't care what type, *Gary*, as long as it has a hose. It can be one of those round red things with the silly faces for all I care."

"A Henry."

"A who?"

"It's... oh, nothing."

Kevin snorted. "You have less than forty-five minutes to get to Homebase before it closes. Again, use your credit card. When you've bought it I will call you with further instructions." He hung up.

Brooker just stared at me. "A *vacuum cleaner*," he said. "Is he having me on? Why does he want me to get a vacuum cleaner? Does he want me to... *clean his house*, I don't..." And then he put a hand to his head. "Oh God - the hose... He's going to handcuff me and whip me and get the hoover to suck me off."

"I doubt that's what he's planning."

"Then what?"

"I don't know." Although I had an idea.

I don't care what type, Gary, as long as it has a hose.

But before I could think it through further, Dawn called again.

"Steele, I have him."

*

"He's at a private lock-up," Dawn said. "Or at least, he was as of a minute ago. He stayed there all through the conversation."

I sat up straight in my seat. That was more like it - a solid lead. "What's the address?"

She gave it me. "I checked the rental agreement and

it's not registered to Kevin, that's why I didn't know about it."

"Who's it registered to?"

"Some guy who doesn't exist by the looks of things."

Fake name, probably fake address - what did Kevin keep in that lock-up? Obviously something he didn't want traced back to him should it be discovered.

And possibly Alex.

"Thanks Dawn, heading there now."

As I drove Brooker said, "Do you think this is where he's holding Alex?"

"Well I left my psychic powers in Scotland, Gary, but it stands a good chance. He's got to be holding him somewhere."

"Oh please God I hope so..." He'd pressed his eyes shut and raised his head as if to a heaven he'd never see.

I nodded to myself. "I hope so too."

Of course, Kevin could have had the boy locked in the boot of his Peugeot, but I wasn't going to say that in front of Brooker. Besides, it was unlikely. By the sounds of it Kevin had been driving around town, scouting out prospective places for the little shopping trips he'd been sending Brooker on. Even if he'd gagged Alex the boy could still have made a real racket by kicking the boot to bits. A passer-by would surely raise the alarm. And Kevin would have thought about all that.

He was a psycho, but he was also very far from stupid.

So. Given everything, this lock-up was the place he'd been keeping Alex. Which is why when we arrived, the first thing I did was draw my Glock.

Kevin's car was nowhere to be seen.

I turned to Brooker and put a finger to my lips. "*Stay behind me.*"

He didn't protest, just stared at the gun with wide jealous eyes and then followed me to the shutter door.

It was padlocked shut from the outside, and my heart began to thump a bit harder.

Kevin had left and locked up after himself.

The question was, had he taken Alex with him?

I set the Glock down and picked the padlock, then retrieved the gun. "Open it," I told Brooker, because I couldn't do it with my sling-arm.

The shutter rattled up.

Brooker said, "*Oh Goddamn,*" and bent forward, his face in his hands.

Alex wasn't there.

But he had been. There was a chair in the centre of the room with a roll of gaffer tape on it. That hardly constituted evidence, but I was pretty sure a forensics team would find traces of Alex's hair on it or maybe his fingerprints.

In the corner of the lock-up was a table overloaded with old computer towers and hard drives. Bet the evidence on those was quite compelling too.

"Oh Alex..." Brooker pulled at his hair, and then kicked one of the computers clean off the table and screamed, "*Kevin! Where the hell is my son?*"

"We'll find him," I said. Kevin *wants* us to find him.

"So what do we do now?"

I looked at my watch. Just after half 7. "We go and buy a bloody hoover."

*

We arrived at Homebase with just ten minutes to spare. A closer call than either of us would have liked.

Brooker ran into the shop and came out just before

closing time holding a large box.

"You *did* buy a Henry," I said as he reached the car.

"It kept staring at me." He put it on the back bench and then slumped into the passenger seat. We sat there in the car park for a while. "Do you have a clue what all this means, Steele? Because I don't."

"No idea," I said.

"Should I call him to say I've bought it?"

"Kevin said he'd phone you when the purchase appears on your account."

And he did call only a few minutes later. He sounded jovial, his voice all high and light. "Going well, Gary, going well."

"I want to speak to my son."

"Soon, I promise. I just have one last thing I want you to pick up."

Brooker groaned, and I couldn't blame him. "I'm sure the shops will be shutting…"

"Oh, I don't need you to go to a shop. Are you still in the Homebase car park?"

"Yes."

"Well look over at the exit, as if you're going to drive out. You see that row of bushes on the left?"

"Yes?"

"Walk over there."

"W-walk over there?"

"Yes, but stay on the phone. I've left you something under one of the bushes. I want you to go and get it."

BROOKER

It would be Alex's finger, I knew it, I'd seen enough movies, Alex's finger in a matchbox or something, and as I walked towards the bushes my legs felt weaker and weaker until I thought I might have to crawl.

I held the phone to my ear even though neither of us spoke, and all I could hear was Kevin's breathing and it sounded like it came from inside my head.

Steele had come out after me - I guess he thought it was Alex's finger too and wanted to shoot it or something.

"Have you found it yet?" Kevin asked, and I had this image, this image of Kevin chopping Alex into little bits and eating him, and maybe his finger was the only part of him left. "It's quite big."

And I thought, his head, he's left me his head.

I reached the bushes, and there was no severed head and there was no severed finger.

There was a statue of an elephant.

"Is... is this it?" The knot in my stomach loosened and I broke out in goosebumps. "The... the elephant?"

"Yes."

Oh thank God... I collapsed to my knees, clutching my chest and gave a bark of shaky laughter. "It's just an elephant..."

Steele crouched down beside me to get a better look, a frown on his face.

"I want you to bring it with you," Kevin said.

I didn't even bother asking why. They obviously meant something to Kevin, but he was a wackjob. "Where am I going?"

"The old stone quarry, using the closed access road.

The gate will be open. Understand?"

"Y-yes..."

"Good. Bring the handcuffs and the vacuum cleaner and the elephant. I'm waiting. And Alex is with me."

My heart took a tumble. "Is he okay?"

"Of course he is. Now, what car did you take?"

Oh goddamn. "I er..."

Me and Steele started looking round the car park, but it was now past closing time and the only car left was Steele's black Mercedes.

"Oh it doesn't matter," Kevin interrupted. "It's too dark to see now anyway. Just make sure you come alone. I don't want to see that fat man who punched me, or any other of your *associates*. Just you. You know what will happen to Alex if you don't." And he hung up.

It took me by surprise. "But what do you want? Kevin? *Kevin!*" I frowned at Steele as I put my phone away. "Does he want money? He didn't mention money, did he?"

"No, I don't think he wants money. Come on." Steele began walking back to his car.

I picked up the elephant statue. It was about the size of my hand, but heavier than I'd imagined. Must have been made of metal or something. "We know where they are now, right?" At the disused quarry - what were they doing there?

"I just need confirmation from HQ, but I think he was probably telling the truth, yes."

We got back in the Mercedes and I put the elephant statue in the bag with the whip and handcuffs.

Steele's phone went - it was that woman again who did all the phone trace stuff.

Her voice came over the hands-free speaker system.

"Steele, I've got a fixed position again. Kevin West is at a disused quarry about five miles east of you."

"Thanks Dawn," Steele replied. "Kevin's told us to meet him there. Can you send a map of the area to my Merc's touchscreen so we can see it?"

"Yes, and I'll flag his position for you. Just a sec…"

Steele moved closer and peered at the screen as a satellite image of the quarry appeared. I tried to make sense of it but just ended up confusing myself.

"See it?" The woman asked.

"Aye," Steele said, "thanks."

"The blue flag was Kevin's position when he called. Sorry, I don't have authorisation to pull a live satellite feed."

"Don't worry, I can work from this. I need an overlooking position."

"Okay. I'm just pulling up a topographic map so I can see the contour lines, hang on." She paused a few moments, then said, "Presumably you want to be somewhere he can't see you, but you can see him."

"Yes. I have binoculars. And a sniper rifle."

My stomach leapt at that. I thought, there you go Kevin you crazy bastard, that'll sort you out.

"Okay - what about here?" A red flag appeared on the map, a few hundred metres west of the blue one. "You're four metres higher, and even better you're in a clump of trees."

"Perfect. Send the GPS coordinates to my car - we need to make a move."

"Will do. Good luck."

Steele hung up. Turned to me. "Time to go."

I swallowed. "Are you going to shoot Kevin?"

"Aye. It looks like I might have to."

"Good."

Steele didn't reply, just stared at me with a sour look on his face for some reason.

"Are we going there now?"

"No," he said. "You heard Kevin. He expects to see you drive up the access road alone. We can't go and get your BMW from outside your office – it's too risky. Kevin will want to know how you got it back and the police are probably watching it. And you're not having my Merc. So first we're going to have to steal you a car."

STEELE

We headed in the general direction of the quarry. No time to go out of our way. Kevin would be expecting Brooker in less than half an hour so we had to get this done quickly.

Brooker went through the items Kevin had told him to bring. "The elephant statue, the Henry Hoover, the handcuffs and the whip." He shook his head to himself. "What does it all mean?"

He was wrong on one point though.

During the last conversation Kevin had said *Bring the handcuffs and the vacuum cleaner and the elephant.*

He hadn't mentioned the whip at all.

Why? Because it was window dressing. The whip didn't matter. It was the handcuffs Kevin wanted. The vacuum cleaner was window dressing too.

I don't care what type, Gary, as long as it has a hose.

Kevin didn't want the vacuum cleaner. He wanted the hose.

But most of all, he wanted revenge.

You need to steal a vehicle, and you need to do so without breaking a window.

Because a broken window would scupper everything.

Kevin had set up a clever little trap, and Brooker was going to walk straight into it without the slightest idea. The loan shark caught, trapped, and little Alex Brooker, nothing but shark bait.

And only me able to stop it.

But what the hell was the elephant for?

Brooker was turning the statue in his hands, muttering to himself. "It has little ears," he said. "Is it Indian or African elephants that have little ears?"

"Indian, I think."

"So it's an Indian elephant. Maybe it's something to do with India. The Taj Mahal?"

"What could this possibly have to do with the Taj Mahal?"

He scowled at me. "I don't know, I'm just trying to solve this puzzle, alright? Wait... isn't there an Indian god that's an elephant?"

"There's an Indian god with an elephant head."

"Maybe that's it."

I rolled my eyes. "Aye, Gary, he's calling you a god."

"*No*, maybe he's saying that *he's* the god, that's why he can order me around."

"Maybe." It seemed to me that Brooker and Kevin probably *both* had god-complexes. "Maybe it's something much simpler."

"Like what?"

I shot him a sideways glance. "Elephants never forget."

We came across a network of deserted back streets, and I pulled up in one that had a run of four parked cars. They were around the corner from the houses to which they presumably belonged. Out of sight.

I would be quiet and I would be quick.

"Pass me my toolbag from the glove box."

Brooker did so, and I opened it and rummaged around. Stanley knife, spare lock pick, oh, there's my bump key. I found the screwdriver and took it out. "Now I need you to hold Henry."

He raised his eyebrows. "Okay... why?"

"I need something from my seat locker."

He followed me out of the car, circled round and took the hoover box off the back seat. "Something to help steal the car?"

"Aye. My slim jim."

He frowned. "Isn't that a sausage? *Holy shit.*"

I'd flipped the bench, revealing the array of weaponry.

Brooker took a step back and almost dropped Henry. "I knew it! You *are* a secret agent... Jesus, and I thought I could kill you..."

I said nothing, just reached in and pulled out the slim jim, a thin strip of spring steel about two feet long with a hooked end. "Stay here. And do *not* go anywhere near my weapons." I slammed the seat bench shut and held his eyes for longer than necessary to show him I meant it.

Brooker nodded, put Henry down on the bench, shut the door and got back in the passenger seat.

I hurried over to the four parked cars. Chose the one that looked the oldest, a rusty green sedan. Less likely to have security measures. Forced the hooked end of the slim jim between the car's window and the rubber seal, caught the interconnecting rods that operate the door.

The door opened in less than ten seconds.

I got in, used the screwdriver to pry off the steering panel. Connected the two wires to complete the circuit and touched it to the starter.

Spark. The engine turned over and then grumbled to life.

Less than thirty seconds to get in and get going.

I turned round in the street, and that's when I saw.

"Oh shit," I said.

BROOKER

I didn't see the Land Rover come up behind the Mercedes, I was too busy watching Steele break into what must have been the oldest piece of junk he could find.

I'd just thought, He's surely not expecting me to drive *that,* when I heard the roar of an engine behind me. And when I looked up into the rear-view mirror I only had a brief image of glaring headlights before the Land Rover smashed right into the goddamn boot.

"Christ!" I flew against the glove box, felt like I'd broke a couple of ribs.

And I smacked my goddamn nose again. It was like my head exploded.

Had the Land Rover done it on *purpose*?

First Steele rams into the back of my Porsche and then these arseholes...

Oh GOD

These arseholes had just jumped out of the Land Rover - two of them, men dressed in suits - the driver and a man from the back seat.

One of them had a crowbar, and he appeared at the driver's window and

Whump

he tried to smash the goddamn glass with it but somehow it didn't break and he bounced away and I think might even have fallen over.

At some point I started screaming. Screaming's like crying - only for babies or women - but I couldn't help it.

The other man tried the door handle, but thank the Lord Jesus it didn't open, the Mercedes had locked me

in, and then the crowbar man appeared again and
Whump
he tried again to break the window and again the window didn't break, and I sat there flinching and yelling and not knowing what to do.

The crowbar man paused before taking another swing and peered in at me. He said to the other one, "That's not him."

Because they weren't after me - what had I ever done? - they'd come after Steele, of course they had, this was his Mercedes wasn't it? They'd probably been ginger ninjered too, just like I had, and wanted revenge.

But they didn't get it, because at that moment they were ginger ninjered again.

STEELE

They were Carlucci's guys, obviously, and they thought they'd got me. Except they were trying to break bulletproof glass with a crowbar and I wasn't even in the Merc.

I was in a put-putting little rustmobile aiming straight for them with my foot to the floor. The engine squealed as I cranked up through the gears with a left arm feeling like molten lead.

The two men heard me coming. I was making enough noise.

One of them ran. The other pressed himself against my Merc's driver door, trying to make himself as small as possible.

Not small enough.

I steered into him, just a glancing blow, crushed him between the rustmobile's right wing and the Merc's door, knocking off a wing mirror each from both cars and then driving on.

Samuel Dalton would not be happy with that.

Then I ran down the runner. No way I could let him live – he would kill me without a second thought if he got the chance.

He hadn't got very far. Tried to dart around the back of his Land Rover but didn't make it. Bounced off the rustmobile's bonnet and over the roof, doing some fancy cartwheels. I think he landed on his head.

I skidded to a halt, spinning the car back round. Got out.

The cartwheeling guy would be doing no more cartwheels, but he could still crawl.

"Hey," I said.

He rolled over onto his back. Reached into his jacket.

I shot him in the head.

The guy crushed against my Merc was already dead. He'd collapsed in a heap, leaving a long red mark down the dented door. I holstered my gun, grabbed him by the collar and hauled him a couple of feet away from the car.

I left the severed wing mirrors where they were.

Changing lanes was going to be interesting.

I unlocked the Merc with my key and found Brooker sitting half in the footwell and still screaming.

"Gary."

"Arrgh... *Arrrrgh*..."

"*Gary.*"

He looked at me, like he'd snapped back from his stupor. "A-are they dead?"

I nodded. "We need to go."

Brooker didn't seem to hear. "He thought I was you... He thought I was you..."

"They were following the Merc. I screwed up. I didn't notice."

"But they're dead, right?"

"Aye. Now get out of the car."

He did so, shakily, as if he was getting out onto an alien planet. I wondered if anyone else had seen this side of him, this scared, shaking, helpless Gary Brooker. I doubted it.

But then again no one else had kidnapped his son.

I pointed at the rustmobile. "Get in and follow me. *Now*, before more Carluccis show up."

That got him moving.

I drove for five minutes, checking my rear-view mirror every other second to make sure Brooker hadn't gone wah-wah and driven into a ditch. He kept up, and when

I pulled over he parked behind me, looking as pale as the moonlight.

"Leave the engine running," I told him as I got out. "Don't try to turn it off."

"But what happens if Kevin wants me to turn it off?"

"I seriously doubt he'll want you to do that."

The Merc's boot was quite crumpled but it opened. I pulled out the bedsheet, already stained with Little Carlucci's blood, and cleaned my driver's door with it.

Brooker looked ready to throw up at any moment.

"Come get your stuff." I passed him over the dark blue bag with the whip and the handcuffs and the elephant, and he made a second trip and put Henry Hoover in the back.

I looked at my watch. "We're running late. Kevin will start to wonder where you are." I hesitated, then put a hand on his shoulder. "Are you still with me, Gary?"

He blinked. "What?"

"Alex is counting on you. I need you to focus. I can't have you freaking out."

One thing was for certain – I couldn't save Alex without Gary's help. I didn't like it, but there you go. This guy had tried to kill me, and was partly responsible for the deaths of at least two others. But I needed him.

Jesus. We needed each other.

He took a huge breath. Nodded. "I'm okay."

"You are?"

"Yes."

"Good. Then let's go get your son back." I led Brooker to the back of my car. "I'm going to set up out of sight. Which means you're going to pull up to Kevin alone."

"I'm not happy about this…"

Well you should have thought about that before you killed his dog. "I'm going to give you a mic so I can listen in on whatever's going on." I popped the seat locker again, but this time Brooker didn't even seem to notice what I had in it. He made no reaction, anyway.

I withdrew a tiny microphone from a side compartment and clipped it to Brooker's suit lapel. I turned it on and wore the corresponding earpiece. "Say something."

"What?"

"Good, that's fine. Just remember to turn your speakerphone on if he calls you again."

"How will you talk to me?"

"I won't. I'll call you when this is over. Now, do you know where you're going?"

"Yes. The disused quarry..."

"Aye, the main access road. Do you still have that pay-as-you-go phone, the one you used to call me when you were at your office? The one Kevin can't trace?"

He nodded, bringing out an old-style pink mobile.

"Good. Wait for me to call you on that before you go down the access road, which I'll do when I'm in position. Do not go down the access road before I've called you, okay?"

"Okay." He looked just about ready to faint.

"Try and do what he says, and don't do anything stupid." And with that I got in my Merc, uploaded the GPS coordinates Dawn had sent into my satnav and headed for the quarry and that kidnapped little boy.

BROOKER

I drove to the quarry feeling like I was going to be sick any minute. At one point I almost had to pull over. My mouth had gone so dry swallowing was impossible, and my head felt like a helium balloon.

I tried not to think about it, but my mind kept showing me his face, Kevin's face, laughing and laughing, and at a red light I pressed my eyes shut for as long as I dared and prayed.

Please God, I don't know if you're there, but if you are please look after Alex.

I thought about the things I'd done, the people I'd hurt these past few years.

I thought about what I'd put Melissa through.

And I thought, would it have been so bad if we'd been poor? If I'd done what Melissa had suggested and picked up some office work or something. Yes, we might have lost the house and the car and the nice holidays along with my job.

But perhaps we wouldn't have lost each other.

I remembered Alex as a little boy, playing football with me in the garden on a summer's afternoon. Sausages were cooking on the barbecue on the patio, where Melissa sat drinking with her parents and watching us play. Everyone was smiling and laughing and life was good.

Back before the banks crashed and I lost my job and my wife and my son, life was good.

Please God, I don't care what happens to me, but please look after Alex.

I pulled onto the access road and stopped to wait for Steele's call.

And just like Kevin had said, the gate stood open, open like the gates of hell.

STEELE

I left my Merc by the copse of trees and fought my way through to the vantage point at the edge of the tree line. Assembled the Arctic Warfare Covert Sniper Rifle in the grass, lay on my stomach and looked through the night-vision scope. Everything came out green.

Kevin's blue Peugeot was side on, its headlights cutting through the dark. He'd driven to the end of the access road and turned round, so as to be facing Brooker when he drove up. He pointed left, putting Alex in the passenger seat between me and him.

Alex had been gagged with what I assumed was gaffer tape - had probably been cocooned in it, although I could only see the top of his shoulders and head. But he was alive.

At least that was something.

I called Brooker on his pink pay-as-you-go. "I'm in position, and I can see his car. Kevin's behind the wheel and Alex is in the passenger seat. He's alive."

Brooker gave a strained cry of relief. "Can't you shoot him? Shoot him now? Please…"

"I can't - Alex is in the way."

"But can't you…"

"This isn't Call of Duty, Gary. Now get down here." I hung up. Looked back through the scope and waited. Waited for Gary to arrive and for this to be over so I could go home and find one of those damn Robotik Golden Bunnies before Wednesday.

Then Brooker arrived.

I saw his headlights first, and then the old rustmobile resolved. Luckily the darkness hid most of the dents and scratches I'd recently given it.

"I'm here, oh God oh God..." Brooker whispered to himself, his voice coming scratchy through my earpiece. The car stopped a few metres from Kevin's front bumper. "What does he want me to do, get out?"

And then his phone rang. It came through clearly. I hoped Brooker would remember to put the phone on speaker.

He did. Answered. "Alright, what now?"

"I'm glad you came," Kevin said.

I focused the rifle scope back on the Peugeot. Kevin had his phone in one hand and held something to Alex's throat with the other.

"Of course I came," Brooker said. "I want my son."

"And you will have him. But I need you to know that I currently have a knife to his throat."

Ah, so that's what it was. Brooker began burbling.

"Be quiet, Mr Brooker, it's only so you do as I say without trying any... funny business."

"I won't try anything, I…"

"Good. Now listen. I want you to leave the engine running and put the handbrake on. Did you bring everything I instructed you to bring?"

"Yes."

"Good. Get out, but don't hang up the phone. And don't come anywhere near my car."

"Okay." Brooker climbed from the driver's seat and the interior light came on.

"Put the vacuum cleaner on the ground," Kevin said.

Brooker fetched it from the back seat and did so. "I... I bought a Henry, I hope it's okay..."

"Open it."

"Open it?"

"Yes. Get it out of the box."

Gary paused, and I could tell what he was thinking – *am I going to have to hoover his car?*

It took him a couple of minutes to rip the box open, not having a knife to assist the process. He'd set his phone on the ground and retrieved it now. "Okay?"

"Show me the hoover," Kevin said.

Brooker must have been thinking this was the most bizarre kidnapping ever. He lifted Henry out and set the vacuum on the dirt. "I think it only comes in red."

"Show me the hose."

There we are, I thought. The hose. The real reason for the purchase. I looked at the exhaust pipe on the rustmobile, rattling and chugging thick black smoke into the night.

Brooker still didn't understand. He lifted the hose as if entertaining the crazy whim of a toddler, apparently without realising that Kevin didn't care less what the hose looked like, he just wanted Brooker's fingerprints on it.

"Okay," said Kevin. "Now the elephant. Do you have it?"

Brooker fetched it from out of the blue bag. "Here. It really is a lovely..."

"Throw it on the passenger seat."

Again Brooker looked confused, but he did as asked. "Oh... it fell on the floor..."

"Leave it, that's fine. Now there's just the handcuffs."

"Er, there's the whip as well..."

"We don't need the whip, just take the handcuffs out and throw the bag in the back."

Brooker did so. He held the handcuffs in his free hand and looked down at them.

"Take them back to your car," Kevin said.

I heard Brooker swallow, it was that loud. "Okay..."

"Get back in, but leave the door open so the light stays on. I want to see. Put one cuff on your right wrist."

Brooker paused for a moment, then did what he was told.

"Now feed the chain through the steering wheel and cuff your left wrist so you're handcuffed to it."

"But... but my phone..."

"I'm sure you can manage. I'd better hear the cuffs click."

Brooker juggled his mobile as he threaded the cuffs between the bars of the steering wheel and clicked them over his hands. He bent his head to his mobile. "Okay... now what?"

Kevin laughed, a sound as cold as a Norwegian fforde and totally void of humour. "Now you watch your son die."

Of course this was how he'd planned it. What better vengeance could there be for his dog? I still had no shot, of course. Brooker began burbling again.

"There's no use, Mr Brooker," Kevin said. "I'm going to kill him and you're going to watch, and then you're going to go to prison for his murder."

Brooker pulled against his cuffs. "*What?* No... you can't..."

"You decided to run away with your son. You hit Melissa over the head with the elephant statue and kidnapped him."

Ah, so the elephant statue was what Kevin had knocked Melissa out with.

Brooker *still* didn't get it. "I... what?"

"The statue has her DNA on it. Bits of skin and blood. It also has your fingerprints."

He got it. "You bastard..."

"You even rung Melissa to tell her you'd done it. But then you realised... running away was no good. Where could you run? There was only one way out, and if you couldn't have Alex, then no one could. So you tied Alex up and handcuffed yourself to the wheel after fixing a hose to the exhaust."

"What? I don't..." He looked at Henry Hoover. He got that too.

Oh Henry.

"Alex will be dead," Kevin continued. "But you'll survive. You'll make a frantic phone call to the police. You've changed your mind. And they'll come and save you but it'll be too late for your boy. And you'll go to prison for his murder, and you'll know what happens when you *screw with Kevin West.*"

Kevin got out of the car, hauling Alex out with him. The boy was totally wrapped up in gaffer tape.

Brooker screamed, pumped the gas, and wrestled like an electrocuted man.

Kevin held Alex close, threw him onto the Peugeot's bonnet, lifted up a cushion and placed it across the boy's face. He wasn't going to slit his throat, of course. Suffocate him. The irony was a post-mortem wouldn't show carbon monoxide poisoning, and they'd find threads of the cushion in his throat. I guess Kevin hadn't thought of that.

But not everyone's a professionally trained killer like I am.

I still didn't really have a shot. Kevin bent over Alex, until they were almost one, a wriggling worm in the glare of Brooker's headlights. I swore.

Brooker bucked and writhed and eventually screamed,

"Steele, *do something!*"

He hadn't meant to expose me, but it had the desired effect. Kevin stopped weighing down on the cushion and looked up - straightened, in fact, into my sights.

I pulled the trigger.

BROOKER

It was like my heart was being torn in two. Alex lay barely ten feet from me. I had to watch whilst that bastard killed him and there was nothing I could do, and I strained against the handcuffs until I thought the steering wheel must pop off, the steering wheel or my hands, and I couldn't take it any longer and I looked out of my open car door into the trees where Steele must be and I took a huge breath and I bellowed, "STEELE DO SOMETHING!"

Kevin heard me and looked up. I heard a *crack*.

But Kevin had already ducked, disappearing behind the Peugeot's bonnet. I reckon I even saw the bullet ruffle his hair.

What I'd have given to see it blow out the back of his head instead.

"Run!" I yelled. "Alex, run!"

My son rolled himself off the bonnet and somehow landed on his feet. Kevin had wound him up in duct tape, and he waddled away in Steele's direction like a penguin.

The gunshot must have cleared my head a bit. I stuck my right arm between the bars of the steering wheel, giving my left hand enough room to reach the gear stick. I put it into first and dropped the handbrake just as Kevin charged out from behind his car after Alex.

I stamped on the accelerator and the old rustbucket kangarooed forward and clipped him. Kevin fell, and the still-open driver's door smacked him clean across the side of the head and knocked him flat.

"Run, Alex!" I screamed, as the car smashed into the bonnet of Kevin's Peugeot and stalled. "Run!"

Kevin began climbing to his feet, but I swung my legs from the car and kicked him down, stamped on him, pinned him there, my arms straining against the steering wheel.

Shoot him! I thought. Why aren't you goddamn shooting him?

Kevin pulled a knife from his jacket. The one he'd been holding to Alex's throat just minutes ago. I tried to kick him, but he grabbed my leg and used it to pull himself to his knees.

Come on then you weird psycho bastard.

He stabbed me in the stomach. Once, twice, making an animal mewing sound. I didn't feel a thing. I don't know why. It should have hurt, I know it should have hurt. I saw the knife go in. I saw the blood come out.

I raised my legs. I could have kicked him away. But I didn't. Instead I wrapped my legs around him and pulled him close, pinning him to me as the knife came up down up down, in out in out, and I didn't feel a thing. I think Kevin might have even forgotten about Alex altogether. It was just him and me, like it should have been.

And everything started to go dark and quiet and that was just fine.

STEELE

Alex was still in the way of my shot. He waddled towards me, blocking Kevin and his dad from my sights. But I saw Brooker wrap his legs around Kevin and hold him there, even as he was being stabbed, and it actually panged at my heart.

And then, mercifully, finally, Alex lost his footing and went down flat on his face. Disappeared beneath my crosshairs. I pulled the trigger. Hit Kevin in the back, where his heart was. The round did its job.

Kevin slumped, went limp, and slid down Brooker flat onto the road.

I'd already sprung to my feet and sprinted down the gentle slope towards them, drawing the Glock from my hip. Alex had rolled onto his side and bucked there on the ground, unable to even sit up. His eyes went wide when he saw me.

I transferred the gun to my left hand and ripped the gaffer tape from his mouth. He moaned, began sucking air in rasps.

"It's okay," I said. "You're safe." And then, "Don't go anywhere - I won't be a moment." As I said before, rescuing people isn't my forte.

I hurried to the rustmobile. Blood turned the road red. Kevin lay on his back with his glazed eyes staring at the stars. My bullet had ripped through his heart and burst out his chest. I looked at Brooker, who lay against the driver's seat, held upright only by his handcuffs. Possibly the bullet had gone straight through Kevin and into Brooker's right shoulder. But he had too many stab wounds, there was too much blood, and I just couldn't tell.

He was still alive, his chest rising and falling, blood pouring from him like a red waterfall. He stared at me. Managed, "A-Alex?"

"He's fine." I holstered my gun. I wasn't going to need it, not now.

"I'm going to die, aren't I."

I nodded.

Brooker nodded back. He had gone the colour of sour milk. But he smiled. "I helped though, didn't I?"

And I smiled back. "Aye. You did good."

"I have... thirty grand in a r-red rucksack under the desk in my office. And f-five more at home in a wardrobe... can you get it to Melissa..."

"Yes."

His breathing slowed. He said, "Thanks, Steele."

"That's not my real name." But he didn't hear, because he'd already gone.

*

I unwrapped most of Alex, until he went freaky and tried to kick me to death, after which I left some of the gaffer tape on. Me trying to assure him seemed not to make a bit of difference. I don't know how much he'd seen of what went on, but he kept screaming for his dad until he finally tired himself out. I half-carried half-dragged him under my right arm to my car.

I didn't tell him that his dad was dead. I don't know why. Perhaps I thought it wasn't my place. Or more probably, I didn't want to deliver the bad news.

Everyone's a coward in some way or other.

And deep down I thought Alex probably already knew.

I called Andrews as I drove, told him what had happened. He said 'Jesus Christ' a few times, but I could hear his relief. Not just at having Brooker and Kevin the low-lying psycho out of his hair, but having me out of his hair too. I didn't blame him.

There were two police cars outside Melissa's house when I got there. Halfway through the journey Alex had begun sobbing his seven-year-old heart out, and didn't stop for ten minutes. He had gone to sleep afterwards, amazingly, a kind of half-doze interrupted by whimpers and snuffles.

Perhaps he'd awake and consider the last few hours a bad dream. But I doubted it.

I pulled in, got out, gently lifted Alex from the passenger seat.

Melissa came rushing outside. She began crying, wrapped her arms around Alex, and then around me as well.

"Thank you," she whispered, and kissed the ginger fuzz on one of my cheeks. I don't know how she could stand to do that, either.

"Mommy, am I safe now?" Alex yawned, swept up into his mother's arms and snuggled there.

"Yes, darling, yes." Melissa looked at me, her eyes sparkling with tears. She mouthed 'Gary' and raised her eyebrows, which I guess made it a question. *Gary?*

I shook my head. Mouthed 'dead'. Subtle, I know.

Melissa barely reacted. She looked down, and then back up at me, then nodded. 'Okay', maybe. Or even 'good'.

Two policemen and two policewomen emerged from their cars. Perhaps I was the crazy father who'd kidnapped the boy and hit the mother. But I showed them my LV licence and they disappeared again.

Melissa invited me in. Actually, she insisted.

We unwrapped Alex properly, completely, and the boy screamed whenever the tape came free from his bare skin. Melissa cradled him and shushed him, and like a baby he went back to sleep. It wasn't even 10 o'clock, but he'd probably sleep for hours.

Melissa carried him upstairs, leaving me in the living room. The house she was renting was small but well-furnished. The fire was on. She had a blanket draped over the settee, and I assumed she'd been huddled under it these last couple of hours, just sitting there with all sorts of terrible scenarios playing through her mind.

Pictures on the mantelpiece showed Alex on a bike, eating ice cream, and his last three birthday parties. Gary Brooker was in none of them, and was now out of her life for good.

She came down a moment later, wordlessly crossed the room and hugged me again, tighter, pressing herself against me, whispering in my ear, "Thank you for saving my son."

She squeezed my bad shoulder a little too tight. I held her back with my right hand and eventually stepped away. "I said I would," I said.

"Can I get you a beer?" She smiled. "Or something stronger?"

I shook my head. "Thanks, but I don't drink."

"You don't drink when you're... working?"

"I don't drink at all. Haven't touched a drop of alcohol for years."

She raised her eyebrows. "Why's that?"

"It's a long story. I'll have a cup of tea, though, if that's going."

"Of course."

We sat on the sofa and drank tea and ate biscuits, and

we talked. I told her everything. About Kevin being the real kidnapper, about making Gary phone her to confess, about the 'little errands' he sent us on and even about what had happened at the quarry.

She listened in near silence, her mouth open and her brow knitted, asking the odd question but generally letting the story flow. When I'd finished she said, "So this Kevin West tried to *frame* Gary?"

"Aye."

"Gary had killed his dog?"

"Aye. With a brick."

She rubbed her face with her hands. "He nearly got my son killed."

I sighed. "Aye. Gary really did pick on the wrong guy."

She stared at me. "So it's lucky the right guy came along when he did."

Dear God, she was coming on to me. Had she unbuttoned another button of her blouse whilst in the kitchen?

"Do you have children, John?"

"No."

"Are you married?"

My heart beat a little faster. "No."

"Oh." Her eyes bored into me like drills. She lifted her coffee cup and sipped, staring at me from over the lip. "So... is there anyone special in your life?"

"No."

"No one?" Another sip.

"No."

She raised her eyebrows. "You need to find someone and settle down."

And I said, "I don't settle easily." I drained my tea and stood up. "I'm heading back to Scotland first thing tomorrow. And I need to sort some things tonight, before the police get too involved. Sorry, I have to go."

She looked taken aback. "Oh - okay... I just thought..."

"It's not you." Oh Jesus, as if I just said that. "Sorry, I..."

"No, don't apologise." She looked at the floor. "Go, if you have to."

"Okay." I paused. "I don't suppose you have a key to his house, do you?"

"No."

"Never mind." I crossed to the front door.

She got up after me. "I thought Gary was taken care of?"

"It's not that easy. Thanks for the tea."

She frowned. "Well, you have my number. Perhaps you'll give me a call later."

I managed another smile. "I'll do that." But I never did. "I hope Alex is okay."

Then I opened the front door and walked out into the night.

*

I drove to Brooker's office. His BMW was the only thing parked outside, although I was pretty sure the circus would arrive soon. He had thirty grand in cash hidden in a rucksack somewhere inside, and I wanted to find it before the authorities got here and started complicating things. Salvage was mine to do with as I liked, after all.

I let myself in and climbed the stairs.

The red rucksack was where he'd said it was – under the desk. He'd obviously taken it out of the safe when planning to run off, and then Kevin had called and I'd got involved and he'd had to leave it here.

I opened it. Bingo. Bundles of cash wrapped up with elastic bands. No doubt his takings from previous scams. I didn't count it, but had little trouble believing there was thirty grand in there. I zipped the rucksack back up again and left.

Still five grand to collect.

There was a chance the police would already have arrived, but when I got there Willow Drive looked deserted. They were probably still cleaning up at the quarry.

This time, instead of parking down the street, I pulled onto Brooker's drive next to his beat up Porsche.

The security light came on as I crossed to the front door. I picked the lock in fifteen seconds, wondering if the woman over the road was at her window watching me do it with her nose to the glass.

Brooker had an alarm. I followed the beeping to the understairs cupboard and pulled the wires out of the alarm box. It stopped whining. Easy.

Nice house. Not huge, but he'd done okay for himself, swindling people. Except for ending up stabbed to death, of course.

I went upstairs to the master bedroom first. I figured he liked to sleep with his money nearby. In the bottom of the wardrobe half hidden by shoes was a large brown envelope. A few more bundles of cash inside. The five thousand, making thirty-five grand overall.

Quite a nice going away present.

I was about to shut the wardrobe when something caught my eye.

Hidden right at the back behind Brooker's hanging shirts, a cardboard box containing...

"That bloody jammy bastard."

A golden Robotik Bunny, all nice and new and cellophaned. I wondered who he'd had to threaten to get it, or who he'd had to rob. No doubt Alex had put it on his Christmas list, *ordered it*, probably - *"I want it I want it I want it!"* - and he'd go mad if on Christmas day it never materialised.

I bet Melissa didn't even know Gary had it. It was a present designed to cement Gary's place as the favourite parent, and to hell with Melissa.

I'd been looking for one of the damn bunnies for weeks, and now I held one in my hand. I thought of Melissa and Alex and sighed. Oh well. Life's a bitch.

I took the envelope and the Robotik Bunny, left the house and got in my car. Set them both on the passenger seat.

Then I drove away.

*

I got back to my hotel room at about half ten and shoved the chest of drawers in front of the door. I'd phone Sam Dalton in the morning, as even he, a chronic workaholic, must have gone home by now. I was pretty sure he'd be in tomorrow even though it was a Sunday, because he was expecting me back.

I checked my left arm. The wrench had missed the gunshot wound, which thankfully hadn't opened up. My shoulder and chest were purple, but I didn't think I'd broken my collarbone, so that was something.

I dry swallowed some more aspirin and fell into bed in just my boxers, having stripped and left my clothes on the floor by my bed. If I'd done that back in the SAS, before becoming John Steele, I'd have been verbally torn apart. But at that moment I didn't care. I didn't remove my make-up or change my bandage, I just got between the covers and despite my arm feeling like a burning, fractured, twisted tree branch I fell asleep almost instantly.

I dreamed, but on waking the dreams faded as quickly as a shadow in sunlight, and I let them go and just lay there for a while. 9 o'clock came and went. If I didn't get up soon I'd miss breakfast.

I had a two hour drive back to London, and now only three days left to find that damn golden bunny.

I hadn't kept the one Brooker had bought for Alex, of course - it'd have reminded me of him every time it came down to the kitchen table for breakfast. And I hadn't kept the money either, but I'd have hoped you'd know that.

I'd gone straight from Brooker's to Melissa's again. You should have seen her eyes light up when she saw me. Except all I did was lay the rucksack and the bunny at her feet, handed her Gary's logbook and said, "Your husband cheated a lot of people out of a lot of money. You'll find all his dealings in there."

She looked down at the logbook with a frown. "What do you..."

"There's thirty thousand pounds in that rucksack, and an envelope with five more. Gary's dealings. I trust you to make it right." I started to walk away, turned back. "Don't lose that golden bunny. They're a nightmare to get your hands on." And then I left.

The whole episode had made me paranoid, though. When I was driving back to my hotel from Melissa's I noticed a green van in my rear-view mirror. Most of the time it was just a pair of headlights in the dark, but it tailed me for a good number of minutes.

Of course, I'd been tailed all day - the black Land Rovers, Cousin Antonio's red Ferrari – so I was bound to be paranoid.

But that *green van*.

It turned left when I turned left and right when I turned right. It followed me over roundabouts and across junctions. Of course, it must have been heading *somewhere* and there was no specific reason to believe it was following me. But still. I couldn't shake that feeling. So I was quite relieved when at another junction it slowed behind me and flashed another car through, and then turned off. I watched it go in my mirror. The green van had **JACOB'S REMOVAL SERVICES** stencilled on the side in white.

Calm down, Steele, I told myself. Not everyone in the world's out to get you.

When you have a job like mine, though, it pays to be vigilant.

And the line between vigilance and paranoia is a thin one.

Anyway. It was Sunday morning and the job was done and I was still alive, so that was good.

I'd phone Sam Dalton when I was on the road, which would hopefully be within the hour.

I didn't shower. I'd have to go through the deep cleanse anyway after signing out of HQ, erasing John Steele until the next contract, and I didn't want to reapply my make-up to keep the ageing ginger Scotsman going just for the sake of the debrief.

Luckily, I'm not a big sweater. I sprayed my underarms and dressed in jeans and a white T-shirt I'd worn only a couple of times. Re-slung my left arm. It had stiffened up again, but the gunshot wound had begun to close properly. I'd have to get it checked out again at HQ's medical centre, but I wasn't worried.

I packed away my clothes, tablet, silenced Glock and holster into my overnight bag, on top of Kevin's cash envelope. I hadn't seen the extent of the damage to the Merc in daylight, but I fancied HQ would need all of the money to put it right.

Breakfast time.

I'd check out after I'd eaten. It'd be good to get home again.

I shoved aside the chest of drawers and went down to the dining room. Full English: bacon, eggs, sausage, mushrooms, beans, toast, hash browns - the only way to start the day. I used my left hand gingerly to assist with the cutting.

Eating alone in a restaurant bothers some people, but not me. Not when I'm playing this character, anyway.

There were a couple of tables of business men and women, probably here for a conference or team building or something, and a family of four. I had chosen a secluded table away from

them out of habit and tackled my breakfast. Not bad. Eggs a little soggy, but the bacon was crisp.

One of the business conference tables stood up. Four men in suits. Walked towards me without looking at me, without speaking, two of them walking faster than the others. The first two reached my table and circled behind me, reaching inside their jackets.

Before I could even think about reacting I felt something cold and hard press into the back of my head and one of the men hissed, "Don't move. Don't make a scene."

I stopped with the fork halfway to my mouth, inched my head round to check that they really were holding a gun barrel to my head (I'd previously held someone up with a Biro). Yep. A gun, definitely, held close to his body so no one else in the room would notice.

The other two men reached my table.

"Put your hands on the table, Mr Steele. Including the one in the sling." The man who had spoken scooted onto the opposite bench, and smiled at me.

I put my hands on the table. "I think you've got me mixed up with someone else."

"I don't think so. You stand out."

That was true. I shrugged.

One of the men sat down on the bench next to me, shoved me along and patted at my hip.

"I'm in jeans and a T-shirt, you can tell I'm not armed."

"Better to be safe than sorry." He took my knife and fork and set them on the table.

The man opposite said, "Mr Carlucci would prefer us to bring you alive. But he made it quite clear that dead would also be acceptable. So don't try anything funny."

Oh brilliant. "Mr Carlucci?"

No doubt also known as Papa Carlucci.

"You have upset him greatly. As he shall explain. Stand up, please."

"I don't think so."

"You don't think so?"

"No."

The one behind me pressed the gun harder into my back, and the man opposite said, "Are you not understanding the situation?"

"I'm not understanding your accent."

"You're very funny." But he didn't laugh. "As I said, Mr Carlucci said dead would also be acceptable, so maybe we just shoot you here."

"I already had this conversation with Cousin Antonio. You're not going to shoot me here. You have a room full of witnesses. You'll all go to prison for a very long time, and I don't think you want that."

The guy smiled. "There will be no witnesses after we kill them all."

I paused. Shit. If he was bluffing he was very good at it.

He said, "We will kill everyone in this room, including the children, and then we will burn this hotel to the ground unless you come with me now."

He wasn't bluffing.

I stood up.

"Good," said the guy opposite.

The one who'd sat next to me took my arm and led me out into the aisle. Someone else took my left arm in its sling.

"Do you mind? I got shot on Friday."

The man squeezed my bandage and the pain made my head swim. "Walk."

They were more professional than Brooker's boys had been. I had a gun pressed to my back and both arms held fast as they marched me out of the hotel and round to the rear car park.

Here they gave me a more thorough frisk down, but they turned up no weapons because I had none. Just my wallet, car keys and my phone, which the older guy kept. One of them pulled off my sling and handcuffed my hands behind my back, wrenching at my shoulder and bandage.

Jesus Christ this wasn't going well.

Theirs was a black Land Rover with tinted windows. I got in the back with a guy pointing a gun at me from the next seat. Someone put a bag over my head and everything went dark.

Okay, think. I tested my cuffs. Tight, of course. I had the lock pick hidden in my watch, as well as a spool of wire garrotte and a short blast of CS spray, but trying to lock pick whilst blind and with a gunman sitting next to me was risky. I still had my shoes, so that was something.

We drove for half an hour, maybe, but I didn't really have a clue. 'Put your hand on a hot stove for a minute and it seems like an hour. Sit with a pretty girl for an hour and it seems like a minute' said Einstein of his famous Relativity. I didn't have my hand on a hot stove, but boy was I uncomfortable.

We stopped eventually, and I heard a mechanical whirring, like the sound of an electric garage door or something. Then the Land Rover edged forward a short distance, stopped, and the whirring reversed.

Doors opened. Someone dragged me from the car and pushed me onwards, again, two people holding either arm.

The ground felt flat and smooth. A floor, and there was no breeze, so we were inside. It wasn't warm, though, and our footsteps echoed, so I imagined a large open shed of some sort, like a warehouse or storage facility.

They led me through a door. Some people cheered, like it was my birthday or something. Jeered, actually. Men in a mob. I tensed my muscles, expecting to be hit, but no blows came.

The ones holding me pushed me down onto a chair and then pulled off my hood.

I blinked into the lights. We were in some kind of industrial unit. A group of twenty or so men stood in an arc staring at me. Some of them wore suits. Some wore more casual hardmen clothes and stood with folded arms and leers.

And on the floor next to me, lying in a pool of blood, a man who'd been recently executed by the look of him. I recognised him. Or rather, I recognised his teeth. One of Carlucci's own small-time dealers. My first point of contact, killed for his unwilling hand in all of this.

*

Sergeant Jane Lane had told me about Arnold 'Keys' Mullard when I first arrived in town, two weeks ago at the start of the Carlucci contract. Back before my left arm was useless.

We'd already checked out the plans and surveillance footage of the Carlucci drugs den. A half dozen SAS could have stormed it in ten minutes, but I didn't have half a dozen SAS. It was just me, and I wasn't about to go in all guns blazing and get myself killed at the foot of the stairs. I needed a different approach.

I needed *inviting* in.

Lane had been gathering intelligence on the Carluccis and their drug pushers for years, and she suggested Keys. "He's the smallest of the small fish - we've only ever been able to pin him for possession. But he'll be anxious to make a good impression. Maybe go up in the ranks a step or two." She pushed Keys's mugshot to me across the table.

I could see instantly where he got his nickname. He

was all teeth. They were like piano keys, except with bigger gaps. He was young, maybe twenty. Had a short fuzz of black hair. "Where can I find him?"

"Corner of Main and Bridge Street. He usually hangs there."

"He'll be wary of approaches from strangers. He might think I'm an undercover cop."

She just stared at me, arms crossed tight across her chest. "Well I can't do anything about that, can I? This is your case now, you'll have to convince him."

I sighed to myself. "This isn't *my case*, sergeant..."

"No? Well it's certainly not mine anymore."

Oh boy, I thought. I don't think Sergeant Jane Lane is overly pleased I'm here. "This isn't about *taking over*, sergeant. Look, you've done a good job..."

"Obviously not good enough, or you wouldn't be here."

"That's not true. Okay, we can't put them in jail because of their arsehole lawyers, but we know they're guilty. That's not in question. It just means our judicial system is not working as well as it should. You have proven their guilt beyond reasonable doubt – I wouldn't be here if you hadn't."

She thought it over for a moment, her lips pursed. Eventually she said, "Don't worry, he won't think you're an undercover cop. You look too much like a druggy."

I took that as an olive branch. "Hopefully that'll come in handy. Do I call him 'Keys' or will that offend him?"

"No, call him Keys. Everyone does. Say you've heard he's the man to see - that'll stroke his ego."

I knew what to say. I'd been a ghost for seven years and during that time been undercover on many occasions. But I didn't say that to Sergeant Lane. No point ruffling her up any more than she already was. No matter how I spun it, I'd basically come in and taken over the case she'd been working since 2009. So she wasn't exactly thrilled at me being here, and I needed her on side. I needed her help.

I studied the picture of Keys again, although I didn't particularly need to. He'd stick out. Or at least his teeth would. Out his mouth.

"And your boys will give us some space? I don't want one of them to arrest us both."

"I'll tell them to leave Keys well alone."

"Thanks." I pocketed the picture and stood. We shook hands. "Good to meet you."

Lane didn't say it back. I think she tried to, but she couldn't get her mouth to work.

No one's ever pleased to meet me, not if they know who I am.

I can't blame them.

I drove back to my Travelodge and changed into something fairly respectable. An old suit, to look like a businessman. More camouflage, to go with my face.

I put on the jacket that in two weeks' time would have a bullet hole high in the left sleeve. I left it unzipped. Wore the SIG Sauer P226, the current MOD police pistol for a change. Just in case. At the bottom of my overnight bag, rolled up tight and wedged between clean pairs of socks, was a ball of £20 notes. I took four of them, stuffed them in my jacket, and then got a taxi to Main Street.

The fare cut into my eighty quid, but that was okay. I got out at the top so I could walk down to the intersection with Bridge Street and scope out the area.

Mid-afternoon. It'd begin to get dark soon.

Drizzle wet the streets. I pulled my hood up. Not a nice neighbourhood. Many of the frontages were boarded up, deserted, dead. Even the grass in the verges was patched and yellow, stringy and uncut, as if the council had long ago given up on this place.

No one stood on the corner of Main and Bridge Street, except for me, and I didn't have any drugs to sell. I scouted the surrounding roads, thinking maybe Keys would be sitting in a car watching the corner, or maybe the Carluccis would have someone else sitting there watching Keys, but I saw no one, in a car or otherwise.

I backed up against the nearest building - the rear end of an office block - and waited. It was bloody cold, that was for sure. I don't much like the cold. Fingers go numb. So do ears, but you don't pull triggers with your ears.

In the half hour I stood around a couple of people passed me, but none of them was Keys. I guessed he was on a break or something.

I wandered further down Main Street, inspecting the boarded up buildings and avoiding the litter. And when I turned round again I saw Keys standing on his corner. Smoking. Probably only tobacco, although I wouldn't be surprised if I found the fruity smell of weed in the air when I reached him.

He noticed me after a moment and watched me approach. I wondered if he smoked the cigarette between the gaps in his teeth.

"Are you Keys?" I asked.

He inhaled deep and then blew in my direction. Cannabis. I held my breath. It wouldn't do to cough on it.

"Who wants to know?"

"I want to buy some of your product."

He summed me up. The grooves and pinch to my skin made me look forty-five. An unhealthy forty-five. He checked out my suit. "Don't know what you're talking about, mister."

I pulled out the roll of twenties. "My boss is new to the area."

"So?"

"He likes his parties."

Keys looked up from the money. "Well good for him."

"Ecstasy helps him keep going. And I heard your product is the best."

"Well you heard wrong, man."

"That's a shame. Word on the street is that you're the guy to talk to. You can get things."

He paused. "Yeah?"

"That's what they said. But if you're not the right guy I'm sure I can find someone else to take my boss's money." I began walking away, still holding the money ball.

I got about five steps when Keys said, "Hey, wait!" I turned round and he said, "Your boss wants E, right?"

"Aye."

"Why don't he come himself?"

"Why do you think? Him getting busted buying drugs wouldn't do him any good, would it? Now," I peeled off £60 and brandished it at him. "Can you help me or not?"

Keys pondered for about a second, then he took my money, counted it, made it vanish into his coat like a magician and his hand reappeared holding a small bag of white tablets. He counted three of them into another bag and handed it to me. "Best in the country," he said, which was probably true. I'd been sent in to destroy the Carlucci business, after all. "Your boss should be very happy."

I took the bag and made it disappear into my own coat. "If he is I'll be back for more."

"There's always more. I'm always here." He grinned at me. Oh God those teeth.

"Then I'll see you around."

And I did. I spent the next day doing more research on the Carluccis, and then two evenings later I went back to the crossroads of Main and Bridge Street, this time with £140.

Keys stood where he had promised, on his corner, spliff in his mouth, walking back and forth because the nights were getting colder. He saw me and stopped. Nodded. "Your boss liked our product, then?"

"He did. Said it increased his productivity."

"What did I tell you, man? That's like, what being high can do, man. Increase your projectivity and shit."

"Uhuh."

"It's just that society's against us, man - this stuff, like, enhances your life."

"Aye." Except it usually takes over and then ruins it. First the muscle tension, nausea, blurred vision, teeth clenching. Then memory loss, depression, psychosis, damaged nerves and long-lasting brain damage. I pulled out the wad of cash. "How much will one-forty buy?"

Keys looked around furtively, and then took the money and flicked through it. That grin again. "Your boss has good taste, man. Seven pills."

"As I said before, his social circle expects it. And money's not really an object for him. So?"

Keys fished in his pockets and brought out everything he carried. "Man, this is all I got on me. I only got six - I didn't think..." He began to peel a twenty off to give back to me.

I raised a hand. "Keep it. See it as a tip for having to wait around in the cold."

The grin. Well, I needed him onside for what was to come.

"Thanks, man," he said.

"Can you get more for two days' time? Tuesday night? My boss wants £200 worth."

"Oh yeah, there's always more."

"Good. 9pm. And my boss may have a proposal for you." I walked away, letting my words sink in. I flushed the tablets and called Andrews directly.

Tuesday night would be the kicker.

*

I arrived at 9pm on the dot Tuesday evening, this time pulling up in my Merc. Keeping up appearances and all that. Keys looked wary, almost like he might scarper, and then he saw me get out and showed me the grin again.

"Hey, nice car, man."

I wondered whether to tell him my name wasn't 'man'. "It's my boss's. I have to pick him up from a conference."

That impressed him. He had his hands in his pockets, probably playing with the ecstasy bags. "I got the extra. Mr Carlucci's pleased with how I'm doing. I mean, with what you're buying."

I laughed. "Don't worry, kid, you should be proud of yourself." I showed him the money. "Two hundred."

And Keys said, "Yeah."

And then three men came out of an alley further up Bridge Street.

It was dark, and they appeared from the shadows and made a triangle around us, quickly and with precision.

I folded my money away again and sighed.

The one in the centre had a shaved head like a potato. He said, "Giz us it all," his words all mashed together like English wasn't his first language.

The other two backed up his demands with equally inaudible demands of their own.

Keys swore and pressed himself against the building behind him. "Hey guys, you don't want to…"

"Shuddup," Potato Head said, and drew a flick-knife with a blade four inches long. "You giz us ze money and drugs and we no kill you." He waved the knife in my face. "Uzzerwise…"

"You kill us, aye, I got it," I said.

"Hey," said the guy on the left, who had a face like a chipmunk. "You speak fonny."

Oh, the irony. I couldn't even be bothered to point it out.

"You don't know who you're messing with," Keys said in a small voice. "My bosses will kill you…"

"We kill you!" said Potato Head. "Giz over your money!" He waved his knife again.

"Okay, okay…" I raised my hands. "Be cool." Reached my right arm across my body, to my left inside jacket pocket. "Just getting my wallet…" I wasn't getting my wallet. I was just setting up my arm for an elbow jab, smashed out into Potato Head's jaw. Your elbow is probably the strongest part of your body. His jaw cracked and then sagged.

Poor Potato Head. He made some kind of gargle in his throat and then collapsed unconscious into the road. I launched myself at Chipmunk, who hadn't yet realized how their mugging attempt was going.

This was back when I had the use of my left arm, remember, and I drove my fist into his stomach. Heads are hard. Easy to break a hand. Stomachs are soft and spongy, and very effective disabling targets. Houdini died after being punched in the stomach before he'd tensed his abs. I don't think I killed Chipmunk, but he went down all the same, winded, doubled over, *oofing*.

The third guy ran at me and tripped over Chipmunk. I kicked him on the way down, just to make sure. He hit the road hard. Groaned.

Chipmunk crawled away from me, holding his stomach, gasping for breath.

I stood on Potato Head's flick knife and said to the two still conscious, "Help your friend up and get out of here."

Keys regained some of his confidence and shouted, "And if we ever see you again we'll kill you!"

Chipmunk and the other guy staggered to their feet, pulled Potato Head up and held him between them.

"We're so sorry..." said Chipmunk, "he made us do it..."

"Shut up and get out of here. And be thankful I didney kill you." It'd been a close thing. The only reason I hadn't was because it'd complicate things with Keys and the Carlucci brothers. Ordinarily a guy who pulls a knife on me doesn't get the chance to regret it later. I might have spared the other two, but not Potato Head. I've seen first hand what knife violence can do.

They staggered away, dragging Potato Head under the

arms.

"Jesus, man," Keys said to me. "You nailed those guys..."

I pulled out my money again. "You should tell your boss about them. They probably won't be back, but you never know." I handed him the money. "You have what we agreed?"

He pulled out a bag of ten white pills, each stamped with the letter C. "Yeah, man."

I took the bag and gave it a casual glance. "Good. My boss wants to make a deal with your boss."

Keys looked wary. "He does?"

"Aye. He has a six day business trip planned. Lots of users. He wants a lot of your product."

"Okay - how much?"

"Ten grand's worth."

Keys's eyes lit up. "You ain't jokin' with me, man?"

"No."

"*Ten grand?*"

"Aye."

"That's like... like..."

"Five hundred pills."

"Jesus, man. That's what I'm talking about!"

I nodded. "It's a lot of money."

"You said it, man!"

"There's one proviso - he isn't willing to do that big a deal on the street."

Keys frowned, and then nodded sagely. "Could get ripped off."

"Aye. So he wants a meeting."

"With the Carluccis?"

"Aye. In a safe place."

Keys spluttered a bit. "But, I mean, they don't

normally see anyone..."

"They don't usually have a guy looking to buy ten grand's worth of product. Put it to them. This is just the beginning. There'll be much more in the future."

"I-I'll try and make it happen..."

"I'm sure you will. I'll come by this time tomorrow for your answer." I turned and left, got back in my Merc and drove away.

∗

Wednesday. 9pm. Keys had a friend with him, a mean-looking guy in a leather jacket. Not a customer - back-up, in case Potato Head came back with reinforcements. Which meant Keys's friend probably had a gun.

I parked my Merc a little way away, and the guy in leathers put one hand on Keys's shoulder and reached into his jacket with the other.

Oh great, a jumpy guy with an itchy trigger finger.

Keys said something to him, and his hand halted inside his coat and stayed there. He stared at me as I got out. Older than Keys by twenty years. More professional. More hardened. One of the Carluccis' more favoured dealers.

I raised my hands and my eyebrows. "I'm the guy," I said.

"The guy?"

"The guy with the money. I'm sure Keys told you."

"I did," said Keys.

The man took his hand back out of his leather jacket, leaving his gun behind. "Your boss is having quite a party from the sounds of it."

"Six day business trip."

He noticed my accent. "In Scotland?"

"No, down here. I don't live in Scotland anymore. It'd be a bit of a long drive." In fact, I've never even *been* to Scotland. The weather's too bad.

"Keys said ten grand."

"That's right."

"Ten grand cash. No funny business."

"I have it in a briefcase all ready to bring."

He frowned. "Will your boss not be coming himself?"

"No. He has an image to uphold. And he doesn't want anything to do with... the purchasing of the product. He leaves that to me."

"I heard what you did to those guys last night. The ones who tried to rob you both."

I shrugged. "My boss needs someone who can take care of things."

"I see." He thought it over. "Okay, listen. Friday, 10pm. 24-29 Tower Road. Do you need to write it down?"

"No."

"Okay. Come alone. Come unarmed. Understand?"

"Aye."

"If we find so much as a pair of tweezers on you we'll have you pissing blood for a month."

"I don't pluck my eyebrows."

"The Carluccis are expecting ten grand in cash. You bring exactly that, because they don't like time wasters. Got it?"

"Aye. Ten grand. Cash."

"Good. Bring it Friday."

And of course I did. But as you know none of us got round to spending any of it.

*

Keys lay on his back in a pool of his own blood, his head tilted towards me. An overturned chair lay beside him. I guessed he had been sitting in it before the gunshot had taken him in the chest and knocked him over backwards.

I blinked again in the harsh lights. The men who had removed my hood had joined the rest of the mob, and they stood in a horseshoe a few feet from my chair. Cousin Antonio stood with folded arms, smiling at me.

A door opened, and in walked Papa Carlucci.

The room fell silent, except for the aging Italian's footsteps. He smiled. "What? Surprised we found out your name, eh?"

'Eh' to rhyme with *yeah* not *yay*.

"You're very clever." With no one behind me, I sprung the lock pick from my watch and began working it on my handcuffs.

"We had to kill the boy there," Papa said, and nodded at Keys, "I'm sure you understand."

"Not really. All he did was sell me some of your drugs, like you paid him to."

"He led you to us."

"It's not like he killed your sons."

Papa screwed up his face. "No. *You* did that. You blew them up with a bomb in a briefcase."

I gave a small nod. "I remember."

"I'm sure you do. And I will make you *pay*."

Not if I can help it. My left cuff clicked, and I slowly freed my hand, holding the free cuff in my right fist to stop it dangling. They'd patted me down for weapons, of course, but only for *conventional* weapons.

The Mexican Cartel make prisoners remove their shoes. My captors had neglected to do this. But they wouldn't have much chance to regret it.

"Oh, and another thing," Papa Carlucci said. "We have your wife and child."

*

I went numb all over, except in my chest, which felt like it had been smacked with a wrecking ball. *No...* I thought, *impossible.* How could they possibly know - HQ didn't even know...

And my head went all swimmy, my vision distorted, the world tilted and spun and every sound went woolly.

"You take my family. You will watch as I take yours."

"You can't have..." I gasped. "They're... I mean..."

"You don't believe me? I call them?"

I'd forgotten all about my shoe, and my handcuffs. And it was almost like John Steele was gone and I was just... just...

Papa called someone on his mobile, said something in Italian. He passed the phone to Cousin Antonio and said, "Hold this to his ear."

Antonio came over and held the phone to my ear, pointing a gun at me with his other hand. Although all thoughts of escape had evaporated, burned away by Papa's words.

We have your wife and child.

Someone said, "Hello?" through the phone. A woman.

I just sat there and listened.

"Hello?" she repeated. "Who's there?"

And the clamp around my heart eased up and I could breathe again, and relief rushed through me. I said, "Melissa."

"John? What's happening? Some men came and took me and Alex from our house - they had guns..."

We have your wife and child.

No they didn't. They just thought they did.

"Melissa," I said, "where are you?"

"I don't know - in a storeroom? There are barrels, big barrels…"

Papa said, "Enough!"

Cousin Antonio took the phone away, handed it back and joined the end of the semi-circle.

"You have it wrong," I said.

"I don't think so. We were watching you. We saw you take the boy round last night."

Oh goddamn.

"She's not my wife. The boy's not my kid. Let them go, they're nothing to do with me."

"You would say that."

"I am saying that. All I did was pick Alex up and take him back to his mother. I went to a hotel afterwards, for God's sake."

"Her neighbour said you were separated."

"They didn't mean *me* - her husband is Gary Brooker. Her name is *Melissa Brooker*…"

"She hugged you," one of the guys said. "I saw it with my own eyes. She threw herself at you."

"Her son had been kidnapped, and I'd rescued him…"

Papa raised his eyebrows. "Well, they are having a bad day, aren't they."

"It's the truth." I remembered my shoe, and tucked my feet under me so I could reach them, pulling the heel of my left foot free. It would not do to have Melissa and Alex in here when the shooting started.

I checked the room again. The men stood in a tight semi-circle facing me, the door through which I'd been led behind them. That wasn't an option. They'd be surprised for a couple of seconds, but I wouldn't have enough time to sprint the length of the room to the door without one of the survivors shooting me in the back.

To my left, ceiling-high shelves of car parts, like at Stockson's garage. Again, nothing going. Potential weapons a plenty, but I was planning on taking a gun from one of Carlucci's guys.

To my right, the cabin of a truck on blocks. And a door in the wall. That would be my target. I didn't have a clue where it went, but didn't very much give a damn. Got to go now.

I said, "If you let them go now I'll think about not killing you."

He laughed. I knew he would. I was lying anyway. I was going to kill him whatever.

I twisted the heel of my left shoe until it cracked. Inside the small carapace chemicals would be mixing. I felt for the pin with my nail and prised it free. Seven seconds.

I positioned the shoe so it hung loose on my toes. Then I counted to three and kicked it at Papa Carlucci.

It flew off the end of my foot. A perfect arc. Papa caught it. Said, "If that's supposed to be an act of defiance, I'm not impressed."

And then my shoe exploded in his hands, blowing out his chest and his head off his shoulders.

*

Not a big explosion - it had been designed only as a modified suicide pill - but big enough. A few of Papa Carlucci's nearest guys got thrown aside, de-limbed, as dead as he was. The others ducked instinctively.

I launched myself out of my chair and threw myself at

the nearest guy on my right. He was the one who'd sat opposite me in the hotel dining room at breakfast, the one who'd said he would kill everyone in the room including the children. I punched him as hard as I could, the empty cuff wrapped around my fist like a knuckle duster and I think I fractured his skull.

He went down and I plucked his submachine gun from his hands as he went. A Beretta M12. Italian, of course. Fired into the nearest guys, who had only just begun to raise their weapons. They dropped them and fell.

The others broke ranks, scattered. Some were screaming. Cousin Antonio took cover behind a work bench and overturned it, yelling at the rest of his men.

I didn't stop to retrieve a second weapon, I sprinted to the grounded truck and threw myself behind it.

Some of the guys returned fire and the windows blew in. Bullets screamed against the bodywork. I looked over at the door and hoped it wasn't locked. The truck would provide enough shelter for me to reach it, but I'd look a right fool if it didn't open.

I pulled off my other shoe and hurled it at the gunmen. They scattered again, dived away from it, expecting it to blow up like the other one. Quite funny really, because it was only a shoe.

So now I was in my socks. Not exactly ideal, but things were looking better than they had a minute ago.

I shot a short burst at the door handle. The wood shredded and the door drifted open. I sprinted through it. Nearly slipped over on the concrete floor. Nearly got splinters in my feet.

But made it through into a corridor. Walls off-white, old and worn, institutional. A suspended ceiling. Carpet on the floor, thank God. I turned right and headed what I hoped was deeper into the building. Whatever it was.

I passed an open door on my left - an office. I barely slowed. The Italians would be running after me any second, and I was low on ammo. Submachine guns fire 500 or 600 rounds a minute - that's nine or ten every *second*. And the magazines hold just 30 rounds or so. Do the maths. Hold your finger on the trigger for just three or four seconds and the clip's empty. Forget your action movies where the hero seems to have unlimited ammo. I had maybe half the magazine remaining and no spares.

I turned another corner, so at least they wouldn't have a straight shot at my back. Came to a steel door. Nowhere else to go. I tried the handle. Unlocked. I wouldn't have to waste any more ammo on the tumbler, at least.

No one inside. No one to shoot and relieve of their weapons.

The room was a kind of bare-walled garage. There were two vans parked in front of a shutter door, which presumably led outside. The vans were green, and had **JACOB'S REMOVAL SERVICES** stencilled in white on the side.

Oh you have to be joking...

Easy enough to hide bags of ecstasy tablets in the bed of a removal van. So that green van *had* been following me last night. Yes it had turned off long before I pulled into my hotel, but not before it had flashed another car through first. The second car had also been with the Carluccis and had taken over the tail. I should have known. I'd thought about exactly that technique whilst following Jermaine the blob on Friday night.

It's much easier if you have a friend in another car helping, because after a while you can turn off and let them take over. No one ever suspects a second car.

There were voices in the corridor behind me now. I ran to the door in the opposite wall, opened it, holding the M12 high. An ante-room, with a guy at a desk filling in a form or something. He stared at me, went for the gun on his desk.

I shot him in the face. The rattle in the small room was deafening and my ears rang.

His handgun was a Beretta 8000. Semi-automatic. 15 rounds if the magazine was full. I picked it up with my left hand, and it felt like it weighed a ton. I could barely raise it, let alone aim it steady, so I stuck it into my waistband for when the M12 ran dry.

God I hated only having one arm.

His mobile phone lay next to him. I grabbed it and stuffed it in my pocket, and then thought about getting the hell out of there.

Voices and shouting followed me as I crossed the office and threw open the door in the opposite wall. Another empty corridor. I hurried down it, throwing open the doors that I passed, hoping to muddy my trail.

A kitchen, empty, followed by a store cupboard of some kind, and then a fire door. I pushed the bar and leant against it and the door opened up on an alley. A chain link fence. The back end of some more old buildings. Nothing to tell me where the hell I was.

I could have run out of there, of course, but I wasn't going to leave Melissa and Alex, even though they weren't my wife and child.

I left the fire door open. Perhaps they'd think I'd escaped.

I kept on down the corridor, the gunshot wound in my

left arm burning, my ears ringing, and I was pretty pissed over the fact that I didn't have any shoes.

And then a little further up the corridor a section of the actual wall opened out and a guy stepped into my path.

I don't know who was more surprised. Luckily, I already had my M12 raised, and I blasted him off his feet before he could do it to me.

There was an actual secret door in the wall. I wouldn't have noticed it if the guy hadn't walked through it. It was hiding a long, narrow chemical laboratory.

Bingo.

The Carluccis made their MDMA in an industrial unit leased to a removal company. It was set up to produce ecstasy on an industrial scale. Rows of glassware, huge metal vats and barrels, some kind of vacuum pump. No one was currently working in it. They were probably all out hunting me. Even the chemists.

Except that one guy. He had been told to stay behind. And he'd had his own M12 in his hands when I'd shot him. I swapped my gun for his, hoping he had more ammo.

And thought about what Melissa had said. *I don't know - in a storeroom? There are barrels, big barrels...*

The guy had been told to stay behind. Why? Because he was guarding something. And in the corner of the lab, a partitioned off room, about the right size to store all the chemicals needed in the Wacker process, or whatever the hell it was called.

I went into the lab and called, "Melissa?"

And she replied, "John!"

Yes, in the storeroom alright.

The door might be locked. The guy I just shot had

probably been guarding them. Would he have locked the storeroom door after him? Yes, if they had a chance of opening it and getting out. But if they were tied up in there, probably not. I didn't know which would be worse.

The storeroom door opened.

Advantages: don't have to waste precious moments hunting through the guard's pockets for his keys. But have to spend precious moments untying them instead.

Melissa and Alex were tied with ropes to two chairs. Not ideal.

The voices in the corridor outside got louder. Perhaps they had found the guard.

There was no other door in the storeroom, and no time to free Melissa and Alex and get back out through the lab. We'd never make it.

Goddammit.

I put aside the guard's M12 and shoved one of the barrels to the open storeroom door. Took out the Beretta handgun and shot a hole in the lid. It burst through and came out the side near the bottom. A sticky pale yellow liquid began gushing out. Safrole. Oil from the root-bark or fruit of the sassafras tree, the fundamental ingredient in MDMA.

I tipped the barrel over and the safrole spread out from the doorway across the laboratory floor.

"What are you *doing?*" Melissa hissed from her chair. "Get us out of here!"

I slammed the storeroom door closed, and the only light came from a dying bulb in the ceiling. "No time, they'll be in here soon."

I shoved another barrel against the door, bracing it, picturing Carlucci's guys venturing slowly into the lab.

"Mommy, that man has no shoes," Alex said, his face red and tear-streaked.

"Where are your shoes, John?"

"I threw them at the bad guys. One of them blew up."

"The bad guy?"

"The shoe. And then the bad guy." I finished moving another barrel and then ran to Alex and Melissa and untied them. "Lie flat on the floor behind the barrels."

"But…"

"Just do it. I'm going to call for help." I flattened myself between them, knowing Carlucci's guys would just fire at us through the walls, which would not protect us for long. Actually, the barrels would probably do a better job.

I fished the mobile phone I'd stolen from the guy in the office out of my pocket.

"That's your plan?" Melissa whispered. "To call for help?"

"Do you have a better one?"

"No, but, I'm not…"

"Even if we're lucky, there's still six or seven of them about."

"But you're a…"

"What? I'm not Rambo. I'm going to call my HQ-" That number I know off by heart, "-and they'll get a local armed police response here in ten, fifteen minutes."

The first voices came from in the lab. They were close.

And then I realized that the phone required a password. "Oh Jesus. Jesus Christ."

*

"Well can't you hack it or something?" Melissa said when I told her.

"Aye, in about ten seconds if I had a decoder or a lead to connect it to my own bloody phone."

"Do... do you have your own phone with you?"

I stared at her.

She shrank a little. "Okay - and... and you can't break the password by yourself?"

I rolled my eyes. "No." Then threw the phone away.

The guys knew we were in here - I'd heard them talking outside. And one of them had fallen in the safrole and slipped away cursing. The oil would make it hard for them to get at the door, and the barrels on our side would make it difficult to open. They'd just slip and slide with no purchase on the floor. But they'd get in eventually. The real obstacle for them would be this: who'd want to be the first one through a door when a crazy Scottish gunman waited inside?

I checked the mag in the M12. They came in 20, 32 or 40-round magazines, and this was a 40, thank God, although half a dozen or so were already missing.

Some more of Carlucci's men slipped over. More swearing. Someone fired at the door and it shuddered, coins of light dotting the metal above the barrel, holes blasting out of the barrels by the door and those lining the walls, leaking chemicals all over the floor.

We were out of the view of the door, but still.

Alex put his hands over his head and began sobbing.

I needed a new plan. Quickly.

A couple of the ceiling tiles had been blasted free by the gunfire and tumbled to the floor, revealing the metal T-hangers they rested in.

A suspended ceiling. And what's more, I could see far along the duct space above. *Over* the storeroom wall, because the wall didn't climb all the way up to the structural beams of the roof. The partitions had been built up *beneath* the suspended ceiling.

Which meant we could go over them.

They'd stopped shooting through the door. Someone said, "If you come out we promise not to shoot you."

Pants on fire. One of the coin-sized discs of light in the door blotted out - some fool slushing through the safrole and putting his eye to the hole, looking in.

"Maybe we got 'em," someone else said.

I picked up the handgun and shot the guy peeping in. Possibly through the eye, definitely through the face. Bloody idiot deserved it. What did he expect?

Pressed myself into the corner as the return fire came, peppering the door some more but the angle never troubled us.

Whilst they destroyed their own stock I pushed up the ceiling tile above my head, grasped the top of the back wall and hoisted myself up to look over. A short dark space and then the main structural, exterior wall. But there was another room beyond this one, and right then I didn't care what was in it.

I was pretty sure the tops of the intersecting partition walls would hold our weight.

"Hey," I hissed, "this way." And used the nearest barrel as a stepladder to climb into the roof cavity, lying on top of the storeroom's back wall. I reached down my right hand.

Melissa scooped Alex up, pressed herself into the corner and hoisted him towards me. I grabbed his arm and pulled him into the darkness, setting him next to me on the wall.

Melissa used the barrel as I'd done and joined me on my other side as gunfire ripped into the storeroom at intermittent intervals. "*Now what?*" she whispered.

"We go over the wall." I turned away from the hole I'd created and set about creating another one on the other side of the partition. I dug my fingers into opposite sides of a tile and lifted it up, peeping down into the patch of light below.

Another storeroom, although this one contained cleaning products and a vacuum cleaner and nothing illegal or drug-related.

I slipped through the hole I'd made in the ceiling, landing as lightly as I could and gripping the M12 should I need it.

No one there.

"Okay Melissa." I set the M12 on a shelf and raised my arms so she could lower Alex down to me. Then she joined us and took back Alex, who had gone white and probably into shock.

"Stay close to the wall and behind me." I picked up the M12 again. I needed an automatic weapon for what came next.

There was just one door, which I opened with a left hand that felt stuck on the end of a lump of wet cement. I'd been in no fit state for climbing through ceilings.

The corridor was empty. I moved back up it, the lab through the wall on my left, hearing murmured voices and the occasional cough of gunfire. Alex and Melissa came quietly behind me. I don't know whether the boy knew how important it was to remain silent, or whether he was physically unable to make a sound. Either way, he didn't even whimper. Just walked like a zombie, his mouth hung open and his eyes vacant, withdrawn deep within himself.

I came to the laboratory's secret panel, still ajar, and I

peeped around it, leading with my gun.

Six guys left, all of them facing the storeroom and more or less in a clump. Cousin Antonio in the middle. They'd thrown some rags over the safrole from the overturned leaking barrel and stood in a tight arc round the door, probably wondering why we were so quiet and if it meant we were dead.

"Antonio," I said.

He turned, and I held the trigger down and hosed them all, and less than four seconds later the gun clicked empty and the six of them lay dead. I threw the M12 aside and drew the pistol. Turned to Melissa and Alex. "Come with me."

The fire escape still stood open as I'd left it, so I led the two of them out through the back streets until we saw a main road at the mouth of the alley, and I let them go on ahead just in case someone came out of the MDMA lab after us.

Lucky I did. That's probably the only reason I didn't end up shot, because then the armed police showed up.

A member of the public must have heard the gunfire and called it in. Not surprising, really. There had been a lot of shooting.

A squad of armed cops, complete with masks and bullet proof vests, appeared at the mouth of the alley right in front of us, and the only thing that stopped me shooting at them on instinct (and them at me in return) was the fact that Melissa and Alex stood between us.

"Drop the weapon!" one of them yelled, which I did. "Get down on the ground!"

They swept past Melissa and Alex, the squad ingesting them and transferring them onward towards safety. I think Melissa might have told them to wait, that I was one of the good guys, but by then I'd lain on the ground and put my hands on my head. My left arm was agony.

For once I'd actually have welcomed the sight of Sergeant Jane Lane, because at least she knew who I was. But she was nowhere to be seen. This was a different team, and all they saw was a crazy bedraggled ginger hobo chasing a civilian woman and child out of an industrial unit with an automatic weapon.

Someone knelt on my back, seized my wrists and folded them behind me. Paused, presumably on seeing the handcuff on my right wrist. "He's already got handcuffs on him."

"The Carluccis put them on when they kidnapped me," I said. "The drug lords. That's their MDMA lab. My name is John Steele, and I work for the government."

"Okay, Scotty, yes I'm sure you do." The cop put his own handcuffs on me, pulled me to my feet. Another frisked me, but found nothing else because I didn't have my wallet or LV licence on me. One of Carlucci's dead guys still had them. I didn't even have my own shoes. I had the CS spray and spool of wire garrotte in my watch, but didn't think using them would help the situation.

"Can you watch my arm? I was shot on Friday."

"We'll get you seen at the hospital," the cop said.

And then he arrested me.

*

I jumped the queues in A & E again. This time because I was under arrest and had a police escort. They redressed my wound, but that was all. The stitches had held, which was a miracle after what I'd been through. I had a large purple bruise on my chest from where Stuart Stockson the satanic mechanic had hit me with that wrench, but the doctor assured me nothing was broken.

He asked if I was on any kind of drugs. I said no.

But I'd seen enough ecstasy to last me a lifetime.

An hour later I arrived at the local police station. Not the one Andrews ran - I was over the other side of town now, and no one knew who I was. So I demanded my phone call and rang Dalton.

"Steele. I expected you to phone sooner."

"I got held up. By the Carluccis."

Dalton whistled. "I *told* you not to hang around."

"Good job I did. I found Papa Carlucci. Or rather, he found me. And now he's dead."

"He is?"

"Yes, I blew his head off with my shoe grenade."

"Jesus."

"And I killed Cousin Antonio and the rest of their crew, and I destroyed their lab."

"You found their lab?"

"Yes, I'll tell you all about it when I see you. But now I need your help. I've been arrested."

Dalton spluttered. "Arrested? But your ID…"

"I don't have it at the moment. Can you get Dawn to call George Andrews? I'm being held at Southside."

"Yes, I will do, but..."

"Thanks. I have to go - they're making faces. I should get to HQ some time this evening."

The call came through quickly, which I was grateful for. They had found my wallet whilst identifying the bodies and returned it to me with apologies. Someone released my handcuffs, and when they didn't seem to know what to do about the remaining cuff on my right wrist, the one the Carluccis had given me, I sorted it myself with the lock pick from my watch. They didn't know how to react to that.

I found my car keys on the evidence table, and got one of the officers to ring my mobile number just in case my phone was there too. I hoped to hear it buzzing, but the officer told me the damn thing was dead. Hardly surprising. I'd probably damaged it with my shoe grenade or put a bullet in it or something. Oh well.

I left the police station without seeing Melissa or Alex at all. That was probably for the best. If the kid saw me one more time he'd probably scream his head off.

I still had no shoes, and got two of the cops to drop me at the nearest sports shop, where I bought a pair of trainers and came out wearing them.

Then I got a taxi back across town to my hotel. My room key was still in my wallet, and I retrieved my overnight bag, made sure I hadn't left anything behind and checked out.

My Merc was quite badly scuffed up.

Dalton wouldn't be happy.

It had gone 3 o'clock by the time I left for London. Rain clouds blackened the sky, and gusts batted the car. I turned the heating up to full and relaxed in the leather. Put on Classic FM. One of Chopin's Nocturnes. Just perfect.

HQ is in Islington. Often the worst part of a contract is driving into Central London after it's completed. It's such a pain in the arse. But not this time. This time had been complicated.

Complicated by a nasty little loan shark who picked on the wrong guy, a guy who happened to be a psychotic parent-killing sociopath.

I pulled up to the gate of the listed Georgian building

and showed my ID to the armed duty guard.

He nodded me through and opened the gate.

I drove into the underground car park and parked in my allotted bay. Exhaled, pressed my eyes shut. What a weekend. I think I'd earned an extended break.

One of the security team greeted me by name (my code name, John Steele, of course) and asked if there was anything he could help me with.

"Is Sam Dalton still here?"

"Yes sir. He's been expecting you."

"Then please tell him I've arrived as I've lost my phone. I'll be up soon for debrief."

"Yes sir."

As he left I retrieved my overnight bag and the purple gym bag with the Carluccis' cash and set them both down on the concrete. I checked the glove box, under the seats and then the boot. The balled up sheet was still in there, crusted with Little Carlucci's drying blood. I just hoped the plastic liner had protected the boot trim. Blood stains on the actual material would be hard to get out.

And then I opened the weapons locker.

Two SIG Sauer P226 pistols, unused. One Colt Canada C8 assault rifle, unused. And a Heckler and Koch MP5 submachine gun, also unused. One Glock 17 present. The other was in my overnight bag, and I returned it to its slot. I tried to count up how many rounds I'd used. Two on hitman Will Pharell. One on Baldy Baz, between the eyes. One on Stuart Stockson, through the chest. One into the left rear wing of Brooker's BMW. And one on that Carlucci guy, after I'd run him over in the rustmobile.

Six. The one into the BMW had been a wasted shot as

I'd been aiming for his tyre, but still not a bad record.

And lastly an AWC sniper rifle, folded stock. Two rounds fired. One high, the other through Kevin West's back.

I shut the locker, locked the car, and carried my bags into the building, wearing the gym bag like a rucksack and carrying the other in my right hand.

Sam Dalton rose as I entered and smiled. He was an aging black man, his thin hair growing greyer each time I saw him.

I dropped my bags and shook his hand. His handshake was just like the rest of him – strong, firm, resilient.

"Jesus, Steele," he said. "You look like crap. I mean worse than *normal*."

"Thanks."

Dalton perched on his desk. He'd loosened his tie. There were bags under his eyes.

"You don't look so good yourself, sir. Ever heard of sleep?"

"I can go home and get some now you've finished arseing about."

"So can I."

"You got them then? And Papa Carlucci too?"

"Aye. Was nice of him to fly over. You should have police confirmation by tomorrow."

"And you found the lab, too?"

"They took me to it."

"So what the hell happened?"

I told him in order. About meeting up with George Andrews and Sergeant Jane Lane, and making friends with Keys, and taking a bomb into the Carluccis' business address in a briefcase of fake money.

About Jeremy Peters, and how he owed Brooker

money, and how Baldy Baz had beaten him to death so I'd shot him in the face.

About Melissa and Alex complicating things, and Kevin West - *bloody mental case Kevin West* - kidnapping Alex and how I'd had to call a temporary truce with Brooker to rescue him.

About how Kevin had stabbed Brooker to death before I'd sniped him.

And then about Carlucci's guys kidnapping me at gunpoint and taking me to the lab, presumably because that was the only premises they had left after I'd destroyed their drugs den, and how they'd kidnapped Melissa and Alex too because they thought she was my wife and he my son. And how we had escaped, using the lock pick in my watch and the bomb in my shoe.

Dalton listened without asking any questions, and at the end said, "Jesus Christ, what a bloody song and dance."

"There wasn't much singing or dancing."

"The man you shot in the head – Baz – that wasn't self-defence?"

"No. Prevention. The police had nothing on him and he would have killed someone else."

Dalton nodded. "I'll need your report on that in the next few days."

"Yes sir." I took out the envelope I'd taken from Kevin's place and dropped it on the desk. "This should cover the Merc."

Dalton stared at me, weary. "What happened to the Merc?"

"Not much. Just a few scratches. And dents."

He sighed. "Please tell me it's not as bad as last time."

"It's not!" I laughed, because last time I'd almost

written it off. "I promise. Just scratches this time."

"And dents."

"And small dents."

Dalton chuckled despite himself. Looked in the envelope, raised his eyebrows and nodded. "Fair enough. Thanks."

"If there's any left maybe you can buy a new suit."

"The next suit I wear will be my funeral suit, because you'll have given me a heart attack."

"Your takeaway dinners will have given you a heart attack."

He laughed some more. "Good work, Steele. Now go home and give your arm time to heal. You've earned it."

"I will," I said.

I've got secrets to get back to.

*

John Steele is just an illusion. A literal ghost as well as a figurative one. You'll know by now that's not my real name. And the forty-five-year-old ginger Scot is an illusion too. Not even HQ knows my name or what I really look like. Because Licensed Vigilantes are required to disappear like fog. It's what we do, it's what we are. No trace, nowhere.

The man I become on these jobs doesn't exist.

They paid me thirty-five grand in cash. Thirty for the two brothers, an extra five for finding the lab. Again, no paper trail. No transfer to real bank accounts. No way of tracking it. That was on top of what was in the purple gym bag, my salvage, which turned out to be no less than forty-three thousand pounds. Not bad for a weekend's work. Except for the getting shot, and getting kidnapped and almost killed on a number of occasions.

Still. I like what I do, and I'm good at it.

And I'm not dead yet.

I left my wallet with my ID and credit cards and my overnight bag with them. There was nothing personal, and they'd provided it all in the first place anyway. The only thing I took with me were the clothes I was wearing, my locker key and my make-up bag. I needed the make-up bag not only to wash John Steele away, but to bring him back for the next time I walked into HQ.

There were just two things in my locker. A jacket and a single key that opened the front door of my house. I put the jacket on and zipped my house key in an inside pocket.

Then I took my money, all seventy-eight thousand pounds of it stuffed into a rucksack, and got a taxi to a hotel on the other side of London. Gave a random name. Paid in cash.

I had enough of it.

Shoved the chest of drawers in front of the door out of habit. Shaved off my beard. Used the chemical make-up remover on my face and washed it all away. Then I showered, using the dye-removal shampoo to change my hair back from ginger to light blonde. The concealer came off my right forearm and I had my tattoo again, a blue snake winding round a sword.

So when I got out the shower I looked like a totally different person, like me again. A clean-shaven, tattooed, blonde thirty-five-year-old, albeit with a bullet wound in my left arm.

I left the hotel less than an hour after arriving and got another taxi to Euston, where I spent the next two hours on a train heading back north. Not as far as Scotland, though. When I arrived at Birmingham New Street station and bought my connecting ticket I dropped John Steele's Scottish accent and used my own, fairly well-spoken, private-school middle England.

I caught the connection and headed north east, watching the lights whiz by out of the darkness, counting the stations, until at 10:37pm I reached my home town. My heart lifted, though the trials of the weekend were catching up with me, my adrenaline no longer enough to keep me running smoothly.

There was a large 24-hour Tesco a short walk from the station, one with a café upstairs, and I drank two coffees entirely for the caffeine even though I don't even like coffee much, and ate a thick wedge of chocolate fudge cake. I felt marginally better.

And on the way out something along the toy aisle caught my eye. A shop worker putting out a new stock arrival of golden Robotik bunnies.

*

The taxi pulled up outside my house just after 11pm. I walked up the drive, rucksack swung over my right shoulder. I'd managed to fit the Robotik bunny box on top of all the cash, but it had been a close thing.

I didn't even get to use my key. The front door opened as soon as I reached it, and there was Claire, my wife. She threw her arms around me and pulled me inside, the two of us laughing.

"About time you got home, David," Claire said, though she had a wide smile. "Thought you were going to miss Livvy's birthday."

"As if," I said. "It's a whole three days until Wednesday. And look what I found." I unzipped the top of the rucksack to show Claire the present Olivia had been just *dying* for, and over Claire's excited gasp I heard the princess herself bounding down the stairs like an elephant.

My ten-year-old daughter burst into the room in her pyjamas just as I zipped the rucksack back up. "Dad!" she jumped on me, and I tumbled into Claire and we all went sprawling on the sofa, laughing, and even though my arm hurt like hell I held onto both of them and didn't let go.

John Steele is a second life, and these two are what I live for.

John Steele will return in

Devil's Breath

Look out for the new standalone
thriller novel from Matt Walker:

Memories
Unspeakable

*How can you cover up the past
when memories can be bought and sold?*

Coming Winter 2018

30112176R00173

Printed in Great Britain
by Amazon